Someone to Love

THE SEASIDE CHRONICLES

Someone to Love

THE SEASIDE CHRONICLES

KELLY ELLIOTT

Dear Reader,

A note to you before you begin the book. The Seaside Chronicles is NOT a stand-alone series. They are interconnected stories with the siblings' stories being carried throughout the series. The books are best read in order or you may find yourself confused, and this writer does not want that to happen!

You can find out more about the books at the link below.

https://kellyelliottauthor.com/library/#seaside

Now...let's begin with Brax and Harlee's story, shall we?

Chapter One

Braxton (Brax)
Twenty-Five Years Old

I could tell the exact moment she walked into the bar without even seeing her. There was something special about Harlee Tilson, though I could never put my finger on what exactly it was.

Turning, I caught sight of her and smiled. Harlee was my sister Addie's best friend. I'd like to say she was basically another sister to me, but that would be fucked up since I'd had a dirty dream or two about her over the years. Hell, I wasn't blind, and the older she got, the more beautiful she became. I'd even had a major crush on her in high school and had only ended up dating one other person because my thoughts were always on Harlee. But she was off limits. The whole never date…or fuck…your sister's best friend rule. I wasn't really sure who'd made up that stupid rule anyway.

"Is that Harlee Tilson?" Thomas Minor asked as he stared at her. He was my best friend and like a brother to me. "Damn, that girl gets hotter and hotter every time I see her."

I glared at my friend. Never mind that I couldn't touch Harlee, that asshole sure as hell wasn't going to even *think* about touching her. "Keep your eyes and your hands off, Thomas."

He swung his gaze over to me. "Don't tell me you're interested in her?"

1

I laughed. "She's like a sister to me, dude."

Okay, half-truth. I don't have sex dreams about my sisters.

I shuddered at the thought.

Of course, up until my senior year of high school, I *had* always thought of Harlee as a kid sister. Then she grew up, got breasts, and her body developed curves that even a priest would look at twice, and the whole kid-sister thing was thrown out the door. But that didn't mean I had free rein to act on it. The last thing I ever wanted to do was hurt her. She meant a lot to Addie, to my whole family. She was an only child, and her father owned our local newspaper, *The Seaside Chronicles*. I was pretty sure she spent more time at our house than she did her own. That meant no matter how much I wanted to know what those pouty lips would feel like pressed to mine, it was best I kept my distance.

And if Harlee was off limits to me, she was off limits to all of my friends.

I watched as douchebag Roger walked up to Harlee and smiled at her like she was a piece of meat. He worked down at the docks and was nothing but a player, out for one thing and one thing only: sex. He held out his hand and she took it, allowing him to guide her to the dance floor.

Thomas grunted. "Well, looks like I'm too late anyway. Roger seems to have claimed her."

A muscle in my neck throbbed as I watched him put his hands on Harlee. It wasn't jealousy, no...no way it was that. It was the fact that he was a scumbag. There was no way in hell I was going to let him fondle her on the dance floor.

With my fists clenched and an anger that came out of fucking nowhere, I marched over to where Harlee and Roger were dancing and gave him a look that said, "Get away from her or I'll break your neck." Everyone in town knew Harlee and Addie were like sisters, and if anyone tried to mess with my sisters or Harlee, they'd have to deal with me.

Roger lifted his hands and took a few steps back. "Dude, it was only a dance."

"Go find someone else to dance with," I growled as I stepped between him and Harlee. When I turned and looked down at her, those steely blue eyes were staring up at me, wide with confusion.

"Why did you do that, Brax?"

I couldn't help but stare down at her, take her in. Her shoulder-length, wavy hair was pulled up into a ponytail. She was wearing jeans and a light blue shirt that seemed to nip in at her waist, showcasing her luscious curves.

Jesus, Brax, stop staring at her like you're the freaking jerk you just saved her from.

I shook my head and came back down to Earth. "What did you say?"

She looked confused, but a part of her seemed to also be delighted I had stepped in. "Why did you run him off?"

Lord have mercy, I was forever having to tell my sisters and Harlee that guys were out for one thing and one thing only. "He wants to get in your pants, Harlee, and that's it."

Her eyes crinkled at the corners before she laughed. "Brax, you think *every* guy only wants to get in a girl's pants."

I flashed her a wicked grin. "That's because I'm a guy, and I know for a fact that guys are only after *one thing*."

She looked around the dance floor. The music suddenly changed to a slow song, so I held my hand out to her. With a shy smile, she took it. I drew her body flush against mine and tried to ignore the way it instantly heated at the contact.

It's Harlee, Brax. Calm the hell down.

"I love this song," Harlee said as she laid her head on my chest. The gesture shouldn't have made my heart jolt, so I purposefully ignored the ache in my chest.

"A Snow Patrol fan, huh?" I asked.

She looked up and smiled. "Yep. *Grey's* fan too."

With a questioning look, I asked, "*Grey's*?"

She frowned. "Braxton Bradley, please don't tell me you've never seen *Grey's Anatomy*?"

I smiled. "Okay, I won't tell you that."

3

Her mouth dropped open. "Wait, seriously? It's only the greatest show ever. Addie and Sutton are addicted to it; how have you never seen it?"

With a laugh, I shrugged. "No clue, but I'll take your word for it."

Harlee glanced around the dance floor once again.

"Are you looking for someone?"

She snapped her head back to me. "Sorry—it's rude of me to be looking around while dancing with such a handsome lad."

I rolled my eyes. "How's school going? I'd think you were getting close to being finished?"

She sighed slightly, then shrugged. "It's going well, and yeah, I graduate this spring. Not sure why I'm even going. My father is going to give me a job at the paper because I'm his kid. And everyone will think I walked into the position, even though I've been working for the paper since I was sixteen. Trying my best to learn how it all works."

"Harlee, this is Seaside. No one's going to think that. Besides, all the employees who work there know you've been busting your butt for years. We've all seen it. No one would ever call you lazy or undeserving."

She smiled. "Thanks, Brax. That means a lot to me."

With a short nod, I added, "You're getting your degree in marketing, you're going to be a very valuable asset to the paper."

"I guess it'll come in handy if he lets me actually have a job in management."

"I can't imagine why he wouldn't."

She gave me a weak smile, clearly not as convinced as I was. "I guess we'll find out in a few months. How's the fishing business going?"

"Busy. Thomas has been helping me, and it's growing a lot faster than I thought it would. I just bought another boat and hired two more people for when the season starts up again in May."

She smiled. "That's amazing! You always were one of the best fishermen in town. How many championships have you won over the years?"

My chest puffed out a little at her praise. "One or two."

"And he's modest as well, ladies."

"I hope I can keep growing. My dream is to make Bradley Charters one of the best in Maine."

Her expression turned soft, and a strange feeling hit my stomach as our eyes locked. "If anyone can do it, it's you, Brax."

I wasn't sure if she also felt the strange pull that had suddenly engulfed us, but I was obviously starved for companionship if I was reacting to Harlee like this. I mentally decided to make some time to hook up with someone else. It had been too long, and sex was clearly overdue.

Clearing my throat, I replied, "Thanks, Harlee."

Something in her eyes changed, and she opened her mouth to say something before snapping it shut.

"What were you going to say?"

Her cheeks turned bright red. "Nothing, it was something silly."

"Tell me."

She looked away as if trying to gather up the courage, but then clearly caught sight of someone. She quickly shook her head and looked back at me. Her smile was forced. "The guy I'm meeting just showed up."

For a hot second, I thought I saw regret in her eyes. Regret for what, though? Not telling me what she wanted to say, or for meeting up with some guy?

I glanced to my right and saw Douglas McCarthy standing there, smiling in our direction.

"Wait, you're going on a date with *Douglas McCarthy*?"

She pulled her gaze away from him to look at me. "I am. Why?"

Clasping her hand in mine, I navigated us through the crowd on the dance floor toward the bar. Seaside only had three bars. The Salty Dog was where the older crowd hung out. By older, I meant over forty. Mickey's had a nice range of ages, and then there was Sea Dog Brewing Company, where we were currently hanging out. There was always a younger crowd at this bar.

After finally making my way to the bar, I ordered two beers, keeping hold of Harlee's hand the whole time. The bartender carded us both, even though he had gone to high school with us and knew damn well we were old enough to drink. He gave us two local brews on tap, and then grinned when I left him a large tip. It wasn't because I was feeling friendly—more like I wasn't paying attention because my mind was spinning in a million different directions, and I had no idea why.

The only thing I knew was that I wasn't about to let Harlee leave with Douglas. What in the hell was she thinking?

I handed one of the beers to Harlee. "Here, drink this."

She took it and said, "Thanks."

I downed my entire glass while Harlee took a sip and stared at me. "You must have been thirsty."

"I'll take a shot of tequila," I called out toward the bar.

Harlee leaned in and shouted over the crowd, "Make that two."

When I lifted a brow at her, she grinned. "What? I know how to drink, Brax. I'm not a lightweight. I do need to go meet up with Doug, though."

"I don't think so."

Her brows shot up in surprise. "I'm sorry?"

"What in the hell are you thinking, Harlee? Doug? He's the worst of them all."

She rolled her eyes. "Brax, go tend to one of your sisters because I don't need a babysitter, thank you."

When she moved to walk away, I took hold of her hand again. "Harlee, you don't know him like I do."

Her shoulders slumped as she exhaled. "I know, I know. He's only out for one thing."

I shot her a frustrated look. The bartender placed the shots on the bar, and we both reached for one and drank it.

Harlee put her shot glass down hard on the bar. "Maybe I'm in the mood for that one thing. Have you ever thought of that, Brax?"

My entire body heated with a rage that nearly stole my breath. "Not the kind *he* dishes out."

She folded her arms across her chest. "What does that mean?"

I did a quick look around before leaning in. "He likes getting rough, Harlee. He has a reputation, and honestly, I'm surprised you don't know about it."

"A reputation?"

"Slapping women around, tying them up. Shit like that."

Harlee's eyes went wide. "What? You're making that up."

"Why in the hell would I make that up?"

She shrugged. "I don't know. You realize you don't have to play the big brother with me, Brax."

Something in her eyes made me pause. "I'm not, Harlee. Trust me...I haven't looked at you like that in years."

Her mouth dropped open, then quickly shut as her cheeks turned a slight shade of pink. She started to chew on her lower lip. I had to stop looking at it and focus on the rest of her face.

"I'm your friend, Harlee. I care about you, and the last thing I want is for some brute to slap you around because he gets turned on by it."

Her eyes darted down to my mouth and then back up. She looked over my shoulder and indecision washed across her face. I could tell she wasn't sure if she should believe me. "He's coming this way."

I tossed some money down on the bar, took Harlee by the elbow, and started to guide her toward the door.

"Brax. Wait! What are you doing?"

"Letting everyone know you're leaving with *me*."

From the slight tug on my hand, I knew she wanted to pull herself to a stop, but she clearly realized it would only cause more of a scene.

"You *want* people to think we're leaving together?" she asked as I pushed out of the bar and continued toward my Ford truck.

"I only want Doug to think it. I don't give a shit about anyone else."

"In case you haven't noticed, I'm an adult now, Braxton. I can handle myself. And did you ever think that *I* might care? What if it got back to Addie that you and I left the Sea Dog together?"

"Who cares what Addie thinks."

"I do!" Harlee protested, clearly pissed off at me for dragging her out of the bar and away from her date.

We got to the passenger side of my truck, and I looked down at her in frustration before I grabbed her arms and pushed them over her head, holding them tightly. I had to show her what was at stake.

Her breathing picked up as she quickly licked her lips and stared into my eyes.

"You think you can adult your way out of this? What would you do if I pinned you down and forced you, Harlee? It wouldn't take much for me to push you into my truck and take you right here in the parking lot."

"Brax," she said in a raspy voice as something moved across her face I couldn't read. I kept talking, hoping I could make her understand.

"Because that's what guys like Doug do. They like to get rough— and the idea of him putting his hands on you makes me want to kill someone."

The words were out of my mouth before I even had time to realize I'd thought them.

"Brax?" Harlee whispered, confusion sweeping over her beautiful face. My heart started to pound as I looked into those eyes of hers and fought the sudden urge to kiss her. "Are you going to let go of me now?"

Dropping my hold on her, I stepped back and let my eyes sweep over her body. Even in the darkened parking lot, I could still see her perfectly. She wasn't thin, but she wasn't overweight either. She was in that perfect spot right between the two. Her hips were wide—and I was immediately hit with a vision of holding them in my hands while I fucked her from behind.

I shook the image away as I rubbed a hand down my face. "Get in the truck, Harlee."

"No. I drove here, Brax. I'm not leaving my car."

The door to the bar opened, and I looked over to see Doug standing there.

"Get in the goddamn truck," I repeated.

She folded her arms over her chest again. "*No.* I need you to let me handle this."

I sighed, but before I could argue anymore, the dickhead walked up.

"Is everything okay here?" Doug asked as he surveyed what was going on.

Harlee glanced over at him. "Everything's fine, Doug. Brax is being a bit of a brute to get a point across."

Doug looked at Harlee, then at me. A slow smile pulled at the corners of his mouth. "I knew I was right about you. We think the same way, dude. I'm totally down for a threesome if you are."

I wasn't sure who was more shocked. Harlee or me.

She blinked a few times and then said, "I'm sorry?"

"If Brax doesn't mind sharing, I don't either."

I watched as Harlee stared at the guy she was supposed to be meeting for a date. She turned and looked up at me, her expression resigned. I hated that I'd had to prove her wrong. "I'm ready to go, Brax."

I nodded and opened the door to my truck. Before Harlee got in, she said, "Sorry, Doug, I don't think we're a match."

Poor Doug looked as if someone had unplugged him and let the air out.

After helping Harlee into the truck, I shut the door and looked at him. "I'm nothing like you...*dude*. Stay away from her."

He looked confused, then motioned from me to Harlee. "Are you two together?"

I started for the other side of my truck. "You heard me, Doug. You so much as even breathe on her, and I'll rearrange your face."

Once I slid into the driver seat of my truck, I looked in the rearview mirror to see Doug heading back into the bar. I had no doubt he'd be able to pick up someone else to spend the rest of the evening with, and I couldn't help but feel sorry for whoever she'd be. Hopefully someone who knew what the guy was into. Clearly, Harlee hadn't heard the rumors.

Harlee sat next to me, her breathing slightly heavy.

"I hate to say I told you so, but I told you so."

She snapped her head around and glared at me. "He wanted a threesome. A *threesome*! What in the hell, Brax? I can't...I don't...oh my God! Seriously, what is that man even into?"

I reached for her hand and gave it a squeeze. "He's a piece of shit, but I don't think he would take things where they shouldn't go."

She sighed, then slowly shook her head. "I just wanted to... I mean, I knew he was into one-night stands, and that was all I was looking for..."

Her voice trailed off, and that weird pang in my chest came back. I had to fight the urge to rub at it. "Want me to drive around for a bit before dropping you back off at your car?"

With a shake of her head, she asked, "Can we go back to your place? I think I need a little time to clear my thoughts."

I nodded, pulled out of the parking lot, and headed down the main road back into town.

"I don't think he would have forced you to do anything you weren't ready to do," I said. "But like I said, I've heard he likes it rough."

She dropped her head back against the seat. "Why do I have such bad taste in men?"

I decided it was in my best interest to not touch that question with a ten-foot pole.

Harlee let out a bitter laugh. "I'm surprised you don't have anything to say to that."

"Would it make you feel better if I agreed with you?"

I felt the heat of her glare and chose to keep my eyes focused on the road ahead. Silence filled the cab of the truck as I drove to my house. Once I pulled into the driveway, Harlee got out and slammed the door shut, then marched up to the front door. I wasn't sure if she was mad at me or herself. Either way, I wasn't very fond of seeing her angry.

"Do you want to tell me why you're so pissed off?" I asked as I unlocked the front door and she pushed her way in. Once the door shut, she unleashed.

"Why do you do this to me?"

I dropped my keys in the bowl sitting on a small table by the front door. I had made that bowl years ago in elementary school, and my mother had insisted I take it to my new house when I moved in.

Turning to face Harlee, I gave her a confused look. "Do what to you?"

"Drive me insane, Brax. You drive me insane!"

I laughed and made my way over to the bar cart. "I drive you insane? How exactly am I the bad guy all of a sudden? Just because you're frustrated your date wanted me to join in on his little sex party doesn't make me the bad guy."

Her mouth opened, then closed. I looked back down at the bottle in my hand and then poured a shot of whiskey for both of us. I turned and handed her one, and she downed it and handed it back. I filled it again, and she tossed the second back like a pro as well.

She looked up at me sheepishly, and it was the cutest damn thing. "Have you done it before?"

I knew what she was asking but decided to play dumb. "Done what before?"

She huffed and made her way back over to the whiskey to pour another shot. After downing it, she drew in a deep breath. Without looking at me, she said, "Had a threesome."

"No. Have you?"

Turning, she stared at me for the longest time before she answered. "No."

"Do you *want* to have a threesome?" I asked as I sat down in the large leather chair in my living room. My house was an open plan on the first floor, so I had a clear shot of my kitchen and dining room areas. I liked the openness. It made the space feel bigger but also *cozy*. My mother's word, not mine.

Harlee bit into her lip as her gaze fell to my mouth once again. My cock twitched in my pants, and I had to remind myself that this was Harlee. My sister's best friend. Yes, she was beautiful, and if she was anyone else I'd probably already have her in my bed. But she wasn't anyone else. She was...Harlee. And that seemed to be the only thing that mattered.

She slowly shook her head. "No, I don't. Do you want to...um...have one?"

I smirked. "I'm not much for sharing. And if you were mine, there's no way in hell another man would so much as *look* at you that way, let alone touch you."

Her eyes slowly lifted to meet mine. I wasn't sure if it was the alcohol relaxing her, but something had changed. The air in the room suddenly felt like it was charged, and no matter how much I tried to ignore it, the more she looked at me, the more I wanted to bite that lower lip of hers.

Harlee swallowed hard. "If I was yours, what would you do with me?"

So, you want to play this game, huh? Okay, Harlee. Let's see how far you're willing to take it.

I slowly smiled as I thought of all the ways I would explore Harlee's body. I'd take my time and learn what made her gasp, what made her sigh with pleasure. I'd find out what she liked and didn't like. What made her shy and what made her beg for more.

"That's a dangerous question, Harlee. Are you sure you want to play this game?"

She raised a single brow and gave me a challenging look. "Are you afraid to answer it?"

I laughed. "No."

"Then answer."

I sat back in the chair and finished off my drink before I moved my gaze slowly up her body until our eyes met. She seemed to be fidgeting under my perusal, and I liked that I had that effect on her.

I slowly wet my lips with my tongue. "I'd get you naked, lay you on my bed, then explore your body with my hands at first...then my tongue."

Her eyes widened as she swallowed hard.

"I'd discover the things you like and the things you don't like. And then I'd pleasure you until you begged me to stop."

My cock was rock hard in my pants, and I knew I needed to stop talking before we both went too far and did something we'd regret later.

Apparently, Harlee wasn't ready to stop. "And then what would you do, after you made me come?"

I closed my eyes and whispered, "Harlee."

"What would you do, Brax?" Her voice sounded low and sexy. She wasn't daring me anymore; she truly wanted to know.

My eyes snapped open, and the way she was looking at me made me speak the truth. "After I made you come with my mouth, I'd turn you over and fuck you from behind, just so I could grab onto that pretty ponytail of yours and stare at your ass while I took you hard and fast."

Her lips parted and a slight moan slipped free.

That moan changed everything—and I flicked the angel off my right shoulder and listened to the devil on my left. "Do you like coming that way, Harlee? On a man's face?"

She blinked a few times. "I've never...um...no one has ever done that to me."

Jesus, who in the hell were the guys she was dating? "You've never had a guy go down on you before?"

She shook her head.

"That's a damn shame."

Her cheeks turned pink, but I watched as she stood a bit straighter. "I've never done it to a guy, either."

I was immediately assaulted by an image of Harlee giving me head. It felt like a fucking train hit me at a hundred miles per hour. I could be her first.

She moved closer to me and sat down on the sofa. "I'm not very experienced when it comes to sex. I've only had a few partners, and it's all been pretty vanilla."

I chuckled. "Thank God Doug didn't get his hands on you then."

An embarrassed smile tugged at the corners of her mouth.

She looked down at her clasped hands, then back up at me. "I wanted to...I wanted to meet up with Doug to have a mindless..."

"Fuck?" I asked.

Harlee flinched, and I felt like a complete asshole. The idea of her with Doug still made my blood boil, and to know she was simply looking for a night of sex made something in my chest ache.

She closed her eyes, drew in a deep breath, then blurted out, "I want you, Brax. I want you to do all those things you said to me. I want you to fuck me from behind, on top, to show me how to sit on your face and make myself come. I want it all."

I nearly dropped the shot glass in my hand. "Jesus Christ, Harlee."

"And it's not like I'm randomly asking you to do all that to me. If I'd thought you were even halfway interested in having sex with me, I'd have asked you a long time ago."

I scrubbed a hand down my face, stood, and started to pace. "Harlee, what you're asking... I mean, we'd be stepping over a line that I'm not sure we should step over."

She dropped her head before she looked up at me. "Did you not mean any of what you said then?"

My heart nearly fell to the floor. "Yes. I meant every word. You have no idea how much I want you. Hell, I've had dirty dreams about you before."

Her eyes lit up. "You have?"

"Don't look at me like that, Harlee. You should be doing this with someone who means something to you. Someone special."

"You *do* mean something to me, Brax."

I opened my mouth to protest, but the sweet way she'd said that—and the way she was currently looking at me—made me want to haul her into my arms and kiss her senseless.

"Have you been with a lot of women?"

Her question threw me off guard. "Um, I don't think so. I mean, I've had one-night stands once or twice, but I'm not a manwhore."

She smiled. "When was your first time?"

I blinked at her in confusion. Why in the hell was she asking me that? "Seventeen."

"With someone you cared about?"

I let out a huff. "No. She was older. It was at a college party, and when she found out I was a virgin, she wanted to be my first. To teach me how to please a woman."

"Wow. She must have been beautiful."

I shook my head to clear the fog that was building. "No. I mean, yes, she was pretty, but I wasn't about to tell her no when she asked. I was honest with her. I think it turned her on to know I was a virgin. I was scared to death. She was nice, though, and taught me a lot."

"Would you teach me like she taught you?"

I froze. It felt like all the air in the entire house was pulled out, and I struggled to breathe.

When I didn't say anything, Harlee stood. "You said you had naughty dreams about me, Brax. I want you to do whatever you did in those dreams."

My heart hammered in my chest. Who in the hell was this woman before me? For someone who wasn't very experienced, she was about to make me come in my pants.

The idea of being with Harlee was suddenly the only thing I could think of. Focus on. Being the first to make her come by oral sex. Holding that goddamn ponytail while she gave me head. My mouth watered just thinking about it.

But some small, sensible part of my brain managed to speak. "Harlee, do you even hear yourself?"

She looked confused. "You don't want me?"

I let a bark of laughter slip free as I walked over, took her hand, and placed it against my hard dick. "Christ, Harlee. *This* is how badly I want you. I'm so hard it hurts."

Her eyes snapped down to her hand, then she looked back up at me.

"You're Addie's best friend," I said. "She would kill me if I ever did anything to hurt you."

She grinned. "Then don't hurt me."

I closed my eyes because I knew—I *knew* that after tonight that was exactly what would happen. I could see the way she looked at me. This wasn't simply about me teaching her with no feelings involved.

Yet, when I opened my eyes, my breath caught in my throat, and I suddenly wanted Harlee more than I wanted air to breathe.

"Harlee, maybe you've had too much to drink and..."

My voice trailed off when she reached for her shirt and pulled it over her head, then quickly worked at getting her pants off. She stood before me in nothing but white lace panties and a matching bra.

I nearly dropped to the floor, my knees going weak at the sight of her. She was more beautiful than I could've ever imagined. Perfect in every single way. No woman had ever made my heart feel like it was about to pound out of my chest just from looking at her.

That should have been a loud warning signal. All I should do was make her come with my mouth, give her some pointers, then send her along.

Right. Like I had the power to do that now that I'd seen her nearly naked.

I tried to speak, but my throat was dry. My dick strained hard against my pants, and the look on Harlee's face told me she knew I was going to cave the moment she touched me.

"You're so beautiful," I finally managed to get out.

She smiled at me, and when I didn't move, she took a step toward me. She slowly lifted my shirt over my head, then ran her hands down my chest. I sucked in a breath from the feel of the heat of her hands and closed my eyes to keep from touching her back. I wanted to touch her so fucking badly.

It doesn't mean anything. It's been a long time. It's not her touch that's driving you insane.

When she started to unbutton my jeans, my head screamed at me to stop her. This was Harlee. *Harlee!* I cared about her, and I was terrified of what this would do to our friendship once we both came to our senses. At the same time, I realized I had never wanted someone so desperately. I wanted to be greedy. I wanted to take what she was so freely giving to me.

My dick sprang free, and she looked up at me with those big blue eyes. I took her hand and wrapped it around me. "You've touched a guy before, right?"

She nodded as she pulled her hand back, licked it in the most sensual way, then started to move it up and down my shaft. I hissed in a breath and closed my eyes, praying I didn't come.

"Brax, I want your mouth on me. Please."

That was the moment I knew I was truly in trouble—because the only thing I could think of was how much I wanted the woman standing before me.

It turned into one of the most amazing nights of my life. But little did I know how much everything would change between us once the sun came up.

Chapter Two

Brax
Eight Years Later

I looked out from the ferry and stared at the lighthouse that was coming into view. The nerves in my stomach told me I was about to prove myself right today, and I wasn't sure how I felt about that.

The moment I read in the gossip column that the anonymous Ms. Seaside thought the town of Seaside was founded in 1762 and not in 1763, I knew it was Harlee who was writing the articles.

During the single night we'd spent together so long ago, she'd told me all about her research on Seaside. That it had actually been founded in 1762, though everyone claimed it was 1763. Her love of history had been so obvious that night, and when she'd talked about our little town, it was clear how much she loved it here.

Sighing, I pushed the memory away.

I was so sure Harlee was Ms. Seaside that I'd tried to talk my sister Palmer out of searching for the writer's real identity. Luckily, Palmer was too busy falling in love with Mason Bryan to truly pursue Ms. Seaside...and that left me to poke around on my own.

The ferry slowed and started to make its way to the dock. I glanced around at the people onboard. Most were still in their cars, but there were a handful who had parked on the mainland, willing to endure the weather to walk around Lighthouse Island.

The island was a huge tourist spot in the spring, summer, and fall, but it was mostly locals who came out here in the winter—with the exception of a few tourists who weren't afraid to brave the cold. Plus, there was a bed and breakfast on the island that was one of the best in Maine.

The family who ran the ferry, the Anders, had built the bed and breakfast in the early 1800s, and to this day, it was still run by an Anders family member. Kris Jensen—that was her married name—currently ran the bed and breakfast. Her brother, Mitch, took care of the lighthouse, and her other brother, Ron, ran the ferries. Their grandfather had started the ferry with only one boat when he was a young boy. Now there was a whole fleet of them that ran twenty-four-seven during the summer, and with limited hours during the harsh winter months.

Kris's other brother, Chip, drove the pilot boat my brother-in-law Gannon worked on.

I shook my head. Both my brothers-in-law—Gannon and his brother, Brody—had crazy dangerous jobs.

I exhaled and headed to my truck before the ferry got to shore. I'd need to find a place to park it so no one getting off a ferry today would see it and know I was here.

After parking and grabbing a local map from the passenger seat of my truck, I headed into the cold to find a good spot to watch everyone getting off the next ferry. I had a hunch I'd see Ms. Seaside today. If the courier came on Wednesdays to pick up the column—something Palmer and I had previously learned—then that meant Ms. Seaside either came on Tuesday, or first thing Wednesday morning. I'd already tried coming on multiple Wednesdays with no luck, so I was betting that Tuesdays were her drop-off days.

I drew in a deep breath as I stood there and waited for the next ferry. My mind wandered back to the night Harlee and I had spent together. She'd been so damn adamant that she was right about the founding date of 1762 and everyone else was wrong. I couldn't help but smile as I thought about how we'd talked for hours before I'd made love to her again as the sun came up.

I closed my eyes and let the memory take me away.

"Brax?" Harlee whispered, tracing a pattern over my chest while I drifted back to sleep.

"Mmm?"

"Do you regret last night?"

My eyes shot open. "No. Do you?"

She rested her chin on the back of her hand that she'd laid flat on my chest. "Not at all. I've never felt this way before."

The pounding of my heart grew so loud, I swore I felt it in my ears. When I didn't say anything, her smile faded slightly.

Forcing a smile, I leaned up and kissed her forehead. "It was an amazing night, Harlee."

She sat up, covering herself. I didn't like that she felt she had to do so for the first time that night. "Will there be a next time?"

I wanted to say yes, but I couldn't make myself do it. It would be hard enough to walk away from her after the night we'd shared; I couldn't imagine trying to do it after spending more time with her. I wouldn't be able to.

"I thought it was only going to be last night."

The moment I saw the hurt pass over her face, I felt the knife go straight into my heart. I was doing the one thing I said I wouldn't do. Hurt her.

"Oh. Okay. Well, I need to be honest with you, Brax...I feel something for you. I felt it before last night, and now I feel it even more."

My breathing picked up. Please don't say you're in love with me. Please.

"What do you mean?"

She gave me a half shrug. "I really like you, Brax. And more than just in a friendship way."

I sat up, letting the sheet pool at my waist. How was I going to do this? I wasn't ready for these feelings. For love. Harlee was still in college. I was building a business. No...no. I couldn't do it.

Or could I?

Those blues eyes of hers searched my face. It would have been so easy to tell her yes, I wanted more. But I wasn't sure how much more I could give her. And that wasn't fair to her...or me.

"Harlee, the last thing I would ever want to do is hurt you. Last night was beautiful, and I'll cherish the memories for the rest of my life."

Her eyes pooled with tears before she quickly got off the bed and walked out of my bedroom.

"Harlee!" I called out as I jumped out of bed. I reached for a towel and wrapped it around my waist before I found her in the living room, frantically getting dressed. "Harlee, please don't do this."

She pulled her shirt on and stopped. "Don't do what, Brax? Feel like a whore?"

I flinched. "Do you think that's how I treated you last night?"

She slipped on her tennis shoes and looked up at me, regret for the words she said clearly in her voice. "Of course not. I'm angry."

"Harlee, princess...I never promised anything."

She let a sob slip free as she walked over and grabbed her purse. "I know you didn't. But I thought maybe you felt the same thing I did."

I looked away, too afraid that if she looked into my eyes, she'd know exactly how I felt.

She sighed. "Right. Well, I need my car, so if you don't mind giving me a ride back to the bar...or I could call Addie..."

I shook my head. "No. Give me a second to get dressed."

I went back to my room, got dressed, and then found Harlee waiting in my truck. The entire drive back to the Sea Dog, she stared out the window. Every now and then I heard her sniffle, but I wasn't sure what I should say.

Once I pulled into the parking lot next to her car, I softly said her name.

"Harlee."

"Thanks for the lessons, Brax. I'll be sure to put them to good use."

She couldn't have made a more direct hit to my heart if she'd tried.

She slammed the door to my truck, and I watched as she slipped into her car, pulled out of the parking lot, and drove away.

And just like that, our friendship was never the same again.

It had taken Harlee six months after she'd returned home from college to even look at me, let alone speak to me.

I shook the memories away. All they did was make my heart ache and my mind replay every regretful word I'd said to her. I had been so damn confused at the time, not to mention scared.

"It's in the past, Brax," I mumbled to myself.

The wind started to blow harder, and a chill rushed down my spine. I wrapped my coat tightly around me as I stood off to the side of the ferry landing on Lighthouse Island. Maybe Tuesday wasn't the right day. Maybe I hadn't come early enough on Wednesdays?

Watching the small group unload from the ferry, I looked for the faces of the guys who I suspected were runners for *The Chronicles*. I knew the lighthouse might play a part in all of this after Harlee had mentioned it to one of my sisters. I wasn't sure if it was a slip on her part...or a decoy, perhaps. Either way, I was hell bent on finding out the truth. I wasn't going to stop until I confirmed my suspicions about who in the hell Ms. Seaside was.

As of yet, I hadn't seen anyone who looked familiar on the few Wednesdays I'd been there. It would have been easy to give up, but I wasn't the type to quit. So here I was, waiting by a group of trees, holding up a map to hide my face, and acting like a tourist.

A group of people walked off the ferry who all appeared to be together. They moved toward the small museum that was housed on the island. One person—a woman—stepped out of the group and started to make her way up the path that led directly to the lighthouse overlooking Penobscot Bay. She had a hood on, so I couldn't see the color of her hair or her face, since she was looking down at her feet.

Something about her was familiar, so I kept my eyes on her instead of looking back at the small stream of people still disembarking from the ferry. January wasn't a busy time of year, but there were still a few brave souls who came over to visit the lighthouse and the museum.

I pulled my hat down some and started to walk in the general direction of the woman while making it seem like I was going to take another path. Her pace picked up as she drew farther away from the group, and I narrowed my eyes as I watched her.

What was the pull that made me follow this one woman? Maybe it was just because Ms. Seaside was a woman—or so I thought.

Glancing behind me, I saw another small group of people making their way toward the lighthouse. They were close, so if she looked behind her, I was hoping she would think I'd simply pulled ahead of the group I was with, and that I wasn't actually following her.

We all continued the small hike up the hill toward the lighthouse.

As the woman made her way closer to the entrance, I hung back a bit and stepped off the path, making sure I had a clear view of the entrance so I could see her when she came back out. I nearly fell twice attempting to get through the damn snow and out of sight, but I was tucked into the trees enough that I didn't think she'd see me.

When she got to the door of the lighthouse, she paused, then turned and glanced around before stepping inside.

The second I saw her face, my jaw dropped.

"Holy shit," I whispered. "I knew it!"

I nearly fell back on my ass as my suspicions became truth.

"Harlee. It's Harlee."

Stumbling out of the wooded area, I found my way back to the path and quickly headed to my truck. I wasn't sure why I was so surprised to have my suspicion confirmed. I'd known it was her from that one article. Or maybe in a small way, I'd *hoped* it was her. Knowing it was Harlee who'd been taking anonymous jabs at me in the paper seemed to make sense. After all, I could justify her anger. Had it been some random woman doing it, that would've pissed me off.

One simple slip was all it took for me to figure it out. That slip about the year the town was founded. How long would it be before everyone else started to put two and two together? Or she messed up and put something personal in the column? So many people adored Ms. Seaside...but I was positive just as many didn't.

I shut the door to my truck and leaned my head back against the seat. If it was revealed that Harlee was Ms. Seaside, so many people would be devastated. *Harlee!* The sweet do-gooder whom everyone in town called the Princess of Seaside. The person who put on the parades, the fundraisers, the Christmas caroling.

She was the fucking gossip column writer. For months she'd been writing about everyone in Seaside. She'd been writing about my sisters. They'd be devastated if they knew Harlee was Ms. Seaside. Hell, if I was being honest with myself, I wasn't entirely sure how I felt about it either.

Nothing she had written was malicious, but it was still fucked up.

"Jesus Christ, Harlee. What in the hell were you thinking?" I said as I shook my head.

Turning on my truck, I tried to decide if I should take the next ferry or if I should wait. The last thing I wanted was for Harlee to see me and ask why I was here. As far as she knew, I had already given up my search for Ms. Seaside.

I pulled out and backed into another space. It was far enough away that she probably wouldn't see me, but I'd still be able to see when she got back on the ferry. The one she'd taken over to the lighthouse hadn't pulled out yet, as it was waiting for more people to get on.

It didn't take long before I saw Harlee rushing down the path to the ferry. I watched as she made her way up the steps and into the heated cabin. Ten minutes later, the ferry took off back to Seaside.

I wasn't sure how long I sat there, still stunned. A part of me had really hoped I'd be proven wrong and that it wouldn't be her. But it was—and I had to decide what in the hell I was going to do with that information. Confront her? I wasn't sure that was the right thing to do.

"Now what?" I asked myself while I watched the next ferry head over to the island. After everyone disembarked, I drove up and slowly pulled onto the ferry and turned my truck off. I wasn't the least bit bothered as the temperature in my truck got colder and colder. I'd gone numb as soon as I saw Harlee's face. For a moment, I questioned why I hadn't gone back to the lighthouse to look for what she'd dropped off, but I knew Harlee had been the last person in there before Mitch Anders locked it up for the night.

Right before we pulled up to the dock in Seaside, my phone went off. I glanced down and read the text.

Sutton: Harlee is planning a town-wide Valentine's Day dance the weekend before V day. She asked Mom to borrow those hearts we used at the grill last year. Do you mind swinging by the house and getting them out of the attic before Dad tries to find them?

A slow smile spread across my face as a plan formulated in my mind.

Me: I don't mind at all. I'll head over right now and get them.

Day of Valentine's Day Party

As soon as I walked into the large room at the community center, I saw Harlee. She was dressed in a red dress that hugged her curvy body perfectly. Her brown hair was piled up on her head in some fancy updo, or whatever they called it. Curls fell randomly around her neck and face. She wore a little makeup, but not much. She didn't need makeup at all, if you asked me. But it was the red lips that had my dick jumping in my pants.

When she walked, I saw the high slit and her exposed leg, and I let out a low groan. I knew what my dreams would be about tonight—and who would be starring in them. I couldn't count how many times I'd woken up with my dick in my hand after having a dream about Harlee. I always had to finish myself off so I could get some sleep. All the while thinking of her.

Harlee looked around the room and caught my eye. I gave her the slightest nod before I strolled over to the bar. I could feel her eyes on me the entire time, and it took everything I had not to smile.

I ordered a drink and waited patiently. I knew she wouldn't rush over. No, not my Harlee. She'd make me sit here and wait.

Earlier that morning, I'd sent her a text saying I had to speak to her and that it was urgent. She'd texted back to ask what it was about. When I'd said I had some news about Ms. Seaside, I quickly saw the dots bouncing on my cell phone. We'd agreed to talk here, at the dance, since I'd given her some lame excuse about why I couldn't meet her beforehand.

From the corner of my eye, I saw Harlee heading to the bar. She walked up next to me and ordered a shot. I smiled as I finished off my drink.

"Are you free right now?" I asked.

With a quick glance at me, she forced herself to smile. "I am."

"Great. Head out the exit toward the hall with the bathrooms. Third door down on the left is unlocked. I'll meet you in there."

"Is this necessary, Brax?" she asked with a frustrated expression on her face.

"I wouldn't have said I needed to speak to you if I didn't think it was."

Sighing, she turned and headed toward the exit. I finished off my beer, glanced around the room to make sure no one was watching, and followed Harlee in the same direction.

Once I stepped into the hall, I sped up and found her pacing in the small office. I shut the door, and before I could say a word, she spoke first.

"What in the hell is this all about, Brax?"

"I told you. Ms. Seaside."

"What about her?" Harlee asked, her voice dripping with boredom. I knew better. She wanted to know what I knew, no matter how blasé she acted.

"I've been doing some snooping the last couple of months."

Harlee's eyes widened slightly, though had I not been paying extra attention to every detail of her face, I might not have noticed.

"You're not the only one," she said. "In fact, I thought you and Palmer were both working on trying to figure out who it is."

I laughed. "In case you haven't noticed, Harlee, Palmer is a bit busy falling in love."

She sighed and looked away. "I've noticed."

The hint of sadness in her voice almost made me call this whole plan off.

Almost.

"I told her I was giving up the search...but then something happened."

Harlee snapped her head to look at me. "What do you mean?"

With a smirk, I waited a beat before saying, "I think I might know who it is."

She swallowed hard. "You...you do?"

I nodded. "I'm not sure, but Sutton—or maybe it was Addie—remembered you saying something about the lighthouse."

Her face went pale, and I internally fist pumped. One for me. Zero for Harlee.

"I went there on Tuesday a couple of weeks ago."

Harlee nodded, but I could tell it took everything in her to do it in a controlled manner. She tried to talk but her voice cracked, so she cleared her throat and tried again. "Okay, is that supposed to mean something? Tuesday?"

"I've been watching the staff and noticed the same few guys coming and going every Wednesday. So I followed one of them, and they went to the ferry and over to Lighthouse Island. I sat in the parking lot of that ferry drop off for a month, sunup to sundown each Wednesday."

Harlee let out a disbelieving laugh. "You really do want to find this person."

"I do. It's apparent the woman doesn't like me, and I'd like to have a little talk with her."

Harlee whispered, "A talk?"

I smirked. "Anyway, I must have missed her, or she doesn't go on Wednesdays."

She raised a single brow. "How do you know it's a *her*?"

I gave her a look that said she was crazy. "She signs it 'Ms. Seaside.'"

Shrugging, Harlee said, "Could be a way to throw people off."

With a thoughtful expression, I nodded. "Could be. But I hired someone to keep an eye on any woman who entered the lighthouse alone. They saw someone go in, then come back out within minutes after dropping something off. I'm pretty sure it's her."

"Brax," Harlee said, laughing, "that could be anyone. It's a tourist spot."

I decided to throw her off. "They followed her and saw her slip a piece of paper into a small crack in the wall near the steps that led up to the lights." I had no fucking clue *where* Harlee put the article for whoever picked it up. I was purely guessing.

I had to hand it to her, her face showed nothing. Probably because I'd totally made it all up and that wasn't what Harlee did at all.

"Okay, that could be something," she said. "But why are you telling me this? Why was it so important for you to talk to *me*?"

"You're on the inside, Harlee."

She sighed and crossed her arms. "I've said it a million times, Brax: I have no idea who it is."

"Right, but you can help me find her."

"You want me to help you?"

"Find her," I said with a nod.

She stood there for a minute staring at me. I could see the wheels turning in her head, and I knew the moment something occurred to her.

I knew Harlee Tilson better than she knew herself. I had been banking on her coming up with an idea to throw me off, and I was almost a hundred percent positive she just had. She would agree to help me, if only to keep me from finding out she was actually Ms. Seaside.

Christ, can it really be this easy?

Turning, she paced a couple of times before facing me again. "I have a few ideas about who it could be."

I raised a brow. "Okay."

She lifted her chin and pulled her shoulders back. "But this isn't the time or place to be doing this. I'll text you tomorrow morning, and we can sit down together and come up with a game plan."

Hook. Line. And sinker. Oh, Harlee, this is going to be fun.

Smiling, I replied, "Sounds good."

Harlee cleared her throat. "Now, if you'll excuse me, I have a party to host and a special announcement coming up."

Turning on her heels, she walked to the door and nearly ran out of the room after opening it.

I counted to twenty and then followed her.

Harlee quickly blended into the crowd, plastering on that Princess of Seaside smile of hers that made everyone putty in her hands. Even me.

I went back to the bar and asked for a shot.

The bartender, a pretty blonde, slid me the drink. I turned to find Harlee watching me. I lifted the shot, winked, and then downed it.

Chapter Three

Harlee

Tossing and turning from my right side to my left, I squeezed my eyes shut. Then I rolled onto my back and let out a soft scream. I sat up, threw the covers off, and swung my legs over the side of my bed. One quick look at the clock on my phone told me it was five in the morning. With a groan, I stood and stumbled to the bathroom. After a quick splash of water on my face, I stared at myself in the mirror.

"I look like shit." I closed my eyes and tried to take in a few deep breaths. The weight of guilt had been growing heavier and heavier as the weeks turned into months, and then into almost two years of writing as Ms. Seaside. At first it was only meant to be something fun that would draw people back into the paper. I was fresh out of college and eager to please my father. When I pitched the idea to him, he was thrilled. And when it became a hit, he insisted I keep doing it. I had tried to step away several times, only to have him talk me into continuing for a few more months. Those months quickly turned into years. The fact that I kept telling myself I wasn't really hurting anyone was fine—until it wasn't fine. The last year, the guilt had been weighing heavy, and I hated that I was so damn good at lying on the spot to cover up my connection to Ms. Seaside. And now Brax was hell bent on finding out who Ms. Seaside was. What a shit show.

The last thing I thought Brax was going to tell me last night was that he'd found out Ms. Seaside left her articles inside the lighthouse. His information about where she put them was completely wrong, but it was close enough to realize I needed to change my routine. And I needed to throw him off my trail until I could slowly fade Ms. Seaside away. At least, that was the plan—I just hadn't told my father yet.

It didn't take long for me to decide that if I helped Brax, I could easily throw him off the right track.

Despite my exhaustion, I smiled at myself in the mirror. It was a genius idea, if I did say so myself. Poor Brax. I was going to send him on one wild goose chase after another. It would be like taking candy from a baby. I'd feed Brax the wrong information, send him chasing after his own tail, and have a bit of fun while I was at it.

The first thing I needed to do was convince him that Ms. Seaside was on to him. That would be easy enough.

I headed back into my bedroom and picked up my phone. I sent Brax a text, figuring he'd have his phone on silent since it was so early in the morning.

Me: Do you want to meet at Seaside Grill this morning and put our intel together?

I couldn't help but giggle. He had no idea what was in store for him.

I was surprised when I saw the three dots start moving. He replied almost instantly.

Brax: You're up early. What's wrong? Can't sleep?

My heart dropped.

Me: So are you. And no problem sleeping on my end. I woke up to go for a run on the treadmill.

I closed my eyes and groaned at my impromptu lie. I didn't run, but I knew Brax did. If he asked me to go running with him, what was I supposed to do? I'd die a quarter of a mile in. I hated running. Unless it was to get the special edition chocolate mousse cheesecake that Seaside Bakery made every so often. Or if my life was in danger

31

of ending since some crazy person was chasing me with a knife or something.

Brax: Nice! I'm headed to the gym.

Me: Okay, well, do you want to meet up this morning?

I tried to push away the image of Brax working out. Sweating and grunting as he lifted weights.

"God, pull it together, Harlee Tilson!"

Brax: Sounds good to me. What time do you want to meet? I'm free all morning.

I rolled my eyes. "Of course, you are."

Me: Eight too early?

Brax: Not at all. See you then.

I chewed on my lip, trying to ignore the butterflies in my stomach at the thought of seeing him.

It didn't matter that once upon a time Brax had broken my heart; I still got butterflies when he smiled at me. My breath still caught in my throat when he walked into a room, and I still dreamed about our night together. It was one of those moments in your life that you wished you could do over.

It was both the best night of my life—and the worst.

The idea of working with Brax to uncover Ms. Seaside's identity was both terrifying and thrilling. It meant I'd be constantly reminded that he didn't see me as anything other than another notch on his belt. A reminder that I'd been too honest with him that morning after our night together, and he'd rejected me.

I had cried for days...maybe even weeks. Once I'd finally stopped having a pity party for myself, I'd vowed to never let another man make me feel that way again.

The hardest part was getting Brax out of my heart. Easier said than done. Oh, I'd dated and had even been in a serious relationship right out of college. I've had a few one-night stands and had learned how to take control of my own sexual desires. However, the heart wants what the freaking heart wants.

And mine, the stupid, lovesick fool that she was, wanted Braxton Bradley.

"Stupid, silly girl," I whispered as I dropped my phone on the bed and headed to my closet. Regardless of the words I'd said aloud, I knew I would spend the next hour figuring out what to wear for breakfast with Brax.

I pulled up and parked behind Brax's truck. He'd parked about half a block from his parents' restaurant, the Seaside Grill. The walk would give me a few extra minutes to calm my racing heart. I'd always been fine with facing Brax when I knew other people would be with us. Talking to him alone was going to be difficult. I'd spent the last few years making sure I wasn't ever alone with him.

"This will work, Harlee," I said out loud. "You can throw him off the trail. You've been doing this a long time, and Braxton is not going to be the one to take you down."

Brax's intel about Ms. Seaside slipping her article in a crack in the wall of the lighthouse was laughable. I actually put it in a secret compartment that only a handful of people knew about.

During my research on our little town, I'd run across a journal that the old lighthouse caretaker had kept. Mitch, the great-great-grandson of that lighthouse caretaker, had been the one to let me read it. He knew I was a huge history buff who craved learning anything related to Seaside. He hadn't read the journal himself, though, so he had no idea about the compartment.

Walker Anders had mentioned the compartment in his journal, including an explanation on how to find it. The only others who knew about it were my dad and our two couriers. Of course, even they didn't know I was Ms. Seaside. I simply told them when and where to pick up the article. The location changed every so often, though the lighthouse was the place I'd stowed my articles for the past two years. No one was the wiser.

That was until Braxton found out about it. Damn him. And damn Palmer for being so hell bent on figuring out Ms. Seaside's identity.

And damn me for going overboard with Ms. Seaside's fixation on the Bradley family. It had been so easy to do at first, and I'd told myself I would only mention them a few times. But they were such a huge part of my world, and the more I talked about them, the more guilty I became. There were so many nights I sat in my office and wondered why I wrote about the family so much. Maybe I was simply jealous I wasn't a part of the Bradley family, and this was in some weird-ass way how I dealt with it.

Sighing, I shook my head.

And damn *me* for even mentioning the lighthouse.

With a deep breath, I got out of my car and nearly fell on a patch of ice. Karma trying to come get me, no doubt. It was the least I deserved. Once I righted myself, I started for the restaurant.

The bell above the door rang as I walked in, and I glanced around until I found Brax sitting in a booth at the very back of the restaurant. I started to take off my scarf, hat, and gloves as I made my way over to him.

He looked up when I got closer.

With a frown, he said, "You look like you haven't slept in days."

I took off my coat and hung it on one of the hooks attached to each side of the booth. "And you look like someone who…"

Oh, dear God, I don't have a comeback. I always have a comeback when it comes to Braxton. Always. What in the heck is wrong with me?

Brax tilted his head, waiting for my reply. When I didn't say anything, he asked, "I look like someone who *what*?"

I waved him off as I slid into the booth and picked up the menu. "It's too early for this, Brax."

"You're going to let that go without a snappy remark?" Brax asked.

Before I could reply, Ruby approached. If I thought it wouldn't make me look like a total nutcase, I'd jump up and kiss her for her impeccable timing.

"Morning, Harlee, sweetheart. You want your regular coffee?"

Smiling up at her, I replied, "Yep, black, please."

She· nodded like I wasn't telling her anything new, because I wasn't.

"Have you ordered yet?" I asked Brax.

"No," he replied with a shake of his head. "But feel free, I know what I want."

Ruby looked at me. "The usual?"

My stomach took that moment to make it known that I hadn't eaten since lunch yesterday. I had been so busy preparing for the dance, and after my little meeting with Brax, I'd lost my appetite altogether. "I'll take the Seaside breakfast combo."

"You're going to eat all of that?" Brax asked.

I narrowed my eyes at him as I heard Ruby whisper, "You've gone and messed up now, Braxton Bradley."

He looked at her, then at me, clearly confused.

I leaned back and placed my hands flat on the table. "Are you saying I'm fat?"

His eyes went wide. "I beg your pardon?"

"Do you have an issue with my breakfast?" I asked, folding my arms across my chest.

"No." He shook his head, his eyes bouncing from me to Ruby— who also looked a bit peeved on my behalf. "I just meant it's a lot of food, and if you wanted to split it..."

"I don't want to split it, but thank you."

Brax blinked a few times before glancing at Ruby. He tried to smile at her but seemed a bit off balance.

Good. That was exactly where I wanted him.

"I'll take two eggs over medium, rye toast, and a cup of fruit," he said.

"You want the yogurt with that?" Ruby asked.

He nodded. "Yes, thank you."

She smiled at both of us. "Orange juice with your meals?"

Brax and I both answered "yes" at the same time.

Ruby gave us a wink and then headed off to put our order in, leaving me and Brax alone for the second time in twenty-four hours. I felt the urgent need to fidget in my seat, but I didn't dare. The last thing I wanted was for him to think I was bothered by sitting alone with him.

"Okay, so I brought my list. Do you have yours?" he asked as he reached into his pocket, took out a piece of yellow paper, and put it on the table.

"Yep, I've got it right here." Reaching into my purse, I pulled out a list I'd made around two in the morning when I couldn't sleep. I probably should have looked at it once more before I gave it to him. Lord knows who I'd written down. I'd been so exhausted at the time. Still was.

"May I?" he asked, pointing to it.

I pushed it across the table. "Have at it. May I look at yours?"

He nodded as he took my paper and opened it. The last thing I wanted to do was look at his list, but I went through the motions of taking it and slowly unfolding the paper. He stayed quiet, focused on my list, and I peeked over to see his reaction to the names.

"Mrs. Pritcher, our librarian?" he asked with a choked laugh.

I nodded.

His eyes jerked up to meet mine, but before he said anything, he quickly glanced around the restaurant. "And Ruby? You honestly think *Ruby* could be the one writing the articles?"

I gave him a one-shoulder shrug. "Why couldn't it be her?"

"When would she have the time?"

Leaning in closer, I lowered my voice. "Think about it, Brax. She's here every day and hears *everything*. All the gossip. And she probably has people planted all over the place, listening."

His brows pulled in tight. "I don't think it's Ruby."

"Just keep reading, will you?" I said as I glanced down at his list and held my breath, waiting to see my name on it. I took one quick look and was relieved when it wasn't there.

"You have Kimberley on the list," he said. "Palmer said she isn't smart enough to put together something like the column."

I laughed. "Please. She plays stupid simply to get attention."

He stared at me for a moment as if he was letting that bit of information soak in before he went back to my list. "I've got Mr. Hall on my list too."

I internally fist pumped. That would buy me some time, for sure. If he suspected Mr. Hall, I could send him on all kinds of goose chases.

"Kim Werther?" I nearly shouted when I saw the name of one of the most active moms in Seaside on Brax's list. She was into everything, but for all the right reasons.

Brax looked up at me. "What?"

"You honestly think Kim Werther is Ms. Seaside?"

He nodded. "Why not?"

I opened my mouth to say she was too busy being a stay-at-home mother and PTA mom to even bother with silly gossip, but I stopped myself. Now that I let myself think about it, she was actually a great person of interest. She was everywhere, volunteering for everything, and most likely heard a lot of gossip from the other moms.

I shrugged. "I don't see it being someone like her."

"And again, why not?"

"She's a *mom*."

Brax laughed. "What does that have to do with anything? All her 'seagulls' are probably the gossiping moms she hangs out with."

"She wouldn't have time to write a column like that. Think about it."

Looking up in thought, he finally nodded. "Okay, scratch that one off my list."

I dug around in my purse for a pen and found a red one. I drew a line across her name and then read on.

Mrs. Pritcher. Why had he made a big deal about her being on my list when she was on his? "You have Mrs. Pritcher on yours too!"

He smiled. "I was mad that you thought of her as well. She's the one person no one would suspect."

"Totally," I said as I went back to the list—and nearly choked on my own tongue when I saw the next name.

Melinda Tilson.

My head shot up. "My mother, Brax? Are you *serious*?"

He glanced up at me. "What? It's possible."

I dropped back in my seat. "My mom? You honestly think she's Ms. Seaside?"

"Anyone could be at this point, Harlee." He gave me a pointed look. "Even you."

That made me sit up straighter. "Oh yeah, like I could get away with it."

He tilted his head and studied me before nodding. "You're right. I don't think you could do it."

My mouth fell open. "I beg your pardon. And why couldn't I?"

Brax sighed. "Do we have to get into this now, Harlee?"

"Yes. Yes, we do, Braxton. Why couldn't I be Ms. Seaside?"

He smiled. "For starters, you're too nice. You're not called the Princess of Seaside for no reason, princess."

I nearly flinched at the endearment. Brax had called me that the night we'd slept together. Although, sleeping was the one thing we *hadn't* done.

He went on, watching me closely. "And I don't think you have it in you to write about people the way Ms. Seaside does."

I instantly felt a mix of hurt pride and overwhelming guilt. Hurt that he didn't think I had it in me to write the column, and guilt because I was gossiping about the people I loved. In my mind I had always separated Harlee from Ms. Seaside. We were two different people, but it was clear that was no longer the case.

"Whatever. But I can tell you there's no way it's my mother. I've never heard her utter a single bit of gossip." *Unlike her daughter.*

"Not once?" Brax asked with an amused smile.

"Nope, not once. I'm crossing her off your list."

He gave me a one-shoulder shrug. "Suit yourself, but I still think it could be her."

I huffed, then read the next name. "Laney Reynolds, the cashier at the grocery store?"

"Yep," he said without looking up.

"Maybe. I could see that."

"You honestly think it could be Trish?" Brax asked, pointing to another name on my list.

"Just because she works at the port authority doesn't mean any-thing. I've heard her gossiping during women's bible study. *Bible study*, Brax! Who gossips in the Lord's house?"

He gave me a sarcastic look, and I waved him off. "Fine, they all do. But I still think it could be her. She knows everyone."

"It's a small town, Harlee. We all know each other."

I ignored him and went back to his list.

He laughed as he said, "Olivia Newman?"

I nodded. "She's top of my list."

"No, she's down at the bottom."

Rolling my eyes, I said, "Figuratively. I mean, I have a feeling it's her. Call it a gut instinct."

Brax stared at me for a beat too long.

"What?" I asked.

He shook his head and softly said, "Nothing. It's nothing."

Ruby came over with our food, and we gave each other our lists back. We ate in silence for a few minutes before Brax said, "What about Joyce Miller?"

"The music teacher?" I asked with a giggle.

"Yeah. I see her chatting all the time with Mr. Hall. How do we know she doesn't get her info from him, or maybe he's one of her... *seagulls*." He snarled his lip. "That's so stupid."

I cleared my throat to hide my sudden irritation. "What is?"

"The way she writes the whole column. *I've got my ear to the docks. A little seagull told me.* And how she calls everyone her little fishes. She clearly isn't a very educated person."

I nearly broke the glass I'd picked up, my orange juice sloshing inside.

Easy, Harlee. Calm down, he has no idea he's talking about you. Deep breaths.

"That's a little mean, isn't it?"

He looked up at me like I'd said something insane. "Mean? Mean is writing an article about me and calling it 'master baiter.' *That* was mean. Do you know how many of my friends sent me jokes about that?"

I took a bite of toast to hide my smile.

"Weeks, Harlee. For weeks that shit went on. Fucking Brody kept sending me how-to videos on safely jacking off nearly every damn day."

I lost the battle and started to laugh. "How to masturbate?"

"Yes! The bastard."

"Well, I think she's kind of clever with the titles she makes up."

He finished chewing, then set his fork down and took a drink of juice before he asked, "And you're not bothered by the way she takes digs at you for being single?"

I shrugged. "Nope, not at all."

"Well," he said with a sigh, "you're a better person than me. It bugs the hell out of me when she writes about me or my family. She seems to love writing about the Bradleys." He paused for a moment and then looked at me. "Maybe it's because she's close to us."

My entire body shivered, and I prayed Brax hadn't noticed. "What do you mean?"

"Think about it. This Ms. Seaside sure seems to know a lot about my family, and she writes about us often. Why is that?"

Because their best friend is the jerk writing the articles? That was what I wanted to say, but I didn't have the nerve. "Maybe because your family is so well known in Seaside, and with all three Bradley sisters finding love, it gives Ms. Seaside a lot of material?"

A small part of me realized something in that moment. Had I been jealous of Addie, Sutton, and Palmer? Was that why I'd been so focused on them? The thought made me queasy.

He frowned. "Fine, I'll give you that."

I put my napkin down on the table, trying to push the guilty feelings away. "Besides, she doesn't *only* write about your family. Did you see what she wrote about Terri and Tim Hassle? I mean, it sure did bring business to their bed and breakfast, but my goodness."

"Oh yeah, the whole orgy thing she hinted at. Honestly, I don't think she was far off. I like Terri and Tim, but they definitely give me orgy vibes."

"Right?" I said with a giggle.

Brax looked at me and smiled. "This is nice, Harlee. For once, we're not throwing jabs at each other."

I returned the smile and winked. "Don't get too comfortable with my cease-fire."

He smiled, but it didn't reach his eyes. "Noted."

"Who's paying?" Ruby asked as she brought the check over.

Brax pointed to me. "That would be her, since she invited me."

I snarled at him. "Only because you dragged me into this little chase of yours."

"What chase?" Ruby asked.

Brax and I both froze, then looked at each other before looking back at Ruby. "We're trying to find out who Ms. Seaside is," Brax finally admitted.

Ruby nodded, put the check down, and then took our plates. "Have fun with that."

When she walked away, I looked at Brax.

"She," he said as he took my pen and opened up his list again, "just moved to my number one spot."

Chapter Four

Brax

The Seaside Chronicles

February 14, 2023

Rip Tide — Special Edition

Seasiders,

My fishes, I know I don't normally do two special editions in one week, but news on the docks is that we have a shark circling the waters of Seaside.

Take caution, dear shark, you may want to find other waters to feed in.

Fair winds and following seas!

Ms. Seaside

I couldn't wipe the smile off my face as I read the special edition gossip column. Picking up my cell phone, I pulled up Harlee's number. What I was about to do was going to take some serious acting skills on my part. Hitting her number, I waited for her to answer.

"Hello?" she said.

"I think it really *might* be Ruby!"

"And good morning to you as well, Brax. Is this going to be a thing in our newfound friendship?"

"What do you mean?"

"This calling me and shouting out random things?"

I fought the urge to laugh. Damn, she was good. I had to hand it to her. "Harlee, did you see the special edition today?"

She feigned disinterest. "Yes, I saw it."

"It was a warning—to *us*. I think you were on to something when you wrote Ruby's name down."

Laughing, she added, "Or a warning to *you,* since you've been the one digging around."

"I have a partner now, remember?"

With a harrumph, she replied, "Oh, that's right, how could I forget."

"You're not a morning person, are you?"

I was pretty sure she growled. "Why do you think it's Ruby?"

"Because I set her up."

There was a moment of silence before she asked, "You set her up how?"

"By telling her that we were looking for Ms. Seaside. So, she waited a couple of days and then issued this warning. It's so obvious, I don't know how you don't see it."

There was a noise in the background like the sound of a door shutting.

"Are you at work?" I asked.

"Uh, no. I'm at home. That was Thomas. He just left."

An instant rush of jealousy nearly knocked the breath out of my lungs. "Thomas?"

"Yeah."

"Are you two, um...back together or something?"

Harlee let out a bitter laugh. "Hardly. He stopped by to pick up a few things he'd left here."

I nodded even though she couldn't see me. The hardest thing I'd ever had to do was watch one of my best friends dating the girl I was…

I was what? What *were* my feelings for Harlee? I had tried to deny them for so long, I wasn't even sure what they were anymore. I knew I'd hated seeing them together. Truth be told, I hated seeing her with *anyone*. But, at the end of the day, I was the one who'd pushed her away, and I had no right to be upset about any man she chooses to be with.

"Brax?"

"Yeah, I'm still here. Sorry."

"Is…is everything okay?"

I cleared my throat and pushed away the image of Thomas and Harlee together. "Yep, everything's fine. I got a text, and it distracted me."

"Okay, so back to Ruby. You feel like you set her up and she took the bait?"

"Exactly. I think we should concentrate on her first."

Harlee let out a breath. "Okay, if that's what you want."

Something was off. Harlee was being too…agreeable. "That's it? You're not even going to argue with me about it?"

"Nope. If you think it's Ruby, let's figure out a game plan."

I ran my fingers through my wet hair. I'd gotten out of the shower right before going out to pick up my paper. "One of us needs to follow her."

"Psh. Have fun with that."

"Me? Why does it have to be me?"

"Because you're the one who wants to find out who Ms. Seaside is, Brax."

"If my memory serves me right, you also want to find out who she is. Or have you changed your mind?"

Harlee paused, and I could practically hear her thinking. "No, I haven't changed my mind. I'm sorry. I'm just…not myself this morning."

"You're sure everything's okay? Did Thomas do or say something to you?"

"No."

As much as I dreaded her answer to my next question, I asked it anyway. "Are you upset that you're not together anymore?"

She laughed once more. "I'm not the least bit upset about that. Thomas was a nice distraction for a while, and that's it."

It felt like someone had kicked me in the gut, but I ignored it. "Distraction from what?"

She exhaled, sounding so tired. "My loneliness."

My legs almost dropped out from under me. I wasn't sure what I had been expecting Harlee to say, but that certainly wasn't it.

Before I had a chance to reply, she beat me to it. "Ignore me—the day is already starting off badly."

"That's okay. Are you free for lunch today?"

"No, sorry. I've got to run some reports for my dad and start on the marketing plan for spring."

Smiling, I decided to go in for the kill. "Okay, well, I think I'm going to head on out to Lighthouse Island. Maybe I can catch a glimpse of Ruby, or whoever it is who's dropping off the stories."

"It can't be Ruby, Brax. Think about it. She works every day at the grill. There's no way she could leave in the middle of the day and take the ferry over to Lighthouse Island."

"Maybe she has someone else doing it for her. I'm going to go stake it out."

I could hear rustling before Harlee finally spoke. "You know what, my dad just sent me an email. He doesn't need the reports until next week, so it turns out I'm free all day. Sutton doesn't need me at the store until later this afternoon, and I can work on the marketing plan then. It's super slow this time of year anyway."

This was going to be too freaking easy. "Great, I'll stop by and pick you up in thirty minutes, if not sooner."

"Wait—what?"

I hit End and counted.

"One, two, three..."

When my phone rang with Harlee's number, I hit Ignore. "You can run, Harlee Tilson, but you can't hide."

Harlee flung open her door and stared at me with a surprised expression on her face. I'd made it to her house in fifteen minutes.

I plastered on a huge smile. "Good morning. Are you ready?"

She blinked a few times as I pushed past her into the house. It was strange that I'd never been in her house before. She'd been in mine. The night we'd slept together.

Harlee's house was a charming three-bedroom, Nantucket-style home. It was only a block away from the waterfront. The inside was a typical New England cottage built in the early 1930s.

"I've never seen your place," I said, glancing around.

She shut the door and slowly shook her head.

When you walked into the house, there was a small area that had a coatrack right at the door and a large, oversized chair at the window. Next to it was a small bookcase loaded with books. Past the foyer, the space opened immediately into a cozy living room on the left, and a dining room on the right. A few family pictures were placed about the rooms, as well as some paintings and moose decorations sprinkled in. I'd forgotten that Harlee had a thing for moose. The color scheme was mostly white, with splashes of light blue here and there courtesy of pillows or blankets. Even her curtains were white, and they tied onto the rods.

The whole place had a very beachy-type feel. Original hardwood floors added to the charm of the house. When I glanced back into the living room, I saw the original wood-burning fireplace—or at least it looked to be original.

"This place is really cute, Harlee. I like it. Is that the kitchen?" I asked as I headed toward it.

"Um, yeah. Please, feel free to show yourself around, Brax," she stated dryly.

The kitchen was actually a good-sized space. An island sat in the middle, and the cabinets on the lower section were painted a light blue while the uppers were white.

"I like the beadboard on the cabinets here." I pointed to the island.

She crossed her arms over her chest and stared at me. "You didn't really come here for a house tour, did you?"

I glanced over my shoulder at her and winked. "If you're offering, I'd love a tour."

She let out a long, loud exhale. "Fine. This is the kitchen, you saw the living room and the dining room. This way is the guest bedroom." I followed her down a small hall. "Bathroom here. And bedroom here."

Nodding, I stepped into the guest room. "Nice. It's huge. I really didn't think it would be this big. How many bedrooms do you have?"

"Two down here, and I converted the attic into my office."

"Nice. Where's your room?"

Her cheeks turned pink. "You don't need to see my bedroom, Brax."

"I may not *need* to see it, but I want to."

Heading back down the hall, I ignored her when she told me to stop as I opened the door at the end of the hallway.

A king-size antique bedframe and bed sat in the middle of the room. A matching antique dresser was on the far wall, and two small bedside tables, which also appeared to be antique, sat on either side of the massive bed. I glanced around and noticed the beadboard on the ceiling and board-and-batten. The latter was painted the same blue that was in the kitchen, while the upper half of the walls were white.

"This is really nice, Harlee."

"Okay, you saw my bedroom, now let's go."

"What about the bathroom?" I made my way toward it.

"Braxton, no!" she shouted as she shot forward and attempted to grab my arm, tripping over a small rug.

I reached out to help steady her. "Jesus, Harlee. Are you hiding a dead body in the tub or something?"

Her eyes widened in horror. "Worse!"

It was my turn to look surprised. "Is Thomas still here?"

She pulled her head back as she replied, "What? God, no!" Then she tilted her head and stared at me. "Did you think he'd still be here? Is that why you came over so quickly?" A suspicious expression grew on her face. "Were you bothered at the idea of him being here?"

I let out a short bark of laughter. "Don't be ridiculous."

She tossed her hands up in frustration. "Then why are you here, Brax?"

"We're going to Lighthouse Island, remember?" Turning, I headed into the bathroom.

"Brax, please don't go in there. Ugh! *Stop!*"

I walked into the bathroom and was about to comment on the large space...when I saw what Harlee had been so worried about me finding...there, in all its glory, sitting on the bathroom sink.

A vibrator.

I raised my brows and turned to her. "Did I interrupt something?"

She shot me a look. "Yes, you did. Playtime."

My dick instantly went hard. "Playtime?"

She shrugged nonchalantly.

"Don't they say it's better to play with two instead of by yourself?"

Her eyes darkened, and I saw her attempt to swallow. She straightened and lifted her lips into a half smile. "Are you offering to join in on my playtime, Brax?"

Jesus, Mary, and all the saints above. I wanted to tell her yes. Hell yes. I wanted to pick up that vibrator and do all kinds of things to her gorgeous body. Things I had dreamed about for years. Instead, I leaned against the doorjamb and tried to calm my racing heart. What if it was Thomas's visit that had gotten her hot and bothered?

"And before you ask, I wasn't thinking of Thomas," she said.

That made me raise one single brow. Was she a fucking mind reader now? "Who were you thinking of then?"

Her eyes darted to my mouth then back up again. "A girl doesn't have to fantasize about a man to have an orgasm. My hands can do the job on their own and give me just as much pleasure as a man's."

It took everything I had not to react to that mental picture. "I don't know about that, Harlee. I bet I can do a far better job bringing you to orgasm with my hands and mouth than that thing can."

Her cheeks turned bright red, but she kept her mouth pressed into a tight line.

"Do you need to finish? I can wait."

She gave me a coy look. "Did you plan on standing there and watching me?"

God. Give. Me. Strength.

"Hey, if you can perform with an audience, I'm more than happy to wait for you right here while I enjoy the show."

She laughed, shook her head, and walked closer. I slowly inhaled when she stood before me, looking up at me with those big blue eyes. "The urge is gone now, unfortunately."

I felt the side of my mouth lift up slightly. "Why do I feel like that was an insult?"

She lifted up onto her toes and placed her mouth next to my ear, and I had to fight the urge to touch her. Her warm breath tickled my neck as she whispered, "Because it was, Braxton. Now get the hell out of my bedroom so I can get dressed."

Chapter Five

Harlee

Brax stared at me for the longest time before he pushed off the doorjamb and headed out of my bedroom. Once I heard the door softly click shut, I reached for something to hold myself up.

I brought my hand up to my chest, only to feel my heart pounding. I closed my eyes, swallowed hard, and slowly shook my head. "That was insane."

For some strange reason, I got the idea that Brax thought I'd been horny after Thomas's visit. Which was a joke. It was from hearing Brax on the phone. That gravelly voice. I was turned on from picturing him standing in his house, fresh from a shower, insisting he knew that Ruby was Ms. Seaside.

It was also from the idea that Brax wanted *me* to help him figure out this mystery...that he actually wanted to spend time with me.

Ever since that night so long ago, all we did was bicker with one another. When he'd first approached me about trying to find out who was writing the gossip column, I had initially panicked. But once the idea settled in, and I came up with a plan to throw him off his game, I got excited.

The thought of spending more time with Brax was both thrilling and a little sad at the same time. Sad because I still had feelings for the jackass, and normally I was fueled with rage when I thought of that night so long ago. Not lust. This whole renewed lust thing was more recent.

Glancing over at my vibrator, I couldn't help but chuckle. Good thing I had a stockpile of these babies. I had a feeling I'd need them with all the Brax time I was getting.

I put my vibrator in a side drawer with the others in my collection and quickly got dressed and ready. It was going to be a long day if we were heading to Lighthouse Island to wait on Ms. Seaside to show up. Little did Brax know, she'd be with him the entire time.

I wasn't worried about my article because I'd already changed the date, time, and location for the drop-offs. I could easily send the article to my father by email, but it wasn't worth the risk of someone stumbling upon it, nor was that as fun as the cloak-and-dagger game I had going on. Plus, anyone who was smart enough could eventually trace an email back to me. I couldn't have that.

So the new plan was simple. Dinner with my father and mother on Monday nights, and I'd give it straight to my dad when my mother wasn't paying attention. He liked that plan much better as well. He hated paying a runner extra money to head out to Lighthouse Island.

Pulling my hair up into a ponytail, I frowned. A part of me felt bad for Brax. He was going to be wasting so much of his time searching for Ms. Seaside. I met my gaze in the mirror and wrestled with my conscience.

For half a second, I actually thought about telling him that I was Ms. Seaside. But I knew the moment he found out, he'd never speak to me again. And that was not something I was willing to risk. No one could ever find out Ms. Seaside was me. In my mind I told myself I wasn't doing harm, but the idea that my closest friends and family would turn their backs on me made me shiver. So instead, I'd have to run Braxton all over Seaside on false leads.

With a shrug, I whispered, "Oh well. You shouldn't have broken my heart, Braxton Bradley. Revenge is a dish best served cold, after all."

As I made my way back to the living room where Brax was sitting on my sofa, scrolling through his phone, I worked to calm my racing heart and steady my breathing. Being close to him without anyone else around was doing strange things to me.

"Coffee?" I asked, making my way into the kitchen.

"I could use a cup."

"Have you eaten breakfast?" I grabbed a pod out of the basket and put it in my Keurig.

When he didn't answer, I turned to look at him. He was staring at me. One glance into those eyes and I was transported back to the night we'd spent together. He had the same look of hunger in them now as he did then.

Did Brax...want me? Surely not.

But then why was he looking at me that way?

With a tilt of my head, I asked, "What's wrong?"

He seemed to snap out of whatever trance he was in and mumbled, "Nothing. How about we swing by Maine Bakery instead? That way we can catch the early ferry and get right to the island."

"If that's what you want. Who's driving?"

Clearing his throat, he said, "I'll drive. Make sure you grab your hat and gloves in case we want to get out and walk around."

Letting out a groan, I replied, "I'm not really looking forward to this, you know. Please tell me we're not planning on sitting in your truck all day? It's freezing outside."

Brax led us through the house to where he'd hung up his coat. Putting it on, he said, "I would think you'd be desperate to find out who it is. She seems to be targeting you lately."

I liked how he ignored my question about the truck. I shrugged, then allowed him to help me put my own coat on. I tried to disregard the way it made my chest flutter when his fingers brushed the back of my neck as he draped my scarf around me. "I don't really care what she says about me. My dating life, or lack thereof, is none of her business."

Brax raised a single brow. "You don't care in the slightest?"

"Nope." Smiling, I asked as we stepped outside, "Does it bother you what she says about you?"

He threw his head back and laughed. "Hell no. I don't care what she says about me."

I folded my arms over my chest. He was such a liar. "Then why were you and Palmer so hell bent on finding her? And you still are, I might add."

He paused for a moment. "I just want to know who it is. The curiosity outweighs everything else. I have to admit, I was hoping she'd be young."

"Why?" I asked, now *my* curiosity was getting the better of me. Even though I knew I would regret asking.

He tossed me a wicked smile. "I do have a thing or two to prove to her."

My stomach did a little flip as my mind instantly went to all the things Ms. Seaside would *love* for Braxton to show her.

With a shake of my head, I whispered, "Stop that."

"What was that?" Brax asked.

"Nothing. I need coffee and food before I pass out."

Five hours.

Five hours we had been on Lighthouse Island, and I'd fallen asleep three times, only to have Brax yell out, "I think that's her!" One time, I sprang up so fast I was pretty sure I strained a muscle in my neck. And I was freezing. The bastard brought a blanket so he could keep his truck off most of the time, but it wasn't helping much. He'd even brought a Thermos of hot tea for me. The gesture was sweet, but I would never admit it to him.

"Come on, let's get out and take a walk up to the lighthouse."

I dropped my head back onto the seat with a groan. "Brax, no!" I didn't even care that I sounded like a five-year-old who wasn't getting her way. "I'm sick of sitting here. No one is coming, and I can't feel my toes."

He scanned the people walking off the ferry. "Yes, you can. I literally just turned off the truck, Harlee. I had the heat blasting for like thirty minutes. Besides, I have a feeling she'll be here. I know it."

I giggled. Oh, she was here all right.

"What was that?" Brax asked, clearly distracted as he peered through his binoculars.

"This is a waste of time. I already texted your mom, and she said Ruby works every Tuesday. It's not her, Brax."

"Fine, if it's not Ruby, then we'll find out who it is." He got out of his truck, grabbed his coat from the backseat, and shut the door.

"What did I do to deserve this?" I whispered to myself. "Oh, that's right. I spent the last several years gossiping about the people in the town where I grew up. If this isn't karma, I don't know what is."

I pulled my coat from the backseat and got out. Once I had my hat and gloves on, I followed Brax toward the lighthouse.

"Keep an eye out for anyone who's alone," he said.

I smiled reluctantly. Brax was totally getting into this, and I had to admit, it was kind of a turn-on to see this side of him. Goodness, when the man put his mind to something, he completely went after it.

A sudden pain hit my chest, and I couldn't help but feel sad that he never wanted *me* enough to pursue me so ardently. I quickly pushed that bullshit thought away.

"I still don't think you can be sure it's a woman." I looked down at the prints I was leaving in the snow, purposely trying to make a pattern with the way I walked. It was something I'd done since I was little.

"What in the hell are you doing?"

I slammed into Brax and nearly fell on my butt. "What?" I asked, confused. The heat from his hands on my arms surprised me. How could I feel his heat through so many layers of clothing?

"What...are you...doing?" He glanced back at the pattern I'd been making.

"I'm bored out of my mind, Brax! I want to go home to my warm house and have a bowl of chili."

He lifted his brows. "You made chili?"

I scrunched up my nose. "Well, no, but I could if you take me back home." I waggled my brows, hoping to entice him. "I'll even let you stay for dinner as long as you promise to sit in the corner and be quiet."

Brax shot me a dirty look, then let me go. "No, we're not leaving."

Stomping my foot like a child, I called out after him as he started to head up the hill toward the lighthouse, "Brax! Please? I want to go home!"

He ignored me and picked up his pace. I nearly ran to catch up, slipping every so often and having to steady myself. "I swear, if I fall and break an ankle or something, I will..."

My voice trailed off when I saw a woman throw her arms around Brax as she let out a scream of delight.

I stopped walking and watched the two of them while they spoke. There was something about the familiarity between them that made my stomach feel uneasy. The way he smiled at her. He hadn't smiled at *me* like that in years.

Brax turned, his smile dropping when he looked at me. "Harlee? What's wrong?"

Thinking I must have looked like an idiot standing a few feet away watching them, I plastered on a small smile and said, "I slipped and twisted my ankle. I need a minute or so to work it out."

Brax moved at light speed and came to a stop in front of me. "Are you okay?"

For a moment, I was too stunned by the concern in his voice to form any words. I simply nodded.

"Can you walk?"

"Um." I looked down at my two perfectly fine ankles and nodded. "All good now, I'm sure. Like I said, I just needed a second."

The woman approached us and stood next to Brax, looking at me with a perplexed expression. When our eyes met, I instantly knew who she was. I had detested her for years.

She was, after all, the only woman I'd ever known who'd been in a long-term relationship with Brax.

"Harlee Tilson, right?" she asked with a grin.

Brandi Larson. Ugh.

Of all the women in Seaside, why did it have to be her? She was the older sister of Mindi Larson, who worked for the justice of the peace. And she was Braxton's ex-girlfriend from high school. The one woman everyone thought he would end up marrying because they'd made such a cute couple. Once she'd left for college, though, she'd never looked back—which meant she'd left Brax behind like she did everything else. Addie had told me at the time that her brother hadn't seemed too heartbroken over Brandi leaving. It was the only thing that kept me from completely hating her.

Okay, not true—I still hated her. Maybe it wasn't a very grown-up way to act, but in that moment, I couldn't have cared less. I was allowed to be childish every now and then.

Lord, Harlee. You sound like a teenybop girl jealous over a rival.

If I had to pick, I'd rather see Brandi hugging Brax over Jennifer, his latest fuck buddy.

"Hi, Brandi, how are you?" I asked, giving her a sweet smile.

"Good! I'm great, actually. I just moved back to town."

"For good?" Brax asked.

"Yes! I'm going to be taking over the accounting at my daddy's tackle shop. I got tired of playing on Wall Street and decided it was time to move home."

I wanted to gag. "And what about your father being sick?" I asked.

She snapped her eyes to mine, and it was hard not to notice the flash of anger. "That's what I meant. I'm here to help my father, with him being sick and all, with…um…with…"

Brax raised his brows in anticipation while I folded my arms over my chest. Was she for real? She had no idea what was wrong with her own father? Maybe little Brandi came back to wait for an inheritance.

Harlee Tilson! That is not nice! Stop it!

"Chronic kidney disease?" I prompted, not even trying to hide the fact that I was appalled she didn't know what her own father suffered from.

"Right!" she said as she pointed to me. "I keep forgetting what it's called."

"And you worked on Wall Street? With people's money?"

Brax shot me a warning look, and I simply looked away while Brandi went on.

"He has to be driven in for some treatment each week."

"That would be called dialysis. You do know what *that* is, right?" I asked as I focused back on her.

Brax shot me yet another look that said to pull my claws back in, but I ignored it and smiled sweetly while I waited for Brandi to answer. Had she really graduated from Harvard?

"It cleans out his blood or something gross like that," she stated.

I could have said plenty to that, but it was her father, after all, and I liked Brandi's mom. I caught sight of her walking down to the ferry, not bothering to wait on her daughter. I felt sorry for Mrs. Larson, but I honestly couldn't stand Brandi, and it was solely because she'd once had Brax. More than once, actually. She was not simply one of his one-night stands. He obviously hadn't told Brandi after spending one incredible night together that he wasn't interested in her—like he'd told me.

Brax had gotten the one thing he'd wanted from me. Hell, he'd even warned me about men. How all they wanted was sex. But I'd been so sure there was something more between us that I'd stupidly admitted my feelings to him. Only to have him tell me that it was nothing more than a night he would always cherish and remember.

Always cherish, my ass.

I pushed the memory away and watched Brandi turn her attention back to Brax. She did a little bounce and clapped her hands together like she was back in high school and ready to start a cheer. Yeah, of course, she was also a stupid cheerleader.

There I go being petty again.

"Brax, we *have* to get together for old time's sake," she said. "We can have a little reunion!"

Ugh. Why don't you say 'come on over to my house so we can have sex?'

"I'd love that," he said with a soft smile.

I was reminded once again why I couldn't stand to be alone with Brax. He would never change. *Never.*

How many other women had he spent one night with, making them feel special and cherished, only to walk away without so much as a glance over his shoulder? But with Brandi, it had been different...it *would be* different...and that made my chest ache.

Stupid, silly heart.

Before I could hear them making plans to *catch up*, I blurted out, "I'll let the two of you talk about your little reunion. I'll meet you at the lighthouse, Brax. That is, if you still want to head up. You might want to go and catch up with Brandi now."

The jealous fifteen-year-old inside me almost added, *in the backseat of your truck.* Luckily, the adult woman in me—what little of her was coming out—kept that bit inside my head.

I started to walk off, but Brax quickly grabbed my hand and kept me from leaving. He looked back at Brandi and said, "Maybe we can get the gang together and meet up at the Salty Dog or something."

The smile on Brandi's face fell for one brief moment before she forced it back onto her face. Meanwhile, I was positive I wore a look of utter shock. That wasn't what I had expected Brax to say.

After bouncing her gaze down to his gloved hand around mine, Brandi looked up at me, then back to Brax. "Sure, sounds good. Well...my mom wanted to come over to see the lighthouse for some odd reason, and she's probably back on the ferry by now. I'll let you guys go. See you around, both of you."

I lifted my hand without even thinking and said, "Bye, Brandi."

I cleared my throat and attempted to pull my hand from Brax's, but he held on tighter. I probably could have slid my hand out of my glove if I really wanted to be free of him, but a small, very small—

okay, not that small—part of me liked having him clutch my hand like he was.

"See you around, Brandi," he said right before he started up the hill, giving me a small tug when I stayed rooted in my spot.

He didn't say a word as he marched us up to that damn light-house as if he was on a mission. It was going to close soon. I wasn't even sure it would still be open *now*.

But a minute later, I was inside the lighthouse where the original kitchen had once been. It was still a kitchen, actually, though more modernized for when the current keeper wasn't in the house next door and had to man the lighthouse.

I glanced at the box where I used to place my articles and smirked. If Brax only knew.

He started up the steps, and I pulled on his hand. "Where are you going? The upper levels are off limits. They're private."

Ignoring the rope to keep people out of the upper levels, he stepped over it, and the only thing I could do was follow. I felt like I was in high school again, sneaking into the school to TP our history teacher's classroom. Fun times, those were.

"Brax, this is still a very active lighthouse, and Mitch—you know, the keeper of the lighthouse who's over six-feet tall—will be here any moment. If he catches us—"

"It's automated now, Harlee. Mitch only comes up to this office when a storm is coming."

"It doesn't matter; he'll be back to lock up. He still lives in the attached house, Brax!"

He glanced over his shoulder and gave me a wickedly handsome smile. "I already told him I'd lock up myself."

I tripped over one of the winding staircase steps. "You did what?"

"Thought we could take a look around. When I called him earlier and told him I suspected Ms. Seaside was dropping off her articles here at the lighthouse, he was intrigued. Told me to take my time."

Panic filled my chest, even though I knew I wouldn't be using the lighthouse any longer. What if Brax hadn't asked me to join in on his quest to find out who Ms. Seaside was? What if he hadn't asked me to come with him and instead what if he would have come alone today and seen me entering the lighthouse? If he'd followed and caught me leaving an article? Or worse yet, found one of them afterward?

He glanced at me. "What's the matter? You look like you've seen a ghost."

All I could do was offer him a small smile and a shake of my head.

We were soon in a small room that housed antique furniture—which I suspected all the rooms contained. There was a bed, a small table, a sitting chair, and a bookcase. The level above us housed an office. The only reason I knew that was because I'd toured the lighthouse years ago in elementary school.

Not paying attention to the fact that Brax had stopped, I ran right into his back.

He suddenly turned and grabbed my upper arms...and stared down into my eyes with a look so full of desire and lust, I nearly felt my legs buckle.

"Did you *really* think I would want to hook up with Brandi again?"

I blinked in confusion as I tried to get my thoughts in order. With him touching me like he was, my brain was all discombobulated. "Wh-what?"

He slowly shook his head, then let his gaze drift to my mouth. "You thought I wanted to sleep with Brandi."

I forced myself to step out of his hold. "Well, I thought maybe your current fuck buddy—Jennifer, is it?—might be busy."

An odd expression crossed his face. Was that regret? *Nonsense, Harlee.* I highly doubted Braxton Bradley regretted anything he did.

"I don't have any fuck buddies, Harlee."

I felt a bark of laughter slip free, hating how bitter it made me sound. "Really? That's not what I witnessed on Thanksgiving."

He exhaled and pushed his fingers through his hair before he turned and walked to a small window that overlooked the bay. "I ought to show you right now," he muttered.

I swallowed hard, then asked in a voice barely above a whisper, "Show me what?"

He turned and leaned against the windowsill. A sexy smirk crossed his handsome face before he said, "That the only woman I want to fuck is standing in this room."

Chapter Six

Brax

From the expression on Harlee's face, I wasn't sure if she was angry or turned on by the crass words that came out before I had the chance to stop them. She'd made me so angry with how she'd acted toward Brandi. I'd never in my life seen her be so rude.

Or maybe I was angry with myself...because I was the one who'd brought it out of her.

When she finally spoke, I had to hold back a smile.

"Oh, that's really nice, Brax. Such a romantic way to express yourself. Do all the women fall at your feet with that one?"

I shrugged. "I'm simply telling you the truth the quickest way I know how, since you seemed to think I wanted Brandi instead."

Harlee tried to make herself look angry, but I could see the disbelief in her eyes. I could also see that she wanted me as much as I wanted her—and that made my entire body feel as if it was on fire. The sexual tension in the room was so thick, you could cut the air with a dull-bladed knife.

"A guy once told me that the only thing men want from women is sex. You proved yourself right, Brax. *Again*. If you think I'm going to lean over this bed and let you take me from behind simply because we're alone, you're wrong."

I raised a brow. "You don't want me deep inside of you, right here, right now?"

"Yes. I mean, *no!*" Harlee's cheeks turned bright red. "No, I don't want that. You. Whatever! You brute!"

She shook her head and let out a nervous laugh. Christ, she was beautiful. I wasn't sure what turned me on more. Her spit and fire, or the fact that she was so stunningly beautiful both inside and out.

"Is that what the women you sleep with enjoy?" she snapped. "A man who talks dirty and crude to them?"

"Was that crude? I didn't think so. I was being truthful. Is that not what you like, Harlee? An honest man who knows what he wants—and knows how to satisfy his lovers? You liked it the last time we were together."

Her mouth opened slightly before she clamped it shut.

I took a step away from the window. "Was Thomas a sweet and kind lover?"

She lifted her chin as she crossed her arms over her chest. "As a matter of fact, he was."

Man, she walked right into that one. "And that's probably why you got tired of him." I let my gaze wander over her body before I looked back at her face. "What you want is a man who tells you exactly what *he* wants. And no, I don't want to bend you over and fuck you from behind, Harlee. What I really want is for you to sit on the edge of that bed while I make you come with my mouth. I want to hear you scream my name like you did back then. I want to see if you still taste as sweet as you did before."

Harlee took a few steps back until she bumped into the bed, letting out another bubble of nervous laughter. "Well, that's never going to happen again, and you know why?"

Moving closer, I asked, "Why is that?"

Chewing nervously on her lips, she held out her hand to stop me. I was inches away from her now. I could feel the heat coming off her body.

"Because I'll never allow you to use me as a plaything again, Brax. *Never.*"

My heart felt as if it slammed against my rib cage. I was assaulted by the memory of the hurt on Harlee's face that night, and it was
so real that it felt like we were standing in my house all over again.
The pain was so raw on her face then, I'd wanted to tear my eyes out
so I could no longer see it.

"Harlee, you were never a plaything to me. I...I..." My words
trailed off as I tried to figure out what I wanted—no, what I *needed*
to say.

She waited with her head slightly tilted. "You what?"

Tell her, Brax. Tell her how you really felt that night.

With a shake of my head, I took a few steps back, the right words
eluding me.

I saw it on her face—the moment her heart broke again because
of my inability to be open and honest with her.

"Right," she said. "If you're simply looking for a warm pussy to
sink into, I'm not that woman. Go find Brandi for that."

She pushed past me, and I reached out for her arm, gently turning her so that she faced me again. I backed her up against the wall,
yanking her hands over her head and pinning them there. I could feel
her fast breaths. My entire body overheated, and not because I had a
winter coat on. It was her. It had always been her.

My heartbeat was rapid in my chest, and I wasn't sure if it was
because she honestly thought I only wanted her for a quick fuck, or
because she told me to go find another woman. Either way, I was
nearly blindsided by the mix of emotions. Lust, anger, regret...love,
even? Hell, I didn't know up from down.

"If that's what you really think, then why are you even helping
me, Harlee?"

Her throat bobbed as she swallowed as she managed to say,
"Because I'm a stupid idiot. Or maybe it's because you're my best
friend's brother, and I feel obligated."

That hurt more than I thought it would.

I closed my eyes for a moment and whispered, "I was scared,
Harlee." When I opened my eyes, she was staring at me, her brows
drawn in confusion.

"What are you talking about?"

"That night we were together. Being with you..."

I closed my eyes once again and tried to calm my racing heart before I looked deep into those baby blues.

"Being with you, I felt things I'd never felt, Harlee. It was different, and scary, and I found myself wanting things I'd never wanted before."

"Things?" she whispered.

"Yes. Things like wanting to give up *everything* simply to see your smile. Things like wanting to fall asleep with you in my arms and wake up with you still there. And when you told me you had feelings for me...I panicked. I don't know how else to say it. We were young, you were in college, I was growing a new business and needed to focus on that. I wasn't ready for that kind of commitment, or so I thought at the time.

"I don't really know the why of it, Harlee. But the only way I could think to push you away was to lie. To tell you I didn't feel anything after we made love. The truth was, I felt..." I let out a long sigh. "Fuck, I *still* don't know what I felt. Because I haven't felt it since. All I know is that it scared the hell out of me, and I wasn't ready to face it."

Her eyes darted all over my face until she looked toward the window. The room was darker now, so I knew the sun must be going down. I wanted to grab her and shake her. Beg her to tell me what she was feeling or thinking or...hell, *anything* after I word-vomited all of that after holding it in for so damn long.

"We missed the last ferry," she said softly before she looked back at me.

My heart dropped. All I could do was nod and step away from her, giving us both the space we needed.

Her chest rose and fell with heavy breaths, and I knew my confession had thrown her. Hell, it had thrown *me*. I hadn't been prepared to say any of that. I'd wanted her to think she—that Ms. Seaside—was about to be caught. That I had an in at the lighthouse to maybe make her panic a little.

But the whole thing with Brandi had thrown something off inside me, especially when Harlee reacted the way she did. For a brief moment, I couldn't help but wonder if her feelings were the same as before. I didn't want Harlee to think I was interested in Brandi, or any other woman, for that matter.

Clearing her throat, Harlee pushed off the wall and started toward the steps. "We need to see if Kris has any open rooms at the bed and breakfast."

All I could do was stare at her. I waited for her to acknowledge what I'd said, but when she turned and headed down the steps without another word, I felt a piece of my heart break off.

I deserved it, I knew that, but it still hurt.

The sound of the door to the lighthouse shutting pulled me out of my thoughts, and I finally headed down the steps.

"Harlee! Harlee, wait a second, will you?" I said as I opened the door and set the code to lock the lighthouse.

She glanced over her shoulder at me, already almost halfway down the hill. "I'm tired and hungry and ready to get into a warm house, Brax. I'm over today."

I cursed internally. I had pushed it too far, too soon.

She pulled out her phone and punched in a number as she marched down the hill, across the large parking lot, and toward my truck. The last ferry had indeed come and gone. In the summer, nearly all the ferries ran for twenty-four hours, seven days a week, but toward the end of February, that wasn't the case. Not enough people were visiting from the mainland to the island. Residents who happened to live on the island—and there weren't many—knew the ferry schedule.

I unlocked the truck and started to jog after Harlee since the path was clear of any snow or ice. I got to the truck right as she slipped inside.

Lighthouse Island wasn't very big, but there was a bed and breakfast on the opposite side of the island that Kris Jensen owned. Her family had settled here a few generations ago. There was a rich history to the island, and it played a huge part in the story of Seaside.

Being a black family who was running a lighthouse in the late 1800s had come with a lot of heartache as well as triumph.

Mr. Anders was appointed lighthouse keeper in 1875. He wasn't the first African American lighthouse keeper in America, but he'd paved the way for so many others. It didn't take long for his sons to come up with the idea of running ferries back and forth from Seaside, and the Anders had quickly become a prominent and wealthy family in the area. To this day, they played a significant role in Seaside and on Lighthouse Island.

Not only was Mitch Anders the current lighthouse keeper, but he and his wife, Jen, ran the museum that was located down the road from their private residence. And Kris, the eldest sibling, ran the popular Lighthouse Bed and Breakfast out of the large historical home that her great-grandfather had built in the early 1900s. Although it was packed every day during the summer, winters were less busy. I was sure there was a good chance she'd have a couple of rooms. Even in winter, a lot of her weekends were booked, mostly by locals who wanted a staycation. But there were likely rooms available on Tuesday.

I climbed into my seat and started to speak, but Harlee beat me to it. "They have two rooms available, and Kris said she has lasagna she can heat up for us. I told her we were on our way over from the lighthouse."

"Harlee."

Turning to face me, she met my gaze. "I can't, Brax." She shook her head. "I can't process all of that right now. I'm sorry."

I nodded. "Okay."

"Can we please go to the bed and breakfast now?"

I pressed the truck's ignition button. "Of course. I need to drop the keys to the lighthouse off to Mitch first. He gave them to me in case the code didn't work. He said it works off and on."

After I dropped off the keys, we spent the ten-minute drive to the bed and breakfast in silence—except for me cursing myself out in my head. I replayed everything over and over. I was pissed that

I'd said the things I'd said to her. Not about how I really felt, but the timing. I mean, I was planning on telling her, just not today.

I was tired of pretending like I didn't have feelings for Harlee. Tired of pretending it didn't bother me every single day that I'd let her slip away. I'd *hated* listening to Thomas talk about being with her. Hated it to the point that it nearly made me feel sick to my stomach on several occasions. And this stupid game we played with each other. Who could insult the other first, or better. We'd been playing it for far too long, and I was tired of that too. I knew she had to be as well. It needed to stop.

Tonight, I would tell her that I knew she was Ms. Seaside. Tonight, it would all come to a head, and then I'd have to wait and see where things fell between us. I'd keep her little secret if she asked me to. The last thing I ever wanted to do was hurt her again.

Once we were checked into our rooms, I went downstairs to meet Harlee for dinner. Female voices grew louder as I drew closer to the dining room. I heard Harlee laugh as she walked out of the kitchen holding a large salad bowl.

"Kris, everything smells so good!"

Smiling, Kris entered behind Harlee. "The only other couple staying here at the moment decided to skip dinner this evening, and I'd already made this *huge* lasagna. I was going to save it for lunch, but I'm more than happy to feed two of my favorite people."

I cleared my throat and both women finally noticed me. Kris's warm brown eyes took me in as she shook her head and grinned.

"Braxton Bradley. Still as handsome as ever, I see."

I felt my face heat as I stepped up to her and took the pan of lasagna out of her hands, careful to make sure I kept hold of the dark green potholders. "You always were a big flirt, Kris."

She laughed. "Pot calling kettle black."

My eyes darted over to Harlee, who was smiling. I glanced back at our host. "Touché."

Kris was a few years older than me and had once been married to a guy who was in the Navy. Rick Jensen had come home on leave with Brody one time, gone out to Lighthouse Island after learning about its history, and had claimed he'd met the most beautiful woman on Earth. They'd written each other often after that, and he'd visit Seaside whenever he was on leave. They'd gotten married in the massive backyard of the bed and breakfast that overlooked the bay.

I'd never seen Kris as happy as she was with Rick in her life. But he'd died in Iraq two years ago, leaving her heartbroken. She'd pretty much secluded herself on the island ever since, dedicating her life to the bed and breakfast, and to making sure people knew the heritage of her family and the island. Kris was also a huge part of helping Harlee with all the community activities for Black Heritage Month, both here on the island and back in town.

"Take a seat and I'll pour you both some of my lavender lemonade." She turned and looked back at us. "Unless you want something stronger?"

"Wine?" Harlee asked. It was then I noticed she was wearing different clothes. Kris must have given her some sweats and a sweatshirt to wear. I had a habit of keeping a bag in my truck, so I always had a change of clothes ready, if and when I needed it.

"Wine also, Braxton?" Kris asked.

I shook my head. "I'm more of a beer drinker."

She winked. "Good thing I have some. I'll be right back. Help yourselves to food; I already ate."

Harlee and I both put the food down on the table and looked at each other awkwardly.

"Do you want some salad?" she asked, pointing to the large bowl she'd set down. "Kris made her famous homemade ranch dressing."

"I'd love some. Do you want me to cut you a piece of lasagna?"

She nodded as she reached for a bowl. "Sure, not a big piece, though."

I cut a piece for myself and held it up. "Smaller than this?"

She looked at my plate. "Maybe a bit less."

After handing her a plate, I took the bowl of salad she offered, and we both sat down opposite one another. Neither of us saying anything.

"Here you go," Kris said as she walked back into the dining room. "Beer for you."

I reached for the beer and nodded my thanks.

"Wine for you. I know you like red."

Harlee took the wine glass. "Thanks so much, Kris. I'm sorry we barged in like this."

Kris sat down at the head of the table. "There's no such thing as barging in. I'm always at the ready for guests. And this time of year, I'm more than happy to have someone to talk to. It's our slowest month."

Harlee smiled, then took a bite of her lasagna.

"Did you see the special edition column today?" Kris asked.

I looked at Harlee with surprise. She paused with her fork in the air for the briefest of moments before she replied, "Nope. We've been sitting in Braxton's truck nearly all day, freezing our asses off."

"I had the heater on most of the time, and only shut off the engine twice. Besides, you had a blanket and was warm enough to fall asleep a few times," I reminded her. I glanced at Kris and made a face like Harlee was exaggerating.

Kris looked at both of us, clearly confused. "Why were you sitting in the truck all day?"

Harlee sighed and leaned back in her chair. "Brax is on the hunt to find out Ms. Seaside's real identity. He has a theory she drops her articles off at the lighthouse on Tuesdays."

Kris's brows shot up. "Does my brother know?"

I nodded. "Yes, I told him about my theory. He said I was insane, but he gave me permission to check out the lighthouse anyway."

"And did you find anything?" Kris asked.

Harlee and I glanced at one another. She then looked down at her food as she replied, "No, we got sidetracked."

I nodded. "If Ms. Seaside came today, we missed her." After I took a bite, I asked, "Do you have the paper?"

I could have pulled it up online, but there was something about reading the actual paper. And with Harlee sitting across from me, it would be even better.

Kris smiled. "Yes, let me go grab it."

After she walked out of the room, I looked at Harlee. "What do you think she wrote about this week?"

She shrugged. "Hell if I know."

I had to fight to keep the smile off my face. The little minx knew exactly what it said, because she was the one who wrote it.

Kris walked back into the dining room and handed me *The Chronicles*. I opened it up to the gossip column.

The Seaside Chronicles

February 21, 2023

Sand Barred — Special Edition

Seasiders,

Word on the sand dunes is that our winner of the Catch of the Season—by default, in case anyone needed reminding—Braxton Bradley, has not been seen out and about with a...special friend... on his arm lately. Even I noticed he was without a date at the Valentine's Day dance that Harlee Tilson put on. Yes, my fishes, I was there, but not many saw me. I know how to blend in.

Could Mr. Bradley be losing his touch? Or has he found a special someone and isn't ready to share her with us yet? My guess is he's hiding something, ladies, and this writer is going to find out what it is. I've got my ear to the sand on this one! For the sake of all the single women in Seaside, of course.

As for now, all I can report is that our Catch of the Season is still on the market. Good luck to all the single ladies in Seaside. I'm told he could be a good catch.

Fair winds and following seas!

Ms. Seaside

Slowly, I put the paper down and forced myself not to shoot Harlee a dirty look. I could feel my face growing hot as I stared at the column. Why in the world would she make it seem like I was in the market to settle down? The only reason she was taking aim at me was because I was looking for Ms. Seaside. Well, two could play at this game.

Clearing my throat, I folded the paper and set it down next to me, drew in a deep breath, and then exhaled.

"What did it say?" Harlee asked innocently. "You look...angry."

Kris chuckled. "Oh, I don't doubt he's angry. It seems to me, Braxton, that Ms. Seaside is fixated on you."

I looked at her and forced a smile, not caring that it most assuredly looked fake. "Sure seems like it, doesn't it?"

"What does it say?" Harlee asked once again, this time reaching across the table and motioning for me to give her the paper.

I picked it up and handed it over. She lifted the paper so I couldn't see her face as she read. When she finished, she put it down and scrunched up her nose. "Well, she's kind of right. You *are* searching for something."

This time, I *did* shoot Harlee a dirty look. Glancing back at the paper, I saw in my periphery the corner of her mouth twitch with a hidden smile.

"I don't know if she complimented you or not with that last sentence about possibly being a good catch," Harlee added.

"Not a compliment at all, I'm guessing," Kris said. She quickly looked at me. "But I think you are. I think you'd make a great catch for some lucky lady. It's just Ms. Seaside doesn't seem to like you much."

Harlee snorted. "Meh, I think it depends on what they're expecting from him."

"What's that supposed to mean?" I set down my fork, my appetite suddenly gone.

Harlee gave me a look that could have said a thousand different things, but at that moment, she had her claws out. "Well, it's no secret to the single ladies in Seaside that you're not the type to settle down."

I wasn't sure what hurt more. The fact that I'd confessed my feelings from that night to her and she'd thrown them back in my face, or the fact that she was right. I'd been a coward to push her away.

"Is that so?" I asked calmly.

Nodding, Harlee picked up her wine, but before she took a sip, she added, "Afraid of commitment, I believe the rumor is. Of course, I'm only speaking from experience."

Kris cleared her throat and stood. "I need to check on something in the kitchen."

Fuck putting the truth about Ms. Seaside out on the table. If she wanted to play, I'd play. But not tonight.

I pushed back from the table and looked at our host. "Thank you for dinner, Kris."

When I picked up my plate and bowl to bring it into the kitchen, she stopped me. "Don't even think of doing that. Do you want dessert? I made brownies with chocolate frosting."

"Sure, I'll take one, and another beer if you have it... if don't mind me taking it to my room."

She smiled softly at me. "I do have another, and please feel free to come down to the kitchen and help yourself to more. Take whatever you'd like upstairs."

"Thanks, Kris."

I followed her into the kitchen, got my brownie and another beer. On the way out, I reached for my unfinished beer on the table. I glanced at Harlee, who had an expression on her face I couldn't really read. She opened her mouth to say something, then stopped herself.

"Goodnight, Harlee."

Turning, I made my way back up to my room...where I spent the rest of the evening writing my *own* little piece for the paper.

73

Chapter Seven

Harlee

I lay curled under the covers at Kris's bed and breakfast and stared at the ceiling, unable to sleep.

Why had I said that to Brax? Especially after he'd opened up to me. The look on his face at dinner nearly had me rushing to take it all back. He had finally, *finally* spoken from the heart—and what did I do? I ripped out said heart and stomped on it. What was the matter with me? Maybe I was doing the same thing to Brax that he had done to me. Pushing him away, afraid of what he would do when he found out I was Ms. Seaside.

I did the very thing I was angry at him for doing to *me*.

"Oh God," I whispered as I closed my eyes. "Will you ever learn, Harlee Tilson? Check your stupid emotions at the door!"

After I wrote the latest article, I kept thinking of one thing over and over. If Brax found out I was Ms. Seaside, he might never speak to me again. That was something I wasn't willing to let happen.

I sat up, swung my legs over the side of the bed, and stood. The room was still warm from the blaze I'd started earlier in the fireplace. It was starting to burn out, so I added another log and stoked it a bit, creating larger flames that brought more heat into the room. I walked over to the window seat that overlooked the large backyard and out into the bay. I sat down and brought my legs up to my chest so I could rest my chin on my knees.

I stared out over the water, watching the reflection from the full moon dance across the surface. Then my gaze caught on something moving along the pathway that led up from the water, and I strained to see what it was.

A person, walking up from the beach. Who in their right mind would be out in the middle of the night in the dead of winter?

As the figure grew closer, I gasped.

"Brax."

I couldn't see his face, but something told me I really didn't want to. I knew I'd hurt him, *twice*, after his confession. The first time by refusing to talk about everything he'd said, and the second with the cheap shot about him being afraid of commitment.

"Damn it," I sighed, watching Brax get closer to the house. At least he was wearing a hat and gloves.

Once he disappeared from sight, I stood and walked over to the door and put my ear against it. Brax's room was right next to mine. Which was another reason I couldn't sleep, knowing he was so close.

I heard the steps creak and strained to listen more closely. Then I heard his voice. Who was he talking to this late at night?

I carefully opened my door a bit to hear better. Hopefully he wouldn't be paying any attention as he walked by.

"No, it's totally fine. And I can't thank you enough for helping me out with this since I'm unable to do it, what with being stuck on Lighthouse Island. I really appreciate it."

I pulled my head back. Unable to do what?

"Tomorrow morning sounds good. Yes, I'll text you when I'm leaving the island. Looking forward to it."

The soft sound of Brax's door shutting caused me to carefully close mine and rush over to the wall between our rooms. I pressed my ear to it, surprised at how well I could hear. It was hit or miss with old houses. Some had paper thin walls, others were like forts.

"No, I'm really glad you called. You too. 'Night."

The room next door fell silent, and it took me a few more moments to realize I'd been holding my breath.

The sound of movement caused me to put my ear back to the wall. I couldn't tell what Brax was doing, but when I heard the bed creak, I guessed he was getting into it.

I slowly took a few steps back—and stopped when the floorboard creaked.

Shit. Shit. Shit.

If I could hear Brax's bed, he'd most likely hear the floorboards creak.

Note to self: don't stay here if you want to hook up with someone.

The instant image of Brax taking me from behind, his words from earlier at the lighthouse filling my head, had me covering my mouth with my hand. I closed my eyes and willed the image to go away. Now was not the time to be thinking about his words from earlier.

Turning carefully, I slowly tiptoed back into bed and pulled the covers up. The room suddenly felt chilled.

Who had Brax been talking to? Was it Brandi? Had she called him after reading that stupid article? At the time, I'd thought it would be funny to have all the single women of Seaside throwing themselves at Braxton, but now I realized I'd made a huge mistake. Women like Brandi would be among them, surely. I could tell from the look on her face that she was interested in something more than a friendly get-together with Brax to talk about old times.

I sighed. How could I blame *any* woman for wanting him? He was handsome, smart, successful, and even though I wanted to hate him, I knew he was a good person. He never told anyone about all the volunteer work he did in and around Seaside. Or about the money he'd donated to the homeless shelter, the women's recovery center, and the pet shelter. I only knew about it because I volunteered at each of those places, and I'd seen the checks come through.

"Damn you, Braxton Bradley. Why now? Why tell me how you felt *now*, of all times?"

I sat up quickly as another thought occurred to me. He'd said he wanted to be with me in the lighthouse. Physically, be with me. What about his feelings? Did he feel the same way that he did before?

I suddenly needed to know. Swinging my feet off the bed once again, I looked for the fuzzy socks Kris had loaned me and pulled them on. I was dressed in a large pajama shirt that fell almost to my thighs, which Kris had also let me borrow.

Without a care in the world for creaking floorboards, I marched to my door, opened it, then turned to the right. I stopped in front of Brax's door and knocked lightly. The other couple staying in the bed and breakfast were on the top floor, in the large honeymoon suite, and I doubted they could hear me. I still wanted to be cautious, though, so I knocked lightly once again.

I could hear movement on the other side of the door and when it opened, my jaw dropped. My eyes swept over Brax's nearly naked body. The only thing he had on was a pair of boxer shorts. The images my mind quickly conjured up were insane.

Swallowing hard, I attempted to look into his eyes, but it was so hard not to notice how built he was. Not that he wasn't years ago, but my oh my, had the man upped his workout game. From his broad chest to his chiseled abs, everything about him was...well...it was stunning.

"Is it warm in here to you?" I asked, starting to fan myself.

Brax raised a single brow as he gave me a questioning look. He was probably wondering why I was at his door in the middle of the night talking about the temperature.

"It's so...so warm suddenly," I whispered.

"Harlee, is there a reason you're at my bedroom door at two in the morning?"

"What?" I asked, my mind suddenly filled with all kinds of naughty things I wanted to do to and with Brax.

"You, here, my door. Middle of the night?"

"Right. Well," I started. "I'm here because..." Why was I there again?

He leaned in closer. "Because...?"

I blinked a few times before I shook away the image of Brax taking me against the wall. "Oh! I remember now," I nearly shouted as I placed my hands on his very thick chest and pushed.

Brax stumbled back into his room while I turned and shut his door.

When I spun and saw him staring at me like I'd gone mad, my mind went blank yet again.

What was I thinking? Surely he didn't still feel the same way he had in the past. Or maybe he did, but then had changed his mind after I'd acted like a complete bitch at dinner. Or maybe it was Brandi whom he wanted now.

Ugh. Stop with the jealousy, Harlee. This is not you!

Brax folded his arms over his chest and waited.

"I couldn't sleep," I finally blurted out.

"Okay. And what would you like me to do about that?"

The coldness in his voice told me everything I needed to know. He didn't want me here. It was time to crawl back to my room and forget this ever happened.

I quickly spun around and stared at the door. "This was a mistake."

As I reached for the doorknob, I felt his body against mine. He pressed his hand to the door to keep it closed. A shiver ran down my spine when I felt his hot breath at my ear.

"Did you need something to help you relax, Harlee? I don't have any vibrators, but I can offer my mouth. No conditions, no expectations."

A delicious warmth pooled in my lower stomach. I nearly moaned aloud as I slowly turned and leaned against the door. My breathing increased when I saw he was only a short distance away from me.

Okay. I had two choices. I could leave and forget any of tonight happened. Or...I could take something for myself, for once. After all, he was offering to give me an orgasm without conditions. What woman in her right mind would turn that down? And I knew from experience that Brax knew how to please a woman.

I raised a single brow. "Nothing in return?"

He flashed me a wicked smile. "Nothing in return."

I narrowed my eyes. "You'd actually do that, and not expect to sleep with me or ask for oral back?"

"Trust me, princess, it wouldn't be a hardship on my part to taste you again."

Nearly letting out a moan, I pushed off the door and stepped closer to him as I glanced at his bed.

He took my hand. "Not on the bed. *Here.*"

He dropped to his knees while I fought to keep my breathing under control.

Before I could even get my thoughts together enough to realize what Brax was doing, my sleep dress or shirt or whatever the hell it was had been pushed up, and he'd slipped my panties down. I stepped out of them as if I were in a trance.

He lifted me like I weighed nothing.

"Brax! Oh God..." I gasped when he pushed me against the door. He was going to do this with me *on his shoulders*, up against the bed and breakfast door, his face buried between my legs. I could have come simply thinking about it.

I instinctively threaded my hands into his hair as he blew on my clit, then covered my pussy with his mouth. "Jesus!" I panted, tugging his silky locks before pulling him closer. I wasn't sure what I wanted: more or less. My mind was a blur as I let the pleasure take over my entire body. I didn't care where we were, who could hear us, or what they might think.

All I knew was that I'd wanted this moment more than I'd realized. And not with just any man. I wanted it from Brax. Only Brax.

He pulled back slightly, and when his eyes met mine, I said in a gravelly voice, "More."

With a smirk, he replied, "Gladly."

Then he was there again. His mouth licking and sucking as my entire body trembled from the sheer pleasure of it all.

I would be the first to admit I wasn't a prude when it came to sex. I liked it. A lot. And oral sex was my favorite. But despite that, only one man had ever done this to me before—and it was the same man currently licking my clit like a fucking ice cream cone he couldn't get enough of.

"Brax," I whispered. "I'm going to come…oh my God!"

I pressed my hand to my mouth when my orgasm hit. I had nowhere to go as he continued to punish me in the most delectable way with his mouth. Wave after wave of pleasure rippled through me until I was pushing his head back, no longer able to take the sensation, and unable to hold back my moans of pleasure.

"I can't. No more. Please!" I cried out as Brax finally relented and drew back. The smile on his face was nearly enough to make me beg him for one more lick. I almost did just that before reality set in.

Holy shit! Oh crap. What had I done? What in the world had I been thinking? I'd let Brax give me oral sex. I had promised myself the last time he'd broken my heart that I would never allow him to do it again. But it was only sex…right? It didn't mean anything. At least, I was willing to tell myself that lie. Deep down, I wanted it to mean so much more, but the coward in me wouldn't allow myself to bring that thought up to the surface.

He slowly lifted me off his shoulders and let me slide down his body until my feet touched the floor. He stood, and I had to grab onto him to keep my legs from buckling out from under me. The orgasm had left me spent and exhausted. Not to mention my thoughts were as cloudy as ever.

"Did that help?" he asked.

It was then I noticed I was still panting for air. The last of the tingles from my orgasm slowly drifted away, and I felt such a loss. Was it from the feeling ebbing away or the lack of his touch?

"I think…I think I'll be able to sleep now."

He chuckled. "I'm more than happy to help you out again if you need it."

I straightened up, or at least attempted to. "I don't think I'll be… um…I mean…that was…nice."

"Nice?" he asked with a quirked brow. "Just nice?"

Shaking my head, I added, "Really, *really* nice. I'd say more, but then it would go to your head, and we can't have you thinking you're all that."

This time he full-on laughed. "No, we can't have that."

Reaching for my panties, I slipped them on. "I can say one thing, Brax. You've certainly gotten better at that."

"Repetition will do that."

Trying not to let him see the disappointment on my face—because I'd totally stepped right into that one—I rolled my eyes. "You're such a jerk."

I turned to open the door, and Brax pushed me flat against the surface with his body. He buried his face in my hair and drew in a long breath before moving his mouth to my ear. He bit it gently, and I had to sink my teeth into my lip to keep from expressing my delight at the sensation. I nearly pressed my ass into him but thankfully stopped myself.

"Every woman I've ever put my mouth on I've compared to *you*, Harlee. Her scent, her taste, the feel of her against me. No one has ever come close to that sweet honey of yours...and now that I've had another taste, I want more."

I closed my eyes and focused on breathing. I'd never been with a man who talked like Brax, and I hated that it turned me on so much. I'd also be lying to myself if I said I hated knowing he was with other women, but I wasn't naïve. Hell, I'd been with other men, some for only one night...so why did it bother me so much to hear him admit it out loud?

When I had my thoughts under control, I quietly said, "If you think comparing me to all the other women you've fucked with your mouth will make me want it again, you're sadly mistaken, Brax."

He stepped back enough that I could look over my shoulder. A look of something like regret was on his face. Regret for his words... or his actions moments ago? Or maybe he was disappointed.

I opened my mouth to speak again, but I couldn't think of anything to say. I was so torn and so confused. So I did the one thing I was good at—I ignored my feelings.

Without another word, I opened the door and slipped out into the hall, rushing back to my room before the tears started to fall.

Chapter Eight

Harlee

The next morning, Kris grabbed my hand the second I landed on the last step and pulled me through the house and into the kitchen. The couple who was also staying at the bed and breakfast smiled as we zipped by.

"Anyone need any more bacon? Or biscuits?" Kris asked on our way through.

"We're good!" the woman called out.

Once we reached the small pantry on the opposite side of the kitchen, Kris looked at me. "How did Braxton do it?"

My eyes went wide with horror. Oh my God. Did Kris hear us last night? I wanted to die, right then and there. Let a giant ocean swell come and take me away that very moment.

"I'm sorry?" I asked, my voice cracking slightly.

"How did he get his response to the paper so fast and then get them to print it in *today's* edition?"

Okay, now I was *really* confused. "What are you talking about?"

Kris turned around and reached for *The Chronicles*. "I just got the paper. Ron has one of his guys bring it to me each morning when the first ferry lands. Braxton responded to the gossip column! They printed it where they usually put Ms. Seaside's column!"

A rush of heat swept over me. "*What?*" I exclaimed as I grabbed the paper from her and started to read.

Dear Ms. Seaside,

Your assumption that I'm looking for love couldn't be further from the truth. I am, in fact, happily single, and will stay that way for the foreseeable future.

Perhaps you should focus your attention on someone new. In the meantime, best to keep your guard on high alert.

Yours truly,

The Catch of the Season

I stared at the paper as Kris asked, "How do you think he got the paper to print it so quickly?"

There was only one answer to that question. "My father."

That must have been who Brax had been talking to last night. The only way he could have pulled off getting this in today's edition was to go through my dad, who would have made sure it was in before the print deadline.

"Mike?"

I nodded. "It's the only way he could have done it. He must have emailed it to my father or called and spoken with him about it."

Kris looked back at the paper and chuckled. "I think it was a brilliant choice on Braxton's part to respond."

I snapped my head up to look at her. Was she for real? "Brilliant?"

She nodded. "You don't think so?"

I let out a bark of laughter. "No. I think people will think it's ridiculous and childish."

"What's ridiculous and childish?"

I spun around to see Brax standing there with a smug expression on his face. An instant memory of last night hit me with such lethal force, I nearly stumbled back.

"You're published!" Kris stated as she handed Brax the paper.

While he read, the smile on his face grew wider, and I had to fight the urge to slap it right off. Smug bastard.

Turning, I started to make myself a cup of coffee. I couldn't let anyone know I was bothered, because then they'd ask questions. And really, why *was* I bothered? Because Brax had responded to me? Er... to Ms. Seaside. He had no idea we were one in the same. And I'd pushed his buttons last night. What had I expected?

After pouring my coffee, I turned and leaned against the counter.

Brax looked up from the paper. "Do you think she'll respond?"

"Yes!" Kris replied at the same time I said, "No."

"No? You don't think she will?" he asked as Kris looked directly at me.

I shrugged. "I mean, I guess she could."

"Oh, I hope she comes back with something witty! I think she's an older woman, and you know how they're full of spit and fire," Kris added.

Braxton gave me a see-I-told-you-so look. I shook my head. "It's not Ruby. She works every Tuesday, remember?"

His shoulders slumped. "Maybe she hires someone to drop off the articles."

"Has Mitch seen anything?" Kris asked. "He does man the lighthouse. Maybe he's seen the same woman coming and going."

"He didn't mention that he's noticed anything out of the ordinary," Brax replied.

Kris frowned. "That's a bummer."

Brax's cell phone rang. "I need to take this," he said, hitting a button. "Mike. Yeah, I saw it."

My mouth fell open.

"Guess you were right about your dad," Kris said, looking over at me.

I forced myself to smile at her but didn't say anything.

Brax walked out of the kitchen, and I had to keep my feet planted to the floor so that I didn't follow him.

Kris pulled some blueberry muffins out of the oven, and the smell quickly surrounded me, temporarily causing me to forget this whole mess.

"How did you sleep, Harlee?"

I looked from the muffins to Kris and gave her another forced smile. With some added fake cheer to my voice, I said, "I slept great."

"Was it that sleeping pill I gave you?" Brax asked as he walked back into the kitchen.

If looks could kill, Braxton Bradley would be dead on the spot. My cheeks heated and I had to clear my throat before replying. "No, that didn't help any. As a matter of fact, I think it was a placebo."

Brax huffed a laugh and shook his head. I gave myself an internal fist pump because I knew that laugh. It was forced to make me think I hadn't scored a direct hit.

Kris tsked. "You know, you really shouldn't take someone else's medicine, Harlee."

Brax and I both looked at Kris.

"What?" she asked. "I'm simply saying. It could be dangerous."

Clearing his throat, Brax turned back to me. "Do you mind if we head out? I've got a meeting I need to get to."

That piqued my interest. "What kind of meeting?"

"A business kind."

I wanted to stick my tongue out at him, but really, I was almost thirty-one years old and that was childish. What was it about being around this man that made me lose my damn mind?

"I'll pack you both some blueberry muffins," Kris said as she grabbed a box out of a cabinet. "I pack little meals all the time for people who want to eat on the beach and such."

I walked over and hugged her. "Thank you so much, Kris. What do we owe you for the rooms?"

Waving her hand to brush off my question, she replied, "You don't owe me a thing. I loved seeing you both."

I hugged her again. "I took the sheets off my bed and put them in the laundry basket. If you have fresh sheets, I'll put them on the bed before we go."

Brax finished off his cup of coffee, then headed to the sink. "I'll do the same, Kris. We really do appreciate you feeding us and letting us crash here."

She smiled. "You'll both do no such thing. I'll take care of the rooms. I honestly don't have anything else to do today besides make a carrot cake."

Brax paused. "Carrot cake? Damn, we stayed on the wrong night."

Kris laughed as I smiled. Oh, he really could be a charmer. Probably charmed my father.

Well, Ms. Seaside was most definitely going to reply—and the kid gloves were coming off.

I asked Brax to drop me off at *The Chronicles*. What I didn't mention was how I was marching right up to my father's office to ask him what in the hell he'd been thinking. We'd gotten plenty of letters over the years addressed to Ms. Seaside, and my father had never printed one of them. I had been trying to work out my anger the entire ferry ride back to Seaside. My father knew the history between me and Brax.

I slowly shook my head. That was it. My father knew the history there and probably thought this was the best idea since sliced bread. Well, all he knew was that Braxton had broken my heart.

Brax pulled into the parking lot of the paper and parked in my spot.

"Why are you parking?" I asked.

"We still need to talk about Ms. Seaside. I think she got wind that we were onto her."

"You. That *you* were onto her."

He rolled his eyes. "Whatever. I have a feeling she changed the drop-off location. And after I wrote that response, I'll bet you she'll be even more keen to throw us off now."

"You. To throw *you* off." And he had no idea how correct his statement was.

"The last I remember, you were sitting in the truck right alongside me yesterday."

I sighed. "Because I had a moment of insanity when I agreed to help you find her. Besides, I think I might have an idea of who she is after that article yesterday."

He damn near turned his whole body to look at me. My eyes drifted to his mouth, and I forgot how to breathe for a moment as I remembered what those lips felt like on me last night when I cried out his name.

Closing my eyes, I gave my head a little shake. *Focus, woman! Focus!*

"Tell me."

My eyes snapped open to meet his interested gaze. "Tell you what?"

He let out a soft chuckle. "The clue you think you read, and who you think Ms. Seaside is."

"Oh, yeah. Right. Okay, so in the article, she said she was at the Valentine's Day dance."

His brows furrowed. "That's right, she did say that."

I smiled. "Right. So, that automatically takes one or two people off both of our lists since they weren't at the dance."

"Go on."

"Well, I was mingling with everyone at the party. And last night when I couldn't sleep—"

"Before you came to visit me."

I glared at him. "That was a moment of desperation. It was sex and that's all. Nothing more, nothing less."

He smirked. "But you did enjoy it."

I gave him a one-shoulder shrug. "I've had better." When he silently studied me, I sent up a prayer that he couldn't tell I was lying. "Can we get back to this?"

"Last night..." he prompted.

"Last night, I got to thinking about who was at the dance. Kelsey Roberts was there...and she was carrying a small notepad."

Brax gave me a blank stare—before he dropped his head back and laughed.

"What? What's so funny?"

"Kelsey Roberts? The art teacher?"

"Yes. What makes you think it's *not* her? She was carrying around a notepad, Brax."

"That doesn't mean anything. Maybe she was sketching. Palmer does that sometimes."

"Not at a damn dance! I'm telling you, she's Ms. Seaside. I think we need to focus on her."

Something moved across his face, and I swore I saw the corners of his mouth twitch with a hidden smile. I was pretty sure I was starting to get paranoid.

"You really think it might be Kelsey?" he asked.

I nodded.

Brax rubbed at the back of his neck. "I don't know. I can't picture her as Ms. Seaside."

Shrugging, I opened the door to his truck. "You asked me to help you figure out who she is. I think it's Kelsey. Take that and do what you want with it."

I slipped out of his truck and pulled my hat and gloves out of my pocket, not sure why since I was only a few feet away from the entrance.

Suddenly, Brax stepped in front of me to open the door to the paper.

"What are you doing?" I asked. "I don't have time for this right now, Brax. I need to check in and get some work done. Since I bugged out on helping Sutton at the store yesterday, I said I'd help her later today."

"I'm not here to talk about that. I'm here for my business meeting."

I was positive my jaw hit the floor. "Who are you meeting with?"

"Don't you mean *whom*? Actually, maybe not. I always get that mixed up—when you're supposed to say whom."

"What?" I asked, shaking my head in total confusion.

"I think it's 'you're meeting with whom.' Or maybe I'm screwing up that rule. I better brush up on my English grammar skills."

My heart felt like it lurched up to my throat. "Why would you need to do that?"

Brax looked at me and winked. "Your dad offered me a job."

And with that, he turned and walked toward the elevator, leaving me speechless at the entrance of the newspaper office.

Twenty minutes later and I was still pacing outside my father's office. Brax had been in there the entire time. Once or twice, I'd heard faint male laughter.

The door opened, and I turned to see Brax shaking my father's hand. "I'm honored you've given me this opportunity, Mr. Tilson."

With his free hand, my father slapped Brax on the shoulder. "No need to be formal here, Braxton. You can call me Mike."

I balled my hands up into fists, and it was only when my nails cut into my skin that I realized I was about to draw blood.

"Dad, are you free?" I asked.

My father gave me a once-over. "Didn't you have that outfit on yesterday?"

I looked down and frowned. *Shit*. Deciding it was best to ignore that, I asked, "I have a question about a marketing campaign that's starting tomorrow. Do you have a minute to talk?"

Brax winked at me. "I was leaving. He's all yours."

My father turned to look at him. "Good talking to you, Braxton. Tell Keegan and Barbara I said hello."

"I will, Mike."

There was no way I could miss the satisfied expression on Brax's face as he walked past me.

My father's receptionist, Beth, quickly stood. She was my age and had an appealing girl-next-door look. "Did you need anything, Mr. Bradley? Breakfast? Coffee?"

"Coffee sounds nice, but only if *you're* free."

She giggled and looked down at the floor as she moved her shoe around at nothing.

I stared at her in disbelief. "Did she offer him breakfast and then *giggle*?"

My father grinned. "This is going to be great."

Turning to him, I asked, "What is?"

Beth went on. "It's too early for me to take a break, but we do have a café down on the second floor I can show you."

"Beth, go ahead and take a break," my father said. "And show Braxton around the paper as well. He'll be working for us soon."

When I looked back at Beth, I swore she was going to burst from excitement at any moment. And when I swung my gaze to Brax, he had a shit-eating grin on his face.

After she grabbed her cell phone, Beth took Brax's offered arm. As they started toward the elevator, he asked, "Beth, how do you sleep at night? Any trouble sleeping?"

I stepped toward them, my head feeling like it was going to explode from the blood rushing to it, but my father gently took me by the arm. "Harlee."

His voice pulled me back down from my anger-induced craziness. Spinning on my heels, I marched into his office. Once I heard the door shut, I got right to it.

"How could you let him publish a response to my article, Dad?"

He made his way around his desk and sat. He motioned for me to sit too, but I shook my head.

"When I got the call from Brax yesterday evening, I told him to write something up and email it to me. An hour later, I had it in my inbox. Once I was sure it would get to press on time, I gave him a call to let him know that I loved the idea the moment I heard it."

"Never mind, I think I *will* sit." I flopped into the oversized chair. That was a mistake, because the smell of Brax immediately surrounded me. I tried my best to ignore it. "You actually think that was a good idea?"

He laughed. "Harlee Tilson, you're in marketing. You know it was a good idea. You're letting your feelings for the boy cloud your judgment."

My mouth dropped open for the third time that morning. "I beg your pardon?"

He rolled his eyes. "You forget that I know it's *you* writing those articles. You also forget I was there the day you came home crying your eyes out, telling your mother and me that you hoped Braxton Bradley fell off his boat and broke both his legs. It wasn't hard for us to figure out that he somehow broke your heart."

"He didn't break my heart," I scoffed.

Dad raised a single brow, silently asking me if I wanted to stick by that statement.

"Fine, he broke my heart."

Leaning back in his chair, he said, "Now, whether you want to believe it or not, you've opened up a can of worms by declaring to the whole town that Brax is looking for love. Why *did* you do that, by the way?"

I shrugged. "I dunno. I thought it might be kind of funny to watch all the women in town try to get his attention."

He lifted his hands and made a tent with them while resting his chin on his index fingers. "And you didn't think, if that happened, he might actually meet someone he's interested in?"

"Ha! He's most likely slept with all of Seaside. If he hasn't found anyone yet, I doubt he will."

My father stared at me for a moment before he leaned forward. "Harlee, I'm about to give you some of that bullshit parental advice I said I'd never dole out."

I couldn't help but smile at that.

"Sometimes the things we wish for end up hurting us the most."

With my smile fading, I asked, "What do you mean?"

"You're going to have to figure that out on your own."

Frowning, I replied, "Dad, it isn't really advice if you don't actually tell me something I can understand."

He sighed. "That's the best I've got. Now, I loved the idea of Braxton replying back to Ms. Seaside. It's going to drive the women crazy—in a good way—and drive up readership even more."

"But we've never published anyone's responses before, and now we'll have to."

An evil grin appeared on his face. "No, we won't. You see, that's why I offered Braxton a job."

A sudden feeling of dread swept through me, and I felt my hand cover my mouth of its own accord. I closed my eyes and prayed I was dreaming.

"He's going to be writing a column called 'Friday's Catch.' I came up with that title. Pretty good, if I do say so myself."

I blinked a few times, then put my fingers into my ears, wiggled them around, shook my head, and looked at my father. With a disbelieving laugh, I asked, "I'm sorry, he's going to *what*?"

"Harlee, it's going to be amazing. Within fifteen minutes of the digital paper going live, we had more than a hundred people commenting. They loved it! To be precise, they loved that the—" he raised his hands and made air quotes—"'Catch of the Season' wrote back in response to your column."

I wasn't sure what to say. I knew it was good for the paper to get that kind of attention, and the business side of me completely understood why my father offered him the job. But the other side of me was in panic mode.

"Dad, with Braxton working here and coming and going, it puts my identity at risk."

He waved me off. "Nonsense, Harlee. How many people work at this paper? And not one of them knows you're Ms. Seaside."

Ugh. He had me on that one.

"Harlee, I really think this is going to be a hit with the readers. Take a look at some of the comments, and you'll see. After all, the gossip column was your idea to increase readership, and look how well it's done. Before Ms. Seaside, our print edition was nearly nonexistent. And now, nearly every resident in Seaside has a paper delivered to their door."

I let out a long exhale. "I know you're right. But...do I get to approve his column?"

My father stared at me for half a beat—then started to laugh. Hard. "Oh no! If I left it up to you, his column would fail in the first couple of weeks."

Damn it. He had me on that one too.

I stood. "Fine. We'll see how this little...Friday's Catch thing goes." I headed for the door.

"Harlee?"

"Yeah?" I asked as I glanced over my shoulder.

"I love tomorrow's column."

Smiling, I said, "I learned from the best."

He tipped his head. "That you did."

Chapter Nine

Brax

I sat on Harlee's sofa and looked down at the board she had on her coffee table. There were names and pictures pinned to the surface. Someone on the left side, someone on the right. Smack in the middle was Kelsey Roberts.

Trying not to smile, I studied the board. I knew exactly what the little brat was up to. She was trying to distract me with Kelsey. But it wouldn't work, and I know I would make her regret throwing Kelsey into the mix.

"How long did it take you to come up with this, Harlee?"

She looked down at the board like a proud mother watching her kid score the winning goal. "Not long. It looks good, doesn't it?"

I grinned at her. "You're into scrapbooking, aren't you? Is that how you spend your Friday nights?"

She shot me a dirty look. "I only agreed to do this because I want to know who she is as well."

Little liar.

"But if you're going to keep insulting me, Brax, I'm out. You can figure this out on your own."

Holding up my hands, I laughed. "I'm sorry. It's just so easy to piss you off."

She huffed then stood. "Did you eat dinner?"

"Not yet."

"Want me to order a pizza?" she called out from her kitchen.

"Sounds good to me."

She popped her head out, and I was struck once again by how beautiful she was. Even in her sweatpants and long-sleeve *Seaside Chronicles* shirt. Her shiny brown hair was pulled up and piled on her head, and it bounced around every time she moved. "What kind?"

"I'm good with anything."

She gave a nod. A couple seconds later, I heard her ordering.

I wondered how long she was going to ignore what had happened between us last night at the bed and breakfast. I had to admit, I was surprised when she's called me earlier and had asked if I wanted to come over and talk strategy on Ms. Seaside. There was no way I was going to pass up the chance to spend time with her. Even if I *had* been in the middle of making some repairs on one of my charter boats.

Harlee walked back into the living room carrying two beers. She handed me one before she sat down. "What do you do for work during the winter months?"

After taking a drink, I set the beer down. "Well, if I've had a good season before, I don't have to worry too much, especially if I'm smart with my money. But I do have a few charters for fly fishing scheduled. St. George River can be fly-fished all year round."

"I've always wanted to learn how to fly fish."

Without even thinking, I replied, "I'll teach you."

Her eyes lit up and that made my chest flutter. I almost rubbed at it.

"Would you really?"

"Sure, if you really want to learn."

She smiled. When her eyes drifted down to my mouth, then quickly away, I decided we needed to talk about what happened.

"Harlee, about last night—"

Lifting her hand, she said, "It's okay, Brax."

"No, I was a dick afterward with my shitty comment about practice. I didn't mean that at all, and it's far from the truth."

Her eyes met mine. "Don't try and tell me you're a sweet innocent boy who doesn't give oral sex to women."

"I won't say that, but it's been few and far between."

She raised a brow. "Why? If you don't mind me asking."

I shrugged. "I don't mind at all. It's not something I do if I'm casually hooking up with someone."

"What was last night then?"

"You're different."

She blinked a few times, looking away for a long moment before she focused back on me. "No one has done that to me since...well... since we were together."

A sinking feeling in my stomach made me squirm in my seat. I wasn't sure if her confession should make me happy or not. Had she not wanted me to do it? She'd certainly seemed to enjoy it—or at least, I thought she had. "Because you don't like it?" I asked.

When she looked at me, I realized I was holding my breath.

"I like it, but it felt too... I just haven't been with another man whom I wanted that sense of connection with. It's very personal, being with someone like that."

A lump formed in my throat, and I wanted to say something. But I wasn't sure what she wanted to hear.

"You're different as well. I wanted you to do it, Brax."

I smiled slightly. "So your comment this morning about it not relaxing you was...?"

She shot me a sly look. "If you think I'm going to compliment you right now, Braxton Bradley, you are mistaken."

Laughing, I sat back. "A man can try. Maybe if you give me another shot at it, I can change your mind."

"Another shot?"

"It was the middle of the night, and I was tired. It took a lot of mental energy to write that reply to Ms. Seaside."

She slowly shook her head as a sexy smile grew on her beautiful face. "You poor thing, having to use all that brain power."

"I know, it was terrible."

With a tilt of her head, she asked, "Just curious, but...what would you do to redeem yourself?"

"So it really *wasn't* good?"

"I never said that. You were in the room. Did you not hear me when I came?"

Fuck, this woman is going to drive me insane. "I heard you."

"Then you know the answer to that question."

I moved in my seat again, and her eyes shot down to my crotch and then back up. "Then what exactly would I be redeeming myself for?"

"For the dick comment you made afterward. For deflating the high I was on after my orgasm."

"Ahh," I said, leaning forward and resting my arms on my legs. "Well, I could take that vibrator you have upstairs and use it on you."

"No confidence in your own tools?"

I nearly coughed on my own spit. "I have plenty of confidence. That would be only the start of my redemption."

"Okay, so you'd play with me with the vibrator. Then what would you do?"

Christ Almighty, if my dick wasn't hard as a rock. "I'd ask what *you* wanted me to do."

Her brows rose. "A giving lover. I wouldn't have pegged you as such."

Smirking, I replied, "I can be many different kinds of lover, Har-lee."

Her tongue swept across her lips, and I reached down to adjust myself.

"Problem down there?" she asked.

"I know how to make it go away."

Harlee looked down at the board and took in a deep breath. She exhaled and asked, "What are we doing here, Brax?"

"I think we're talking dirty to each other."

She smiled but kept her eyes on the board. "It's pretty obvious we're sexually attracted to one another."

"You think so?"

Looking up, her eyes met mine. "Is that what you want, Brax?"

I frowned. "What do you mean?"

"Another fuck buddy? Because that's not what I'm interested in."

It felt like a rock settled in the pit of my stomach. I had so many things I could have said to her in that moment. That I wanted more from her than simply sex. That I wanted to see where things could go between us. That I wanted a life with her that I never thought I'd want with any woman. That seeing her with other men nearly drove me fucking crazy. That every woman I ever slept with, I compared to her. Wished they *had* been her.

I could tell her I was a stupid idiot for letting her go that day.

"I'm not looking for that with you, Harlee."

Her shoulders dropped some, and I could see her entire body deflate. "Okay. Well...that's good then."

"Harlee—I meant I don't want you as a fuck buddy. I want—"

The doorbell rang, and she jumped up. "That's the pizza."

She rushed to the door. I sliced my hand through my hair as I mumbled a few curse words.

"I'll go grab us a few paper plates," she said after she got back. "Do you need another beer?" And in a blink of an eye, she was back to acting like nothing had happened between us.

"Do you regret it?" I asked as she set the pizza down on the end table.

"Regret last night? No, I don't regret it."

"Not last night. Our first time together."

Her eyes softened, and she smiled at me. "Not at all. Do you?"

I shook my head. "The only thing I've ever regretted was hurting you like I did."

She chewed on her lip, and I thought she was going to say something else, but then she exhaled and said, "It's in the past. Let's leave it there. And last night...was a moment we shared, nothing more."

"A moment we shared?"

Nodding, she turned and walked to the kitchen. I hadn't been prepared for her to brush off last night like that.

"Okay, so back to the board," she said. "Let me tell you why I think Kelsey is Ms. Seaside."

Everything Harlee said for the rest of the evening was a blur. I nodded, spoke when I needed to speak, and agreed when I needed to agree. When it came time for me to leave, we said our goodbyes... and that was that.

As I made my way to the truck, I realized that this whole plan of mine wasn't working out how I'd hoped it would. Hell, I wasn't even sure anymore *what* I'd wanted by starting this. All I knew was that it was time to change the rules, even if Harlee wasn't aware there were any.

Thomas walked into the warehouse and placed a copy of the paper next to my coffee. "What in the hell did you do to piss off Ms. Seaside?"

"What do you mean?" I looked down at him from the deck of the boat I was working on. It was one of the boats I'd bought early on, when I'd first started the fishing charter, and I was replacing the rod holders.

"I take it you haven't read today's article then."

I wiped my hands on a cloth and stepped off the boat. "Not all of us run to read that damn article first thing every week."

Thomas wore a shit-eating grin. "Well, I think your reply might have made her a tad bit...angry."

Returning his smile with one of my own, I calmly picked up the paper. I had to admit, my fingers had been itching to read it all morning, but I'd kept putting it off.

Grabbing my coffee, I sat down in the metal chair behind my desk. The warehouse I'd purchased not long after starting Bradley Charters was right down on the bay. I had socked a bit of money into it over the years, including putting in two offices—one for me and one for Melissa, who was my business manager, accountant, receptionist, and all-around person who kept me in business. There were two bathrooms, two large bays for working on the boats, and a private area that had a small, combined kitchen, living, and bedroom space. I'd crashed there several times over the years and was glad my father had talked me into adding it. The entire warehouse was heated in the winter, but only the living area and the two offices had AC.

I took a sip of coffee and started to read.

The Seaside Chronicles

February 23, 2023

This Week's Catch

Seasiders,

For clam's sake, the talk around town about our very own Catch of the Season responding to one of my little articles has been something even the seagulls are surprised by. What Mr. Bradley doesn't realize is that it's going to take a lot more than his attempts to find out my identity to pull me away from his...well...let's not say interesting life—that would be going a little far. How about we go with colorful life? Yes, it will take a lot more than some snooping and a reply to my article to scare me away.

Search on, Mr. Bradley. May the best shark win.

Meanwhile, news on the docks is about—you guessed it—our Catch of the Season. Word is, Brandi Larson is back in Seaside. If my memory is correct, Braxton and Brandi were quite the couple back in high school. We won't talk about the time they got caught behind the football bleachers in a rather...compromising position, and Brandi's father nearly broke Braxton's nose. What we will talk about, my fishes, is how Brandi and Braxton were spotted together on Lighthouse Island. Not to mention, he was seen leaving Lighthouse Bed and Breakfast the next day.

Could this be what our Catch of the Season has been hiding? A rekindled love? Oh, I do love a good second-chance romance! Could this be another Adelaide and Gannon Wilson story? I guess we'll have to wait and see.

Although, Braxton was also seen leaving Harlee Tilson's house last night. Our Catch of the Season has been a busy boy, it seems, bouncing from one to another. Let me lean in a little close and whisper: Are we surprised by this? I think not. Maybe he isn't such a great catch, after all.

My ear will be to the sand. Stay tuned, my fishes!
Fair winds and following seas!
Ms. Seaside

I couldn't help it. I laughed.

"You think it's funny? Dude, she's all but calling you a man-whore."

Shrugging, I tossed the paper down and took a long sip of my now nearly cold coffee. "What do I care what she thinks? I'll find out who she is soon enough and reveal her to the entire town."

Thomas grabbed a chair, spun it around, and straddled it. "Dude, you know...if you're interested in Harlee, we've been over for a long time. As a matter of fact, we never actually connected. I mean, she's fun and all, but it was pretty clear she wasn't interested in settling down. Plus, she's a little too adventurous in the bedroom for me."

I nearly crushed the coffee cup in my hand, picturing Thomas sleeping with Harlee. I cleared my throat to keep the anger out of my voice. "What do you mean? Like, she's into kinky shit?"

He shook his head. "Nah. She asked me once to use a vibrator on her before we had sex, but it felt weird. I mean, don't they use those when they're alone? Why would I want to use one on a woman when I could do the same thing with less work?"

I stared at him. I wasn't sure if I wanted to punch the living hell out of him, or explain that he was a stupid motherfucker.

"Dude, you need to work on your foreplay. Have you never played with a woman like that before, vibrator or not?" I asked.

"No," he said, laughing as if I'd asked a stupid question. "Have you?"

Again, I stared at him for a hot second. No wonder he'd had so few girlfriends throughout the years. "Hell yes! It's a fucking turn-on, watching them squirm on the bed while you tease them with a vibrator. Better yet, bringing a woman almost to orgasm, then denying her, only makes it that much greater when she comes with you inside her. You're missing out."

He seemed unsure. "What if she ends up liking that better than you?"

Why did it feel like I was talking to a high school kid about to lose his virginity? "If a woman would rather be fucked by a vibrator instead of your dick, then you're doing something wrong, dude."

He rubbed at the back of his neck and nodded. In all the years I'd known Thomas, I'd never really heard him talk about sex. Was he really not confident in the bedroom? Hell, if that was the case, he needed to go talk to someone—and it sure as hell wasn't going to be me. I quickly changed the subject.

"I'm thinking of taking off next week and heading up to St. George River. Do some fly fishing."

Thomas smiled. Of course, *that* would get him going. Fish. "Sounds like a good time. You going alone?"

"I'm not sure. I might have a client who's interested in learning how to fly fish. They've never done it before."

He laughed. "So you thought it would be a good idea to take them in the dead of fucking winter?"

"I've caught some of my largest fish in the winter. No crowds. It's peaceful."

"The fish are slow as shit cause they're freezing their asses off... just like you'll be."

I ignored him. "This person wants to learn to fly fish, so an empty river would be perfect."

"Brax, you're going to make them hate the sport. Why not wait until spring?"

Without looking at him, I stood and grabbed my coffee cup and headed toward the kitchen. "I have my reasons."

He laughed. "In other words, you don't like him."

"Not true. They simply need to be taught a lesson or two, that's all."

Chapter Ten

Harlee

The Seaside Chronicles

February 24, 2023

Friday's Catch

Dear Anglers,

I've been given an amazing opportunity to do a column about fishing in our local waters and whatever else I'd like to write about. Now, I will admit that I may or may not use this space to occasionally respond to a certain person—Ms. Seaside—who's become obsessed with me. I'm not really sure why she's so interested in my 'colorful' life, but if it makes her happy to write about me, then who am I to stop her?

I'd like to first address the ex. Nothing is going on there, and nothing will, so she can stop sticking her nose in that particular tackle box. And my night at the Lighthouse Bed and Breakfast was indeed a very pleasant stay, but not for the reasons Ms. Seaside thinks. I had a great time catching up with an old friend and eating some amazing food. I even enjoyed a late-night snack. I will say, the snack was my favorite part of the stay.

Now that we've cleared that up, I'll be heading out to do some fly fishing next week. Some might ask why in the world I'd want to fly fish in the middle of winter. I can offer a few reasons why you should head on out yourselves for a few days.

No crowds.

It's peaceful.

And if you're patient enough, you may get yourself a trophy-size fish. I'm hoping to get some wild brown trout. You'll have to wait until next Friday to see how I fared. Until then...

Your Catch of the Season

PS. Maybe what Ms. Seaside needs is to come to me directly, since she likes fishing around. I can show her where all the good spots are.

"Late-night snack!" I shouted as I nearly crumbled the newspaper in my hand. "Obsessed? He thinks I'm *obsessed* with him?!" My father was probably sitting in his office, laughing his ass off. I exhaled and dropped the paper onto my kitchen table. "This is what you get for playing with fire, Harlee."

Starting to pace, I tried to think of what to do. Clearly Brax wasn't going to stop searching for Ms. Seaside. He needed a distraction. But what could I use to distract him? I had already attempted to put him on the trail of someone else, and he wasn't taking the bait.

Taking the bait... Taking. The. Bait.

I smiled and raced to my computer.

The Seaside Chronicles

February 25, 2023

Taking the Bait — Special Edition

Seasiders,

It seems we have a battle of words going on. If Mr. Bradley thinks I'm in any way obsessed, he's letting his ego get the better of him. It appears to this writer, and others who have expressed the same opinion, that it's Mr. Braxton Bradley who seems to be obsessed with little ol' me. After all, he's declared he's searching for my true identity. Perhaps what this writer needs to do is toss out a clue for him. After all, he has been searching for months now and doesn't seem to be getting any closer.

Now, my fishes, in other news, this writer has some info on Palmer and Mason's upcoming nuptials! News on the docks is that it will be a summer wedding. Most likely after her two older sisters, Adelaide and Sutton, both deliver their first little ones. No word on where the wedding will be held as of yet. I'll keep my ear to the sand.

Fair winds and following seas!

Ms. Seaside

The bell above the door at the Seaside Grill rang as I stepped in. I made my way over to the same booth I sat in each time I met Addie, Sutton, and Palmer here on Thursdays and Saturdays. Braxton had texted last night to say he'd be joining us, and that he had news for me. I had to admit my heart nearly pounded out of my chest as I wondered what news he could possibly have to share that warranted him joining us.

"Morning, ladies!" I cheerfully said as I slipped into the booth next to Sutton. Addie and Palmer were sitting across the table.

"Did you see it?" Addie nearly shrieked. "Oh my gosh, this is the best thing ever! The banter between the two of them is *amazing*!"

Sutton sighed while Palmer grinned and said, "I thought Brax had given up the search for Ms. Seaside, so when I saw his first response, I nearly died!"

"It's a good way to flush her out, I think." I smiled up at Ruby when she placed my coffee on the table.

"Usual?" she asked.

"Yep! Thanks, Ruby."

"Harlee, why didn't you tell us Brax asked for your help in figuring out who Ms. Seaside is?" Sutton asked.

I looked at her, confused. "I thought I did."

"No!" all three of them exclaimed in unison.

Addie leaned forward. "Is that what the two of you were talking about at the Valentine's Day dance? Palmer thought you were hooking up."

I nearly choked on the hot coffee I'd sipped. "Hooking up?" I let out a bark of laughter that caused a few people to look in our direction. "Hardly."

"You looked flustered at the time," Palmer stated.

"I was," I replied. "I mean, he cornered me and declared he had to find out who she was. And during the damn party. I was busy!"

Palmer tilted her head. "I wonder what changed his mind?"

"I don't think he ever changed his mind the first time," Sutton said. "He just wanted you to focus on Mason."

Palmer's cheeks turned pink. "Well, I'm glad I did. I haven't ever been this happy."

I reached across the table and squeezed her hand. "I'm so happy for you, Palmer. For all of you. It's about time each of you found happiness."

"What about you, Harlee?" Addie asked. "Don't you want to find someone and settle down?"

All three of them were suddenly looking at me as if I were under a microscope. I had to fight the urge to squirm in my seat. "I mean, yes, eventually. I'd love to settle down and have a family."

"And there isn't anyone you have in mind? Like, oh, say...Brax?" Palmer asked.

"Brax?" I let out a disbelieving chuckle. "*Brax?*"

Sutton reached for my hand. "We know you guys kind of have a past. And Brax told Palmer that he regretted letting someone he cared about get away several years ago."

When I jerked my head to look at Palmer, she nodded. "He did. It broke my heart to hear him confess that. He was clearly in love with someone once, and he let her go because he thought he wasn't ready for that level of commitment."

I swallowed hard. "Did he say he was in love?"

She shook her head. "Not in so many words, but he hinted at it pretty strongly."

Concentrating on my breathing, I tried to smile. "I think you have it wrong. We spent one night together, and that's it. It was so long ago, and we didn't exactly part on friendly terms. At the time, he made it very clear he wasn't interested in settling down with anyone."

Of course, I neglected to tell them I had poured my heart out to him, and he'd all but stomped all over it.

The three sisters looked at each other, then back to me.

"That's it!" Palmer declared. "You're the one he let get away! Harlee, how do you not see it? He hasn't had a steady girlfriend since. And before that, it was only Brandi. Ugh—I really didn't like her."

I blinked several times. "How do you figure it's me, Palmer?"

Addie spoke first. "Harlee, it's pretty obvious he pushed you away because he had feelings for you."

"Lord above, does that sound familiar," Sutton mused. "What is it with men and pushing away women whom they care for? Why are they so afraid of commitment? Is it the idea of only having sex with one woman the rest of their lives, or does a relationship truly scare the bejesus out of them?"

I rolled my eyes. "I think you're all reading too much into this. I agreed to help him figure out the whole Ms. Seaside thing, and that's it. Besides, Brandi's back in town."

Addie huffed. "So? She was never the one Brax was meant to be with, and he clearly doesn't want anything to do with her. He said so in his new article. By the way, your dad is brilliant for making that happen."

I forced myself to nod in agreement.

"I will kick his ass if he goes back to her," Sutton said. "I never liked her. She was always so mean to him."

"She was?" Palmer asked.

The rest of us nodded as Sutton went on. "She belittled him about his desire to stay in Seaside and open his own business. She basically told him he wouldn't be able to make a successful career out of it."

"What a bitch! Yet she came back to work here," Palmer stated while we all nodded again.

"Okay, well, enough of that. Did you read the special edition this morning?" Addie asked with a wicked smile.

"No," I said, then thanked Ruby for my breakfast as she set it in front of me. Eggs, hash browns, and sourdough toast.

"Oh, it's a good one!" Palmer handed me the paper. All I really wanted to do was eat my breakfast, but I played along and pretended to read it.

I looked up at the end. "She offered him a clue?"

"Yes!" the three of them said in unison.

Laughing, I slowly shook my head. "Damn, I really like whoever the hell this is. She has balls."

"I don't think he wants a clue, to be honest," Sutton said.

"Why?" I asked, taking a bite of my eggs.

She shrugged. "I think Brax is enjoying this too much. I mean, he has his own column now because of Ms. Seaside."

"I'm not surprised my father did that," I said. "The response from Brax's initial reply was incredible. From a marketing standpoint, it's brilliant. I'm a little sad I didn't think of it first."

"And he does love to talk about fishing. He might actually enjoy writing. At least, he seems to like to spar with her," Addie added with a look in my direction. "Exactly like he does with you."

I rolled my eyes and did my best to play it off. I couldn't have them comparing me to Ms. Seaside. "Maybe now he'll stop doing it with me. Although, I do like to get a good jab in every now and then."

The others laughed.

"What are we laughing about?" Brax asked as he approached our table. He pulled over a chair from the table next to us and sat at the end of the booth.

"Nothing," we all said.

He raised a brow, looking between the four of us.

"Did you read the special edition of Ms. Seaside's column?" Palmer handed the paper to him. It took everything in me not to watch him read it.

"She's back on you and Mason," he said, looking at his sister.

"It's okay, it's nothing. It's not like we're keeping the wedding a secret. We've actually talked about moving it up and doing something simple."

"Simple is the way to go," Sutton said with a wink. Turning her attention back to Brax, she asked, "You're not even going to comment on how she suggested giving you a clue if you can't figure out who she is in a few weeks?"

I glanced up from my toast, where I'd been intensely focused on spreading jelly, and our eyes met. Something moved across his face, but it was there and gone so fast that I couldn't really pinpoint the emotion. But still, a strange feeling came over me.

He knew something.

What did he know? Had he found out another clue?

"She's playing head games," he said. "She's worried I'm getting close to finding out who she is—as she should be."

The entire time he spoke, he never once stopped looking at me. I forced myself to keep my expression neutral.

"By the way." He pulled his gaze from me. "I asked Kelsey Roberts out to dinner tonight."

My knife slipped out of my hand and clattered against my dish.

"Sorry!" I quickly said as I picked it up.

No one seemed to notice—because they were all staring at Braxton in shocked disbelief.

"You asked Kelsey out? Brax, that's not a good idea," Palmer said. "Mason told me she got super clingy with him when she thought he was into her."

Giving a half shrug, Brax took the offered cup of coffee from Ruby. "I ate already, Ruby, but thank you."

She smiled, then looked at the rest of us. "Anyone need anything else?"

I really wanted to ask her if she could make me a drink, but I had to remind myself I was at the grill, not a bar. Although, a stiff drink right about now would do wonders.

Brax had been looking at me because he was going after Kelsey. The very person I'd pushed him toward.

"I'm good," Addie stated while everyone else agreed.

"I'm not worried about it," Brax finally responded to Palmer, dropping back in the chair and giving her a smirk.

"You should be," Sutton said. "Thanks to Ms. Seaside, every single woman in Seaside thinks you're in the market for a relationship, Brax—even if you said you aren't. Now you're asking out people like Kelsey? Rumors are going to fly."

Brax tossed his head toward me. "Harlee thinks Kelsey might be Ms. Seaside. I need to get closer to her to find out the truth."

"Ouch! What in the hell, Harlee? Did you kick me?" Palmer asked, leaning down to rub at her shin.

"Sorry." I made a face of apology. "My foot was stuck."

"On what?" Brax asked.

I shot him a dirty look. "I think my lace was stuck on the leg of the booth," I mumbled.

He ignored my lame explanation and focused back on the rest of the table. "Anyway, Harlee thinks it could be her, so I intend to find out."

"How? I mean, I know you can charm the socks off of any woman, but do you actually think you can charm her into confessing?" Addie asked with a laugh.

"I'm sure I can work my magic on her."

I coughed hard, then hit my chest when everyone looked at me. "Egg went down wrong."

Addie asked, "Harlee, what makes you think it's her?"

Wiping the corner of my mouth, I sat back and pushed my plate away. "Ms. Seaside said she was at the Valentine's Day dance. I knew everyone who was there. I spoke to nearly everyone, too, and I remembered seeing Kelsey walking around with a notepad. She didn't have it with her at all times, but I saw her pull it out every now and then. Why else would she be carrying a notepad at a dance?"

"I said probably to sketch things, since she's an art teacher," Brax added before he took a sip of his coffee.

Palmer shook her head. "I mean, I like to draw, but I don't think I would have been focused on that during a party."

"Well, we know why *you* weren't," Sutton stated with a wicked laugh.

Palmer stuck her tongue out at her.

"Are we missing something?" I asked.

Waving off my question, Palmer said, "No. You really think it could be her?"

"Wait, wasn't she at the grocery store when Mason's ex was there following you and Charlie?" Sutton asked.

Palmer's mouth dropped open. "She was!"

"Come to think of it," Sutton added, "she was walking into my store one day when Brody was leaving. She even asked me if there was something going on with us, and I told her he was fixing something for me. Oh my gosh! You might be on to something, Harlee!"

Addie fell back in her seat. "Okay, so she happened to be in a few places. That doesn't mean anything."

"Well, when I was making my board of suspects, she was smack in the middle," I said.

The all stared at me with questioning looks.

"What?" I shrugged. "Brax asked for help, and I'm taking my part seriously. I made a board of who I thought it might be, and who Brax thought it might be. Hopefully Ms. Seaside will be one of our suspects."

Brax nodded. "It is a rather impressive board, if I do say so."

Turning to him, I smiled. "Thank you, Brax."

He tipped his head, then winked. "That's your one compliment for the day."

Exhaling in annoyance, I looked back at my three best friends. It was hard to lie to them, but it was something I needed to do. If I kept quiet, everyone would start to suspect something, so I had to play along. "Kelsey seems like the perfect fit. She's well liked in the community. She volunteers in different places, and she's pretty enough to talk to both men and women and get information without them even realizing it. Plus, she's smart enough to pull off something like Ms. Seaside."

They all let my words settle in. Then Palmer said, "One could say all the same things about you, Harlee."

I nodded. "I guess they could."

Sutton laughed. "Like Harlee could be Ms. Seaside."

Palmer rolled her eyes. "I think we really need to take a hard look at everyone."

"I don't know," Addie said. "I'm starting to think maybe we should leave well enough alone."

"And not find out who she is?" Sutton asked.

"What if she turns out to be someone we know? And by that, I mean someone close to us? A friend...or hell, even a relative? In that case, do we really, honestly, want to know who she is?" Addie asked.

It took less than five seconds for Addie and Sutton to both shout at the same time. "Yes!"

My heart started to beat hard in my chest. What in the hell had I gotten myself into? I could actually lose these friendships with this stupid column. Addie, Palmer, and Sutton were like sisters to me.

"What do you think, Harlee?" Palmer asked, causing me to jerk my head up and force a smile. I gave a noncommittal half shrug.

Addie sighed. "Okay. But don't say I didn't warn you guys. This might blow up in our faces."

We all looked around the table at each other before Brax said, "I'm too close to stop now. I'm all in."

Palmer clapped her hands in excitement. "Good! Now—are you really going fly fishing?"

"I am. And Harlee's coming with me."

All eyes were suddenly on me as I looked over at Brax and his shit-eating grin. "I am?"

Chapter Eleven

Brax

The second we stepped into the small cabin, Harlee froze. It was a one-room cabin with a queen bed and small dresser on one side, and a kitchenette and two-person table on the other. A large fireplace sat in the middle of the cabin, with a sofa directly in front of it as well as a large, oversized leather chair. It was freezing inside the place, but it was clean. A fishing buddy of mine owned it and said I could use it anytime I wanted. At this point, I made more use out of it than he did.

"Welcome to our home for the next four days."

"Four days!" Harlee shouted. "You said it was a quick trip up and back. Not four days! I have work, Brax."

"I already talked to Sutton, and she said it was fine since things were so slow at the shop. And your dad thought it was a great idea. He said you'd be able to help me write my article for next week."

She dropped her bag and pointed to herself. "Me? Why would my dad tell you that? I don't know the first thing about writing an article!"

I shrugged, then walked over to the bed and set my bag down. I'd already dropped off all of our fishing gear in the fishing shack, which was actually bigger than the cabin. I'd made Harlee be ready at five in the morning, so we could get an early start. The cabin was only a little over an hour away from Seaside, but I wanted to get some fishing in both this morning and afternoon.

"Maybe because you've been working there for so long, he figured you'd have some advice for me."

I watched as Harlee turned in a circle. "Where's the other bed?"

"We'll have to share this one." I walked over to the kitchen area and opened the cabinet where Nick usually kept some food. It was empty. It took everything I had not to smile. Especially when Harlee started to stutter her words.

"Wha...wha...sha...sha...wha?"

"I'm sorry, I don't speak that language. What are you trying to say?"

"Share the bed? Are you crazy, Braxton?! I'm not sharing a bed with you."

"Why not?" I asked with an innocent smile.

"Why not? Why not?" She turned in a circle again. "Why not?"

I leaned against the counter. "Yeah, why not?"

"We can't. I mean, what if people found out we were up here together?"

Laughing, I asked, "Who would find out? The only people who know we're together is my family and yours."

I watched as her throat bobbed. "What if someone sees us?"

"In case you didn't notice, no one is around for miles."

"For...for miles?"

"Yeah. I don't even think anyone with a cabin on the river lives full time up here."

"What if a snowstorm blows in and there's no one to help us get out?"

I pushed off the counter. "I made sure the weather was good. You don't honestly think I'd bring you up here if there was a chance we'd get stuck, do you?"

She folded her arms against her chest, or at least she attempted to. Her large down jacket made it hard for her to look angry. "I wouldn't put anything past you, Braxton Bradley. This is stupid.

When I said I wanted to learn how to fly fish, I pictured it in a river in the middle of summer where I could soak up the sun. Not in winter with a chance of freezing to death."

"You know how busy my summers are, Harlee. If I'm going to teach you, this is the perfect time."

"I'll freeze!"

Laughing, I walked up to her and grabbed her dropped bag. "Nonsense. I made sure you have all the clothes you'll need for fishing."

"You don't know what size I am."

I lifted a brow as I swept my gaze over her heavily covered body. "I'm pretty good at figuring that out...and I got a close-up look at the bed and breakfast. Remember?"

She snarled her lip at me, but I ignored her.

I tossed her bag onto the bed—and something started buzzing inside.

"What is that?" I asked. "Did you bring an electric toothbrush?"

Her eyes widened as a look of horror moved across her face. She pushed past me and grabbed for her bag, fumbling to open it. "Shit! Shit! Shit!"

Glancing over her shoulder, I caught sight of what she was desperately trying to turn off.

"You brought a vibrator with you?" I asked in disbelief.

Shooting me a go-to-hell look over her shoulder, she said, "I thought I would be in a room by myself!"

Smiling, I took a step back. "I don't mind if you use it."

She turned and put her hands on her hips. "I supposed you'd like to watch as well."

"Oh, back to this conversation, are we? Again, if you're offering, I won't say no."

Harlee put her hands on my chest and gave me a hard push. "Damn you, Brax! Did you know we'd have to share a bed?"

I couldn't help it, I laughed. She looked so damn cute with her nose all crinkled up and her brows pulled down hard. Fuck if she wasn't stunning, even angry.

"You think this is funny?" she said. "I want to go back home. *Now*."

Holding up my hands, I took a step away before she swung and punched me. "Hold on, Harlee. I'm sorry I laughed. Calm down. The sofa is a pull-out bed; I'll sleep on that. There's also a small privacy screen leaning up against the wall over there. You can put it between us."

She raised one perfectly arched brow. "A privacy screen? You think that's as good as a door?"

"It's better than nothing."

Letting out an exhale, she tossed her hands in the air. "I give up. Whatever. It's fine. I don't care anymore."

I could have egged her on, but I decided she was probably about to explode and if I laid any more on her—like the fact that we had no food—she could crack.

"After you unpack, we should head to the grocery store in town."

When she slowly turned and looked at me, the fight-or-flight in my body kicked in. "You didn't bring any food?"

I stuck my hands in my pockets and glanced at her. "To be honest, I forgot about the food."

Her mouth dropped open. "You forgot about food? Brax, how?"

I rocked back and forth on my feet as I looked anywhere but at her. "I was excited about coming up and fishing." When I peeked back at her, her eyes were closed and her lips were moving. I cleared my throat. "Are you talking to yourself?"

Her eyes snapped open, and I almost screamed like a little girl at the look of death she was giving me.

"I'm praying for strength so I don't find something in this freaking cabin to murder you with."

I let out a laugh, and when she looked even more pissed off, I pressed my lips together.

"Smart man," she said as she grabbed her purse. "Since I'm still wearing my coat, let's leave now."

"I don't think anything is open yet, Harlee. Let's get a little bit of fishing in, and then we'll head in. We can eat lunch in town first; I know a great little place."

"I hope you know that protein bar I ate this morning isn't going to last me until lunch!"

I smiled. "I do have some snacks we can bring out with us."

She folded her arms over her chest. "The moment I get cold, we're leaving."

"Fair enough."

"Fine. Let's go fishing."

"I promise you it'll be fun, Harlee."

She harrumphed and stomped her foot like a little girl not getting her way.

I tried not to smile. "If you really want to go back home, I'll take you."

I could feel her turn and look at me. "You'd do that?"

Keeping my eyes on hers, I replied, "If that's what you want, yes."

She remained silent for a few moments before she said, "I don't want to go back home."

Smiling, I winked. "Good. I'm glad. Will you still be using your vibrator, though?"

"Ugh! Braxton!"

My heart was soaring as I watched Harlee walk from the fish shed to the cabin. She was a natural when it came to fly fishing. I would never admit it to her, but she was better than Thomas. Or even Nick. She had picked it up like she'd been fly fishing her whole life.

Once we got into the cabin, I shed my fishing garb and started to make a fire. Harlee opted to use the bathroom to get undressed.

After a minute or two, the door clicked open, and I looked up to see her standing there in sweats.

"Warmer now?" I asked.

She nodded, then made her way to the kitchen area. "Much. Coffee?"

"Please. The hotter the better." Luckily, Nick wasn't so much of a Neanderthal that he didn't have some modern appliances, like a Keurig. After our morning fish, we'd gone into town to eat and pick up some food. At the top of the list was coffee.

I arranged the wood I'd brought in from the shed, neatly stacking it next to the fireplace. I'd made sure to haul plenty of extra so the fire wouldn't go out.

"Is that our only source of heat?" she asked. "The fireplace?"

"Yep. Don't worry, I'll keep it going all night, and there are extra quilts in the closet."

"I take it Nick doesn't come up here much in the winter?"

I chuckled. "I think I use this place more than he does, no matter what time of year it is."

Harlee turned and handed me a cup of coffee. "You really enjoy fishing in the winter? I mean, you didn't do this simply to torture me?"

Giving her a questioning glance, I asked, "Did you not enjoy yourself?"

She grinned like a kid who'd been caught with her hand in the cookie jar. "I had a blast. I honestly can't wait to do it again tomorrow. How is it in warmer weather?"

"Not as peaceful."

She chewed on her lower lip. "It was definitely peaceful with only the two of us out there. And so beautiful. I wish I'd brought my camera. It's funny how we live here our whole lives and take the beauty surrounding us for granted."

"Speak for yourself. I never take it for granted."

She got her cup of coffee and walked over to the large chair to curl up in it. "You really love what you do, don't you?"

"Yeah, I really do," I said with a nod. "I know my parents were disappointed when I didn't show an interest in the restaurant—really, when none of us kids did. But they've always been supportive. They really encouraged me to follow my dreams."

"Was is scary for you to take such a leap? You were so young when you bought your first boat."

I chuckled. "I was scared to death I would fail. The last thing I wanted to do was go back to my parents and say I couldn't make it. I'm glad I never had to."

She smiled. "I know we've had our differences in the past, but I do hope you realize I'm proud of you and your success with the fishing charter, Brax."

It felt like someone reached into my chest and gave my heart a tug. "Thank you, Harlee. That means a lot to me."

She took a sip of her coffee as she looked everywhere except at me. Finally, she asked, "Did you want to make any of the fish we caught for dinner?"

"If you don't mind, I'd like to donate it to a local family I know is having a hard time right now. I already put it on ice."

Something moved across her face before she replied, "I don't mind at all. How about BLTs then?"

"That sounds good. I make a kick-ass aioli. I made sure to get the ingredients when you mentioned BLTs in the store."

Harlee stood. "Okay, you get busy with that, and I'll get the bacon going."

We fell into a smooth routine of making dinner together. Every now and then I stole a glance at her, and I couldn't help but imagine spending every night like this. Harlee and me in the kitchen, talking about our day, and laughing as if we didn't have a rocky past between us. I quickly found myself wishing the night wouldn't end.

Chapter Twelve

Harlee

The easiness of being with Brax made me feel both happy and sad. I could get used to spending my days and evenings with him. I'd never had so much fun as when I was standing in that river with him earlier. When he'd wrapped his arms around me to show me how to cast, it had felt so damn good. It had been the first time in ages that we didn't pick at one another or bring up the past. It was beautiful. And I wanted more days like this. I craved them.

At one point this afternoon, while watching Brax get lost in his fishing, I'd had the strong urge to tell him I was Ms. Seaside. It suddenly seemed wrong for me to keep it from him, and I wasn't sure why. I knew that the moment he found out he'd be pissed. Might never forgive me for it, especially since I was leading him on a wild goose chase.

Call me greedy, but we were finally getting along, and things felt so good between us that I wasn't about to risk losing this feeling.

I sliced the tomato I was holding and drew in a slow, deep breath. I had been dreading asking him a question all day, but I knew I needed to. Brax was taking a batch of bacon out of the pan. There wasn't going to be a good time to ask, at least not in my eyes, so I might as well get it over with while he was distracted.

"How did things go last night with Kelsey?"

He paused for a moment, and I swore I felt my heart jump into my throat. Had something happened between them?

"I don't think it's her," he finally said as he took out the last of the bacon. "I think this is enough bacon, don't you?"

It took everything I had not to demand he keep talking about his dinner last night. Glancing at the bacon, I replied, "Looks like more than enough. Um, why don't you think it's her?"

After he finished putting the bacon on the paper towel, he turned and faced me. "First, she absolutely hates Ms. Seaside. And when I say hates, I mean she really, *really* dislikes her. Second, she had her little notebook with her last night, and she pulled it out to write down a reminder. The woman's memory is bad for someone so young."

"She could be trying to throw you off. I mean, by hating Ms. Seaside that is, and using her notebook in a way that would make you suspect it's not what we think it is, but it really is."

"I'm a little worried I understood that."

I let out a nervous laugh as I pulled the toast out of the toaster oven. "Did you mention the notebook to her?"

"Nope."

Frowning I said, "Not at all?"

"Not at all. She actually let me see it herself when she caught me looking at it. I thumbed through the entire thing. No paper was torn out, and there wasn't a single bit of gossip. Just lists. Lots and lots of lists and little drawings of random things, like birds, the sunset, a tire swing."

"A tire swing?" I asked with a slight chuckle.

Brax nodded and laughed. "Anyway, she's not quite intelligent enough to be Ms. Seaside. She doesn't have the quick wit. Also, when I asked when the town was first formed, she had no idea."

"What does that have anything to do with Ms. Seaside?" I asked.

Looking directly at me, he said, "She mentioned it in one of her articles. The date the town was founded."

I raised my brows in surprise, quickly racing through my past articles to remember when I'd said that. "Did she? Wow, I must have missed it."

"Let's make our sandwiches. I'm starving."

Two hours later, we were both curled up on either side of the sofa in front of the fire. I yawned, then noticed how Brax followed suit.

"Are you tired?" I asked. "Do you want me to get off your bed?"

"No," he said with humor in his voice. "You're fine."

"What are you reading?" I leaned his way to get a peek.

"A book about the end of times. It's about a fisherman who's faced with saving his small oceanside town before a tsunami hits."

I crinkled my nose. "That sounds depressing."

He shrugged. "Thomas told me to read it."

"Ugh, I should have known."

I could feel Brax's eyes on me. "Did you and Thomas end things on bad terms?"

Shaking my head, I said, "No. He wasn't a good match for me *at all.*"

"He said the same thing."

I snapped my head up, and our eyes met. Before I had to chance to ask questions, he went on.

"He said you were too kinky in the bedroom."

"What?!" I exclaimed. "*Kinky*? That asshole wouldn't know kinky if someone spelled it out and showed him pictures!"

Brax lost it laughing. When he was finally able to speak again, he said, "Give him a break, Harlee. He was pretty nerdy in high school, and still doesn't have a lot of experience with women."

I felt my cheeks heat. "If I tell you something, do you swear not to utter it to another soul? Ever? For as long as you live?"

That caught his attention, because he shut his book and moved closer. "Tell me."

Who would have guessed Braxton Bradley was into gossip? I nearly laughed at his excitement. "Promise me you won't tell anyone. Not Gannon or Brody, and *especially* not Thomas."

"I swear."

"Cross your heart and hope to die?"

He shot me a frustrated look. "Are you ten?"

"Do it!"

He crossed his heart and mumbled, "Cross my heart and hope to die."

"Stick a needle in your eye."

"For fuck's sake, Harlee!"

I jumped at his outburst, then laughed. "Fine. Okay, here it is."

He leaned in closer.

"Ready?

"I'm going to murder you if you don't tell me."

I slowly shook my head. "You are no fun at all."

"*Harlee.*"

"Fine! Thomas was a virgin when we started dating."

Brax's mouth fell open, and he blinked as if he was moving in slow motion. After a minute of him sitting there with his mouth gaping, I snapped my fingers in front of his face.

"I take it you had no idea."

"Wait," he said, sitting back and shaking his head. "Are you sure? I mean, how do you know?"

I could feel my face get hot. "He told me. He said at first he was saving himself for his wife, and then as he got older, he figured it seemed too weird, so he always broke up with women before it got to that point in the relationship. It's why we started dating, actually. He approached me and asked if I would be his first. And I thought it was kind of sweet...at first. But he's terrible in bed."

Brax pushed his fingers through his hair. "Holy shit. It all makes sense. It's like...it's like every conversation we've had about women suddenly fell into place. He'd *never* had sex before you?"

"Nope," I said, popping my P.

He looked back at me. "And you agreed to be his first?"

"Yep." Another P pop.

"He'd *really* never...at all?"

I shook my head. "Nope. Never."

"Wow. This is... I don't know what this is. He never said a word to me."

Pulling my knees up to my chest, I asked, "Why would he tell you, Brax? He was probably embarrassed. I'm sure you talked about your hookups plenty."

He groaned and scrubbed his hands down his face. "God, I feel like an ass. I gave him a hard time about not using a vibrator on a woman."

I dropped my legs back down. "What did he tell you?"

Brax slowly lifted his gaze to meet mine. A sexy smirk grew across his face as he tilted his head and gave me a wicked once-over with those hazel eyes of his.

"Oh. My. God. He didn't," I said.

"He did."

"No! Men talk about stuff like that?"

Laughing, Brax nodded. "Said you wanted him to use a vibrator on you, and he was worried you'd like it better than him."

I shrugged. "Well, he was probably right about that. Like I said, he wasn't the best in bed, even when I tried to, um...help him."

"Oh, this is rich. The last thing I want to hear about is your sexual lessons with a man in his thirties who was still a virgin."

I reached over and hit him on the shoulder. "Don't be like that, Brax. How many guys do you know in their thirties who are virgins?"

"I don't think I've ever known any guy older than sixteen who was a virgin."

With pleading eyes, I begged him, "Please don't tell him I told you."

He looked at me, and I could tell by his expression that he wouldn't do anything to hurt Thomas. "I would never say anything, Harlee. He's one of my best friends."

Reaching for his hand, I squeezed it. "Thank you."

He pulled me to him, and I nearly fell into his lap. "I want something from you to keep this little secret, though."

I felt myself grinning like a little girl. I was so giddy and happy, being close to him. "You and I both know you're going to keep it."

He lifted a single brow. "Are you sure about that?"

With a wink, I stated, "Pretty confident."

"Let me watch you play with yourself."

My face instantly flamed. "No," I whispered.

"Let me watch you, and you can watch me. I'll stay here on the couch and won't move."

I felt an instant rush of wetness hit me between the legs, nearly moaning at the visual that popped into my head.

"What if...what if things go too far?" I asked.

He held up his right hand. "Pinky promise."

I chewed on my lower lip. The idea of seeing Brax take himself in hand had me so hot and bothered. Then add in him watching *me* get myself off... It was probably a recipe for disaster. But one I was pretty sure I'd be willing to do anyway.

"That's playing with fire, Brax."

The right side of his mouth rose in the sexiest smile I'd ever seen. "Are you afraid of getting burned, princess?"

My heart hammered in my chest. He was challenging me, and I was never one for backing down from a challenge.

"Not at all," I replied. My voice didn't even sound like my own.

"Stand up and take your clothes off in front of me."

I narrowed my eyes. "I don't do well with orders."

His tongue came out and swept over his lips, and I found myself crawling on top of him. He brought his hands to my hips, and I nearly exploded from his light touch.

"If I'm going to let you watch me fuck myself with a vibrator, I feel like I should be allowed a bit of fun first." He closed his eyes and moaned when I pressed down against his hard length. "The last time I got to see you, I was young and naïve. Not anymore."

I reached for his sweatpants. I pulled down as he lifted his hips with me still sitting on him. It was like I weighed nothing to him. I quickly raised my body up and pulled down his sweats down the rest of the way.

I gasped. "Jesus, you're not wearing anything underneath."

He smirked. "I like to be comfortable."

I stared at his impressive length and had to fight the urge to bend down and take him in my mouth. It watered for a taste of him. Lifting my gaze to his, I replied, "So do I. That's why I sleep naked."

He closed his eyes, and I watched his chest rise and fall. He was as horny as I was, and this whole little cat-and-mouse game we had going on only made it more intense.

The idea that Brax had no idea I was the woman he was looking for both thrilled and bothered me. More so the latter, but in that moment, I forced myself to ignore it.

I wrapped my hand around his length and shivered at the warmth of him. He was so hard and hot. I cupped his balls with my other hand, then ran my thumb over the bead of wetness at the top of his dick.

"If you don't stop," he said, "I'm going to come, and my part of the party will be over before it even begins."

Smiling, I moved off him completely. Before I walked over to the bed, I leaned down and licked up his shaft. The sound of Brax hissing only fueled my desire to please him. And what he wanted was to watch me please myself. That, I could do.

As I made my way across the room, I took off my sweatshirt and tossed it to the floor. Once at the bed, I hooked my thumbs into the waistband of my own sweats and pushed them down, leaning over so my ass was his only view.

"Jesus Christ, Harlee."

When I stood, I glanced over my shoulder to see his eyes wandering over my body. His hand was wrapped around his hard length, and for a moment I was jealous of that hand. I slipped my panties off and reached for my bag, then dug around until I found my vibrator.

I'd never performed like this for a man, and it was thrilling. I knew for a fact I would never try this again. Unless Braxton Bradley asked me to do it. For him. I knew deep down, I'd do anything he asked.

Pushing that thought aside, I propped up the pillows and lay back. With my eyes on Brax, I spread my legs wide. His entire body jerked, and he looked as if he was trying to remember how to breathe.

"I want you, Harlee."

Lifting my finger, I tsked. "That wasn't part of the agreement, Brax. Remember?"

Of course, I also wanted him, but I wasn't about to give myself to him. Not when he held the power to crush my heart again.

I knew I was wet, and as soon as I slipped my fingers inside me, I moaned at the confirmation.

"Do I make you wet, princess?" Brax asked.

All I could do was nod...because this man was whom I thought about every time I slipped a vibrator inside of me.

"Put it inside you."

Turning the vibrator on, I touched it to my nipple first and jerked slightly.

"Holy hell," he whispered as he gripped himself tighter.

"Do you like watching me do this?" I asked, running the vibrator down my body until it was inches from where I knew he wanted me to put it.

"Yes," he said, his voice cracking. "Give me more."

With a smile, I turned the vibrator off, pushed it inside me, then turned it back on. When the little extension vibrated on my clit, the jolt sent me off the bed.

I could hear him panting, could see the way his eyes turned dark as he watched me move the vibrator in and out of me. "Fucking hell. I'm not going to last long."

Pouting, I moved it slower, letting my desire coat the surface.

"Faster. Go faster," he begged.

I did as he asked and watched his own hand mimicking the speed of the vibrator.

"What...what are you...thinking about?" I asked between gasps and moans of my own.

"I'm wishing that was my cock thrusting in and out of you."

I closed my eyes, and I let the image play out in my mind. Brax over my body, inside my body. His mouth on my neck, my lips, my breasts.

Lifting my free hand, I played with my nipple, pretending it was his teeth biting it.

"Harlee."

Snapping my eyes open, our gazes met across the small distance.

"Faster. Fuck yourself faster," he demanded.

I moaned as I obeyed, my body trembling with the orgasm that was quickly building. "Brax. Brax, I'm so close!"

"That's it, princess. Deeper. Faster. Oh, fucking hell! Oh God, I'm going to come, Harlee."

I sat up some, watching as he jacked-off faster. Sweat beaded on his temple, and when I saw his face, I knew he was about to come. My eyes drifted down, and the moment I saw his cum, heard him cry out my name, I exploded.

His name repeated on my lips as one of the most intense orgasms I'd ever had rippled through my entire body.

I dropped my head back, my body trembling while wave after wave of pleasure washed over me.

When it stopped, I pulled the vibrator out. I wasn't even sure how in the hell I managed to turn it off. With shaking hands, I dropped it down next to me. I was panting like I'd run a freaking marathon. And on the couch, I could hear Brax attempting to get his own breathing under control.

"Fuck," he softly said. "That had to be the hottest thing I've ever seen."

I tried to find the words to say I agreed, but all I could do was nod. When I finally managed to look at him, I thought I might be a bit embarrassed. I was pleased to find out I wasn't in the least. Not when I saw the way he looked at me.

He still wanted me. He wanted more than what I'd just given him, and that caused me to smile, because in a way, I had won something. I wasn't sure what it was, but I'd won.

Sitting up, I let out a long, slow breath. "I'm going to go shower."

He frowned ever so slightly. Not going to lie, I was hoping he would ask to join me, but true to his word, he stayed put.

"I'll, um, add more wood to the fire."

I forced a smile. What had I been expecting? Him to fall to his knees and beg? Tell me he loved me and wanted to be with me now and forever?

As I made my way into the bathroom, I turned and looked back before I shut the door. Brax sat there, staring at the fire with an expression I wasn't able to read.

That was the problem with fire. When you played with it, you were always on the losing end.

Chapter Thirteen

Brax

The next three days flew by. Harlee acted as if the first night never happened. I tried to talk about it, but after the third time she changed the subject, I dropped it. We flirted, fought, teased, and even got a little tipsy one night. But nothing sexual happened again. It was as if we were both afraid that the next time we wouldn't be able to stop. I knew for a fact *I* wouldn't be able to stop. There was no fucking way. I wanted her more than ever.

I *wanted* there to be a next time, but the way she so easily brushed off how explosive we were together told me she wasn't interested in more. Not with me. I'd had my chance all those years ago, and now all I could get was a fucking sample. I wanted all of her, damn it.

As we drove down Main Street in Seaside after returning from the trip, Harlee asked, "Are you hungry? We never did eat breakfast, and it's almost two."

"I could grab something to eat before I drop you off. The grill?"

"Sure."

I parked a half a block down from my parents' restaurant. I walked around my truck and opened the door, helping Harlee out.

It didn't take long before I noticed a few people staring. Some whispered. Some smiled. Some openly gaped at us in shock.

"Why is everyone looking at us?" Harlee asked.

Placing my hand on her lower back to move her along faster, I replied, "I have no idea."

Once we entered the grill, we got our answer.

Palmer was the first one to walk up to us. "You haven't seen it yet, have you?" she asked, a look of worry written all over her face.

"Seen what?" Harlee and I both asked at the same time.

Palmer held up *The Chronicles*—and my eyes nearly popped out of my head.

"It's Wednesday," I said numbly. How in the hell had Harlee managed to write a special edition when she'd been with me twenty-four-seven for four days? Had she written it before we left?

"I know! She wrote a special edition!" Palmer confirmed with excitement. Oh, it was all fun and games when she wasn't the one being written about.

Grabbing the paper, Harlee quickly walked over to the counter. She actually seemed surprised, and when she started to read, her face turned bright red.

I read over her shoulder.

The Seaside Chronicles

March 1, 2023

Creating a Wake — Special Edition

Seasiders,

News on the beach is that Braxton Bradley has caught the eye of Seaside's very own darling, Harlee Tilson. Now, this might come as a shock to many of you, since our Catch of the Season has stated that he's not interested in settling down.

A little crab might have informed me that Braxton and Harlee were seen leaving early Sunday morning and have both been out of town since. Coincidence? I think not! The absolute scandal of it all, since Harlee is fresh off a breakup with Thomas Minor...who happens to be Braxton's BFF and works for him. Did I mention scandal?

Could it be true? Could Braxton and the Princess of Seaside be an item? One has to wonder what poor Thomas must think of this new development.

Stay tuned, my fishes...more is surely to come!

Fair winds and following seas!

Ms. Seaside

Harlee's entire body started to shake, and I wasn't sure if she was angry or upset. It was then that I realized she *hadn't* written this column.

If she didn't, who did?

Palmer wrapped her arm around Harlee. "It's not a big deal, Harlee."

She forced herself to smile. "I know. I guess it's a shock, that's all." I could see the wheels turning as Harlee continued to scan the article.

"Harlee, can I talk to you?" I asked softly.

Her head jerked up, and she met my gaze. "What?"

"Can I talk to you, *in private*?"

She shook her head. "Not right now, Brax. Can you do me a favor and take me to *The Chronicles*?"

Frowning, I asked, "Right now?"

Palmer stepped between us. "Harlee, believe me, I know when Ms. Seaside comes at you like this, you want to take up arms and fight. But take a few deep breaths first."

Harlee let out a humorless laugh. "I'm not bothered by it, Palmer. Honestly. I remembered I was supposed to do something before

I left town, and I forgot about it. My father will kill me if I don't get this ad out." Her gaze met mine again. "If you can't take me, I can—"

"I can take you," I quickly said. After kissing Palmer on the cheek, I followed Harlee out of the grill. She practically ran to my truck.

Once we were inside, I looked down to see her hands twisting together.

"Harlee, are you okay?" I asked as I rested my hand on hers. She pulled them away, then let out a breath and smiled.

"Yeah. I guess it was a shock to read that."

I knew for once she was actually telling the truth regarding the column. She was thrown. I hated seeing her like this...and I really wanted to come clean with her.

Lacing my fingers with hers, I gave her a light squeeze. "It's okay, Harlee."

She nodded. "I'm honestly fine, Brax. Like I said, I remembered I needed to meet a deadline for my dad, and it slipped my mind. The article doesn't bother me. I swear. The last thing I care about is what other people think."

I gave her a reassuring smile. "I know you don't care...much. But I also know a small part of you *does* care."

When she turned and looked at me, my breath caught in my throat. She looked so lost. And that killed me.

A few minutes later, I pulled up to *The Chronicles* and Harlee reached for her bag in the backseat.

"Can we talk before you rush off?" I said.

She got out and then turned and looked back at me. "Later, okay? I had a really good time these past few days, Brax. I hope you know that."

Smiling, I replied, "I enjoyed myself as well, princess."

Her eyes sparkled, and she looked down for a moment before meeting my gaze once again. "Bye, Brax."

"See you around."

I watched as she rushed into the building and out of sight.

After sitting there for a few minutes, I pulled into a parking spot. Before I could think about it any longer, I got out of the truck and walked toward the entrance.

I was done running. It was time to tell Harlee everything. And that included how I felt about her.

Chapter Fourteen

Harlee

My heart had been pounding since I'd seen Palmer holding up the paper. I hadn't written a special edition column this week. I'd sent my regular column to my father before I left town, in case we got stuck up at the cabin.

The elevator door opened, and I marched toward my father's office.

His receptionist, Beth, jumped to her feet. "I'm supposed to let your father know—"

I walked by her. "*I'll* let him know I'm here."

"Ms. Tilson!" she cried out when I opened the door and slammed it behind me.

My father looked up from his computer, smiled, then leaned back in his chair and assessed me as I stood in front of him. "Someone isn't happy."

Clenching my hands into fists, I stalked toward him. "How could you, Daddy? How could you rewrite something of mine and publish it?"

"Harlee, take a few deep breaths."

My entire body shook. "No! You took something I wrote—*months ago and never published!*and changed it. Why would you do that?"

He leaned forward. "Have you not seen the response we've been getting to Brax and Ms. Seaside? They're going crazy for it, and it makes for an amazing read. I just gave you a nudge in the right direction with Braxton."

I stood there and gaped at him. "You care more about this paper than you do your own daughter."

"Oh, Harlee, stop that. This is business and you know it. You've spent years gossiping about everyone in this town, including your own friends, and now you have a problem with it? You've even talked about yourself in the column. Why do you have an issue with it *now*?"

I opened my mouth, then snapped it shut before I said something to my father that I'd regret later. I needed to stop and focus on my words.

I closed my eyes and counted to ten. The hand that Braxton had held only minutes ago still felt as if it tingled, and that made my heart ache in my chest. Suddenly, I was so tired.

God, I felt *exhausted*. I was mentally and physically exhausted. All the lying about Ms. Seaside had paid its toll on me, and I was over it. All of it.

I wanted to go back to the cabin. To pretend that none of this had happened. I wanted to wrap my arms around Brax and tell him I still loved him. That I had never *stopped* loving him.

Tears stung at the back of my eyes because I knew I couldn't do that.

"Now that you've calmed down, do you see my point?"

Looking at my father once again, I slowly shook my head. "No, Daddy, I don't see it at all. You stole something that was mine, something I never intended to publish, and took liberties with it knowing I was out of town with Braxton. I write what I want to write. What I'm comfortable writing. I never would have mentioned going away with Brax in an article and made it seem like it was a love triangle between me, Brax, and Thomas. More importantly, I would have never taken *your* words and changed them and printed them without asking your permission. You went *behind my back* and did this."

He sighed and slumped in his chair. "Why do you care so much now, Harlee? This column was your idea. You knew what you were getting into when you started it. At the most, I guess I shouldn't have taken one of the articles and tampered with it—"

"Or published it as me."

"It *is* my paper."

"It's my *life*, Daddy! I get to control it. And it's my column. I get to control what information I put in and what I don't. We both agreed when I started this that you would give me one-hundred-percent ownership and wouldn't censor me."

"I didn't censor you. I added content. And from the comments online, everyone seems to love the idea of you and Braxton being together. What makes *your* private life any different than those of the people you write about?"

I blinked several times. I wasn't sure if I was attempting to keep my tears at bay or clear the sudden confusion that his words had caused. "The difference is, you took an article I wrote and changed it to benefit *you*."

He shook his head. "I also did it for you, Harlee."

I let out a bark of bitter laughter. "For me? How in the world did you do this for me?" I asked, slamming a fist to my chest.

Standing, my father placed his hands on his desk. "You might not want to admit it to yourself, Harlee, but you've never gotten over Braxton. I would go so far as to say you're in love with him—maybe even more than before."

And that's when it happened. The dam broke and the tears spilled free.

My father straightened abruptly and started to make his way around his desk.

I put up my hand to stop him. "Stop. Don't," I whispered.

I was about to open my mouth to say I was finished being Ms. Seaside when I heard a female voice clear their throat behind me.

Spinning around, I gasped when I saw Braxton standing next to Beth. His eyes bounced from me, to my father, before settling on me again.

I quickly wiped my tears away. "What did you hear?" I asked.

Brax said nothing as Beth looked from him to me.

"What did you hear?!" I shouted.

"The only thing we heard was Mr. Tilson saying you were in love with..." Beth's voice trailed off, and all I wanted was for the floor to open up and swallow me whole.

"I'll leave so you can speak with my father," I said, rushing out of the office.

"Harlee!" Brax called after me. "Wait, Harlee!"

I made it to my office and shut the door. I locked the knob, then pressed my back to the door and brought my hand up to stifle the sobs struggling to break free.

I heard a soft knock, then Brax's voice coming from the other side of the door. "Harlee, let me in. *Please.*"

"Go away, Brax," I called out. "If you care anything about me at all...please leave me alone. *Please.*"

I heard him exhale before he said, "Don't push me away, Harlee. Please let me in."

Tears streamed down my face as I turned and pressed my forehead to the door. Everything in me wanted to let him in. Well, almost everything. That stubborn part of my heart that was still hurt from his last rejection kept me from reaching for the lock.

Right when I thought he might have left, he spoke again. His voice was low and close to the door. "I know the truth, Harlee. I know you're Ms. Seaside. I've known it for months."

Stepping back away from the door, I pressed my hand to my stomach and fought the urge to throw up.

"Open the door, Harlee, so we can talk."

I quickly looked around my office. "Damn it," I mumbled. I only had one way in and one way out. Rushing over to the window, I looked down. Not even I was desperate enough to scale down three stories.

I spun around when Brax knocked on the door again and then rushed back over to it.

"You're going to have to leave at some point," he said. "I'll wait here for as long as I need to."

"Shit!" I finally unlocked the door and opened it.

Brax pushed his way in, shut the door, and relocked it behind him.

I backed up a few paces and twisted my hands together nervously. "What do you think you know?" I asked, ignoring the way my heartbeat pounded in my ears.

He walked closer until he was right in front of me. I tilted my head up to look at him and held my breath. When he framed my face with his warm hands, I wasn't sure if I should panic or melt against him.

"I know you're Ms. Seaside. And now I'm going to do the one thing I've wanted to do for a long while now."

A rush of panic swept over me. The moment I had pretended would never happen, the moment I dreaded would happen, was about to rock me to the core. I was going to lose Braxton forever. I deserved it though, that much I knew.

I swallowed hard and then asked in a barely there voice, "Break my neck?"

He chuckled and slowly shook his head...before he leaned down and pressed his lips to mine.

The kiss was soft and sweet, and I instantly melted into him. It didn't take long for things to turn heated as he deepened his kiss.

"Brax," I gasped, pulling my mouth from his. "We really need to talk."

He brought his hand up behind my neck, drawing my mouth back to his. "We can talk later. Right now, I need to be inside you, Harlee."

My knees nearly buckled out from under me as I grabbed onto him. *What did he say?*

"But...you know who I am, and you still..."

He nodded. "More than ever."

All I could do was nod back and whisper, "Okay."

He snickered and quickly swept me up into his arms and carried me over to my desk.

"Anything important on here?" he asked, holding me like I weighed nothing.

"No. Um, I mean, maybe. But I—"

His large hand swept everything off my desk, and I was thanking the stars above I had the one office at the end of the building, away from everyone else. No one would hear the clatter of everything falling to the floor...or what was about to happen.

Setting me on my feet, Brax took his coat off and tossed it to the floor as I worked on getting his jeans unbuttoned.

My hands shook so badly, I wasn't able to unbutton his jeans.

He took my hands in his and pulled them behind my back, giving me a sexy grin. "Let me do it."

I nodded.

Taking a step back, Brax worked on my jeans first, unbuttoning and pulling them down, along with my panties. He knelt and pulled my shoes off one at a time, then divested me of my pants. I stood in my office with the lower part of my body completely naked. A shiver ran up my back, but not from being cold. It was the way he looked up at me, that wicked gleam in his eyes as he stood, lifted me, and set me on the desk. He unbuttoned his own jeans, but didn't pull them down.

"I want to taste you first."

My eyes flew to my office door, then back to Brax. "What if..."

Words failed to form as he slipped his fingers inside me, moving them in and out while kissing along my neck.

"Brax... Brax!"

That was it. I was broken. I couldn't do anything but moan in pleasure and say his name.

"I love hearing my name on those pretty lips of yours, princess."

Dropping my head back so he could get better access to my neck, I reached for his shoulders. I wanted to push him down. I needed his mouth to be where I ached the most. But then again, I wanted him inside me. I was a bundle of horny confusion.

"Brax, I need to come. *Please.*"

I could feel him smile against my skin, and before I could even take a breath, he had my legs spread open and his mouth devouring me.

"Oh God!" I cried out before I pressed my hand to my mouth. I used my other hand to grip the desk as Brax worked my body with his mouth and fingers.

He sucked, licked, and nibbled as I wrapped my legs around him and dropped my other hand to the desk to hold on. I could tell it was going to be a massive orgasm. The tension in my tightly wound-up body was begging to be released.

"Oh, dear God above," I gasped. "Brax!"

He pushed a finger against my rear end while his others found that special spot inside of me. And his mouth... My God, his mouth was doing something to my clit that should be illegal. Two seconds later, I placed my hand over my own mouth again and fell hard. Wave after wave of pleasure unleashed, and I was positive I left my body.

Closing my eyes, I saw bursts of light, one after the other, while Brax never stopped moving his fingers and mouth.

My body was still trembling when I felt his hard tip at my entrance. Snapping my eyes open, I met his gaze.

"I don't have a condom," he said.

"I'm on the pill."

He hesitated. "I've never been with anyone without protection, Harlee."

"Neither have I. But do you really want to stop now and go to the store for a condom?"

"No," he said—then pushed inside me.

I nearly screamed as he filled me, and another orgasm hit immediately. "Braxton!"

His mouth covered mine, swallowing my moans of pleasure as he drove in and out of me like he'd lost all control. I wrapped my arms around him and held on tightly, feeling him grow bigger and harder inside of me.

He pulled his mouth back and looked into my eyes. "I love you."

Tears blurred my vision as I slid my fingers into his hair and grabbed it, drawing his mouth back to mine. But before we bridged the connection, I panted my reply. "I love you too."

The moment his mouth captured mine, he groaned, spilling his hot cum into my body as we both came together.

Three orgasms. Three. How does he do this to me?

Chapter Fifteen

Brax

The second I slid into Harlee's hot, tight pussy, I knew I would lose control. Now was not the time to make love. It was the time to fuck, and I knew it was what she wanted too. Hell, what we both *needed*.

Harlee's eyes widened as another orgasm hit her. Covering her mouth with mine, I swallowed her screams of pleasure while I got lost inside her. Her whimpers, the feel of her tightening around my cock—it was all too much. I was going to release soon, and I didn't care. I needed to be inside of her, be one with her again.

I'd missed her so damn much.

I could feel my release building as my balls pulled up. God, it was going to be the orgasm to end all orgasms.

Jerking my mouth from hers, our eyes met, and I said the one thing I'd regretted not saying so many years ago.

"I love you."

Her eyes pooled with tears, but in true Harlee fashion, instead of letting them fall, she grabbed my hair and tugged my mouth back to hers. Before she kissed me, she uttered the words I had only dreamed of hearing.

"I love you too."

Then our mouths collided into a hot, searing kiss, and I came so fucking hard I thought I was going to black out. By the feel of Harlee's pussy contracting and pulling out every drop of my release, she was coming again too.

When I finally stopped moving and broke the kiss to get air into my lungs, our foreheads were resting against one another. Our chests rose and fell like we had run a marathon. Each breath burned yet felt amazing.

I was still inside of her and wanted to stay like that forever. The way she had her arms wrapped tightly around me, I knew she felt the same.

It was only then that I realized I'd just fucked her only a few offices down from her father's.

Holy. Shit.

"I don't want to move," I whispered.

Her fingers moved lazily as she played with the hair at the nape of my neck. Just having her touch me, anywhere, was fucking amazing.

"Neither do I. Please tell me that wasn't a dream."

I chuckled. "It wasn't a dream."

She was the first to pull back, our eyes meeting. "We have a lot to talk about."

I nodded. "We do."

"Are you angry with me?"

"No."

She chewed on her lip. "About Ms. Seaside, I mean."

"I know what you meant." Glancing around, I saw some tissues on the floor. Reaching for them, I grabbed a few and slowly pulled out of her. Dropping to my knees, I began to clean her body.

Her knuckles were white as she gripped the desk. When I looked up, her eyes were closed.

"Does that feel good?"

She nodded. I knew I could easily make her come again, but I wanted to save some for later.

I stood, and she opened her eyes, then looked down at my still-somewhat-hard cock. She ran her tongue over her lips, and I moaned.

"Harlee, you have no idea how many nights I've dreamed of your mouth wrapped around my dick."

Her gaze shot up to mine, and she smiled. "I can make that happen, you know."

Tucking myself back into my boxers, I zipped my jeans and fastened the only button. "Tonight."

She nodded. "Okay."

"Come here," I said, helping her off the desk.

Harlee held onto my shoulders as I helped her slip her jeans back on.

"My legs feel like jelly," she giggled and stumbled once she let go and stood up straight. Reaching for her shoes, she looked over at the sofa on the other side of her office.

"That might have been more comfortable for you," I said, lacing my fingers with hers and guiding her over to it.

"I wouldn't change a thing. That was incredible."

I winked and sat down, pulling her down next to me. "It did. And I'm already counting down to when we can do that again. But slower."

Her teeth dug into her lip as her cheeks turned pink. I loved that she knew what she wanted sexually and wasn't afraid to express it, but seeing her blush made me fall even more head over heels for her. Harlee might know what she wanted, but there was a soft, sweet side to her. A side that cared so damn much for other people, it was still a little strange for me to wrap my head around the fact that she was Ms. Seaside.

After helping her don her cute little rubber boat shoes, I pulled her onto my lap. Harlee buried her head against my chest, and we sat there for the longest time in silence before she took a deep breath and exhaled.

"My father wrote that special edition article off of one I'd written a few months back. I was never going to print it because it was all made up in my head."

"What do you mean?"

"I'd just broken up with Thomas, and I ran into you on the pier. Do you remember that?"

"After the New Year?"

She nodded as she ran her finger over a pattern on my T-shirt. "I wanted you to kiss me so badly that day. I daydreamed about you pulling me into your arms and...well...like I said, it was written more out of a fantasy than anything. I thought about printing it, but it would have been a blatant lie. My father must have been looking around in my work computer and found it. He changed it quite a bit...and that's what he printed. I'm so sorry, Brax. I'm so sorry for everything."

I pulled her closer and tightened my arms around her.

"When did you find out?" she asked. "*How* did you find out?"

I smiled and kissed her head. "It was an article Palmer showed me. You're actually going to laugh when I tell you."

Drawing back, Harlee looked at me with a soft smile. "Tell me."

"It was when you mentioned the year Seaside was founded. That's when I suspected you were writing the column."

Her brows drew down in confusion. "Why?"

"The night we spent together, we talked about everything and anything."

Softening her face, she nodded in agreement. "We did."

"You told me the town was founded in 1762, but everyone else said 1763, because that was when they officially named it Seaside. But the real year was the one before. So, when Ms. Seaside said 1762, I instantly knew it was you."

She slowly shook her head. "Wow. I can't believe that. I'm usually so careful with what I say. Although, I think I said something about knowing Deacon, and Palmer jumped all over that."

I laughed. "Yes, that's when she came to me to help her find out Ms. Seaside's identity. Anyway, I started to put some things together, and you mentioned something about the lighthouse. I went on a Tuesday, waited all day...and saw you."

149

Her eyes went wide with disbelief. She turned and straddled my lap. "When?"

"Mid-January or a bit later."

"I knew it!" she said, hitting me on the chest. "I knew I was being watched that day! I felt...well, I felt *you*. I don't know how to explain it, but I remember looking back down the walkway because I was so certain you were there. I didn't see you, though."

"I was hiding in the trees."

She stared at me for a moment. "Hiding in the trees." Then her eyes went wide again. "So you knew it was me all those times I wrote about you since then?"

I laughed and squeezed her ass. "I sure as hell did. Even went back and reread some of the older articles. I've got to say, my least favorite is the Master Baiter one."

She brought her hand up to her mouth before she lost it laughing.

"You think that's funny, huh?" I moved quickly and pinned her to the sofa while she laughed until tears trickled out. I couldn't help but laugh along with her.

When she finally stopped laughing, we stared into one another's eyes.

She smiled. "I have to be honest and tell you that I laughed so hard writing that article. Then to hear what everyone said and sent to you afterwards..."

Rolling my eyes, I shook my head. "Fucking Brody."

Harlee fell into another round of laughter. But when I laid my body over hers, it faded away.

"Watching you the other night was one of the hottest fucking things I've ever seen, Harlee."

Her chest rose and fell with a deep breath. "I felt the same way. I wanted you to come into the shower with me so badly."

"You did?"

She nodded. "I thought you weren't interested."

"Far the fuck from it." I leaned down and kissed her. Our tongues danced together in the most sensual rhythm, and I knew if we didn't stop, I'd be taking her again. Chancing it once in her office was bad enough, but twice might be pushing our luck.

When I drew back from the kiss, I ran my finger down the side of her beautiful face. "There isn't a day that's gone by that I haven't regretted lying to you that night."

Her eyes bounced all over my face.

"I knew there was always something there," I said. "I would get so damn jealous when I saw you with other guys. I felt things I couldn't explain. And after making love to you over and over that night...you scared the living hell out of me, Harlee Tilson."

She pressed her warm hand against my face and I leaned into it. "I probably shouldn't admit this," she said, "but I gave Jennifer chocolate laxatives on Thanksgiving."

Shocked, I moved off her, and she scrambled into a sitting position.

"I had to stop three times when I was taking her home that night so she could use the bathroom! She blamed my mother's cooking, said it gave her food poisoning."

Harlee covered her mouth in an attempt not to laugh.

"How much did you give her?"

With a grin, she said, "She ate all six little squares. It kind of looked like half of a Hershey bar."

"What?!"

She shrugged. "I told her it was chocolate from a friend of mine in Australia. I thought she'd take a bite and give it back to me. She ate the whole thing before I could stop her! So really, it was her fault for being a chocolate hog."

"Oh my God, Harlee."

She tried to keep her laugh in and failed. She laughed even harder when I joined in.

"Come here," I said, pulling her back onto my lap. "Where do we go from here? Because I can tell you, now that I have you back, I'm not ever letting you go."

Resting her head on my shoulder, she let out a contented sigh. "Before you and Beth walked in, I was about to tell my father I was done being Ms. Seaside."

I studied her for a beat. "Harlee, you have to keep being Ms. Seaside."

Her eyes widened in shock. "What?"

"If you walk away now, people are going to put together the connection after that last article. No. You need to keep doing it. And I think we need to keep bantering back and forth."

She gave me a disbelieving laugh. "So you want to keep doing the Friday column?"

I gave a small shrug. "I mean, it's kind of cool. I love fishing, and I love teaching people about fishing. Your dad said I didn't have to do it every Friday. Just what worked for me. And I think a few months of us—by that I mean, Ms. Seaside and me—going back and forth will be good for you and the paper."

"Why do I have to keep writing it?"

"If you suddenly stop, people will think one of two things. One, you're Ms. Seaside, or two, you ran to your daddy and complained about her, and he fired Ms. Seaside for writing about you. You need to keep going at least until your dad can transition someone else into the column. As hard as you went after Addie, Sutton, and Palmer... you need to do the same thing to yourself, Harlee. You're practically a Bradley as it is, so it only makes sense Ms. Seaside would target you next."

Tears pooled in her eyes, and I quickly cupped my hands around her face. "Hey, what's wrong?"

She sniffled. "I've always wanted to be a Bradley. I've always thought of Addie, Sutton, and Palmer as my sisters."

"And me?"

"I can honestly say I have never once thought of you as a brother."

Smiling, I kissed the tip of her nose. "Someday, Harlee, I'll officially make you a Bradley."

Her head jerked back as she gasped.

"Too soon?"

She shook her head. "No. Not at all."

Leaning her back onto the sofa once more, I decided to hell with worrying about taking our chances. I stripped Harlee naked, undressed myself, and slowly made love to my woman.

Chapter Sixteen

Harlee

I glanced up and saw Sutton and Palmer walking into the Seaside Grill, locked arm in arm and giggling. Once they saw me, they made a beeline toward our regular booth.

"Morning!" Sutton said as she sat down, then immediately frowned. "Man, pretty soon we're going to have to sit at a table. I can't believe how big this baby is getting, and I'm not even due until July!"

Palmer snickered and slid in next to Sutton.

"Where's Addie?" I asked.

"She's on her way." Sutton looked around surreptitiously before focusing back on me. "She was craving a breakfast taco from Taco Hut."

I laughed.

"Did you see it?" Palmer asked.

I frowned. "See what?"

Palmer rolled her eyes. "Ugh, the paper! The whole reason we meet for breakfast on Thursdays?"

"She wrote about you and Brax. Again!" Sutton stated.

Rolling my eyes, I sighed, "Lucky me, two days in a row. And I thought we met for breakfast because we loved seeing one another."

Palmer waved me off then clapped, a little bit too excited about *Ms. Seaside* writing about me again.

She took the paper out of her bag and slid it toward me.

With a big sigh, I opened it up to Ms. Seaside's column.

The Seaside Chronicles

March 2, 2023

Tide's Out

Seasiders,

Well, I'm not one for saying I told you so, but I told you so. The little bit of news I shared yesterday about our Catch of the Season and Harlee Tilson? Well, it's been confirmed from a source close to both that they did indeed go out of town together.

Is anyone else just as excited about this love match as I am? I mean, the bad boy and the good girl trope is by far one of my favorites. Is it too early to call them a couple and come up with a cool couple name? I mean, Braxlee does roll right off the tongue. Feel free to offer up your suggestions. Maybe we'll do a town vote on it!

A little seagull did in fact clear up that Harlee and Thomas Minor broke up well before the Christmas holiday. Let's hope the latest news doesn't interfere with the working relationship between Thomas and Braxton.

Until next time, my fishes.

Fair winds and following seas!

Ms. Seaside

After reading, I looked up to see both Sutton and Palmer smiling.

"The bad boy and the good girl?" I said. "What the hell?"

Sutton nodded. "Clearly she doesn't know you like we do. I thought that part was funny too. Can you imagine if she knew you were behind the pleasure loft?"

Palmer added, "That's all you got out of that? Hello? She's trying to give you guys a cheesy couple name."

"Is anyone going to address the fact that Harlee hasn't denied she and Brax are a thing?" Addie said as she stood at the end of the table with a piece of cheese stuck to her cheek.

Pointing, I said, "Um, you have evidence of your food betrayal on your face."

She quickly wiped it away and then slid in next to me, making almost the exact comment that Sutton made about her belly.

"Wait, Addie's right." Sutton stated. "Are you and Brax a thing? And who in the hell would confirm it for Ms. Seaside? The only people close to you are right here at this table."

The three of them all looked at each other with accusing expressions.

"Okay, first, I can tell you that Brax and I are..."

They all leaned in closer.

"Together. Multiple times."

Three loud female screams caused everyone in the restaurant to look at us.

"My goodness, what are you girls doing?" Barbara asked as she rushed over to the table.

"Mom! Oh my gosh, you were right! It's official! Braxlee is real!" Palmer whisper-shouted.

Barbara turned and looked at me, a wide smile on her face. "It's about darn time!"

The four of us all said in unison, "What?"

Dismissing us with a wave of her hand, Barbara replied, "Please, it was so obvious the two of you had a thing for each other. I'm glad you both finally gave in to it."

Addie shook her head. "Mom...you've always suspected they liked each other?"

Crossing her arms, Barbara replied, "I *knew*, not suspected. And your brother may have confided in me a few years ago about his feelings for Harlee."

The table fell silent at that. I opened my mouth to say something, then quickly shut it.

"You knew!" Sutton said in an accusing tone. "Mom!"

She shrugged. "I try to stay out of my kids' business. Now, two things. Stop screaming. And the second, never utter the word 'Braxlee' again. That sounds creepy."

Turning to walk away, she stopped and looked back at Addie. "How was your breakfast taco this morning, honey?"

Addie's face went blank as Palmer whispered, "How does she know *everything*?"

"Good morning, ladies." Brax walked up, grabbed a chair, and swung it around to sit at the end of the booth. When he looked at me, he winked. My mind instantly went back to my office. His truck. My bedroom...and then again this morning in the shower. According to Brax, we were making up for lost time, which was perfectly fine with me. I was a bit sore, though. Not that I would tell him that.

"Harlee Tilson, did you just blush?" Sutton asked.

"She totally did," Palmer added.

I shot them the finger and laughed.

"My, oh my, what *could* you have been thinking of?" Addie added.

I decided to give them a taste of their own medicine. "Probably the amazing shower I had this morning."

Brax laughed while the three of them all screwed up their faces in disgust.

"Gross. I did not need that visual." Addie put her hand to her mouth and pretended to gag.

"You were the one who asked, Addie," I said.

"Touché," she mumbled.

Palmer reached for her brother's hand. "We just found out that it's true! I'm so happy for you both. But how did Ms. Seaside get it confirmed? None of *us* even knew."

Brax shrugged. "Maybe someone saw me going into Harlee's house last night and not leaving until this morning."

Addie waved her hand in front of her like a fan. "Man, when you two decide to get together, you don't waste any time."

Everyone laughed.

Sutton reached across the table for my hand. "Well, I, for one, am so happy. Two of my most favorite people have found happiness with each other, and that makes me...it makes me..."

"Oh God, here we go," Palmer muttered.

Sutton started to cry.

"Sutton?" I put my hand over hers. "What's wrong?"

Sniffles came from my right, and I turned to see that Addie was crying too.

"Addie?" I asked.

"What's happening?" Brax looked from sister to sister.

Palmer leaned back and sighed. "I'm never getting pregnant. It makes your hormones too crazy. They both cry at the drop of a hat, I swear."

Brax grabbed some napkins and handed them to his two sisters. "Seriously, why are you both crying? What's wrong?"

Sutton waved her hand frantically in front of her as she attempted to get her emotions in check, while Addie blew her nose.

"It's okay, Brax. These are happy tears," Addie said before breaking into a full sobbing fit.

Brax and I looked at each other with stunned expressions.

"Put me down for no babies, please." Palmer leaned forward and waved Ruby over. "Ruby, do we have champagne?"

Ruby made her way over and started to rub Addie's back. "I don't think so, why?"

"A mimosa sounds really good about now, hold the OJ."

Ruby chuckled. "Should I get your mother?"

Our five voices all said, "No!" at the same time.

Holding up her hands, Ruby took a few steps back. "Sorry it took me so long to get over here. Are you all ready for your drinks and breakfast?"

"I ate already," I said.

"Nothing for me," Sutton said, suddenly perfectly fine and with a smile on her face. "Wait. Can you bring me a pickle and some mayo?"

Ruby nodded as if the request wasn't the grossest thing ever ordered.

Palmer gagged. "I'll just have a coffee."

"Same for me," Brax said.

"Really, Sutton? A pickle and mayo?" Addie asked.

"Yep. It's what the baby wants."

Addie shuddered. "I'm so glad I haven't gotten any weird cravings."

"Excuse me." I turned to face her. "Who texted me two weeks ago at midnight and asked if I could please go buy rocky road ice cream and black beans because Gannon was working. THEN you proceeded to mix them together and eat it, remember?"

Palmer practically turned green. "Yep. Nope. I think I'll stick with my future stepson, Charlie."

Addie put her hands on her stomach and giggled. "Trust me, Palmer. Being pregnant is the most amazing thing you'll ever experience."

Palmer raised a brow. "Even better than making said baby?"

Brax cleared his throat. "This conversation is taking a turn in the wrong direction with your brother sitting here."

"No, nothing is better than that," Addie stated.

Sighing, Brax said, "So, my dinner last week with Kelsey Roberts. No way she's Ms. Seaside."

All eyes turned to Brax.

"I could have told you that," Palmer said. "She isn't on Kimberly's level of never-could-have-pulled-it-off, but she's a close second."

"Who else is on your list?" Addie asked.

Before either of us could answer, Barbara and Keegan appeared. "Kids, we need to have a family meeting. Now, please."

My heart dropped, and I immediately looked at Keegan. He'd had a heart attack a little over a year ago, and I knew I wasn't the only one who went there with my thoughts.

Standing, Brax looked at his father. "Dad?"

Keegan held up both hands. "I'm fine. We're both fine. We have some news we'd like to share with you, and since you're all here, now's the time. If you don't mind, Ruby brought your drinks into the office."

Brax moved his chair out of the way and held his hand out for Addie, helping her slide out of the booth. He did the same for Palmer and Sutton. The three sisters started for the back as Brax held his hand out to me.

"Oh, I'll wait here."

"No, you won't," Brax said.

Barbara looked at me. "Harlee, honey, that includes you."

Turning to look back, Brax smiled at his mom.

"Me?" I asked.

Barbara held her hand out and I took it, sliding out of the booth. "I may not have birthed you, young lady, but you are just as much a daughter to me as my three girls. Now, come on, we have some news to share with everyone."

"I knew it was coming, but I'm still in shock," Sutton said as I helped her unpack a box of shirts she'd gotten in today. They bore the name of her shop, Coastal Chic, along with her sunset logo.

"They seemed so happy about their decision to sell the restaurant to Ruby," I said.

She stopped and smiled. "They did seem happy. And I can't believe they're going to Italy!"

"Can you blame them? Since I've known them, they've been at that restaurant nearly every day, except for when your dad was sick."

Her smile faded some as she folded one of the shirts and stacked it on the counter. "I don't blame them at all. I know this is something Mom has wanted for a while now, especially after Dad had his heart attack. Maybe someday we can all go on a big family vacation."

"That would be fun."

Sutton stopped folding and looked at me. "You and Brax..."

I felt my cheeks heat. "Me and Brax."

She reached for my hand, and I paused in my unpacking. "There's something about you today, Harlee. You have a glow about you."

"That's called having hot sex, Sutton."

Jerking her hand away, she rolled her eyes and laughed. "Gross! That's my brother."

I shrugged. "Not gonna lie, your brother is—"

"Please don't say another word."

Laughing, I let out a long, contented sigh. "I haven't been this happy in so long, Sutton."

"I think Brax is feeling the same way. He looked so happy this morning, and when he saw you, I could see it written all over his face. The way he lit up."

I started to say something, and she held up a hand. "Please don't say it was from all the sex you had."

"Okay, I won't say that. But I *will* say, I think we've both been so stubborn. Maybe me more than him. That night we spent together, I was so hurt when he pushed me away. I mean, I knew I always had a crush on Brax, but something changed when we were together, and I swore he'd felt it too."

Sutton nodded. "The difference is, he got spooked. Lord, doesn't this story sound familiar."

We both giggled.

"How do you think Ms. Seaside knew about you two?" she asked.

"My guess," I said, grabbing another shirt and handing it to her, "is that someone, maybe even Ms. Seaside herself, saw Brax going home with me. We weren't hiding anything when he stood on the front porch and kissed me like he wouldn't see me for months."

Sutton sighed. "Oh, I just love this. My brother with my very best friend. It just makes my heart feel so—ouch!"

I dropped the shirt I was holding. "What's wrong?"

"The baby kicked me! Hard."

"It's a boy."

She rubbed along the side of her stomach. "Either that or a future soccer player. That was the biggest one so far. Speaking of...this might be too soon, but do you want kids?"

"Yes," I replied without even having to think about it. "Brax and I actually talked about it last night. I think it was between when he took me against the wall and when we had a late night-snack before sex on the kitchen floor."

Sutton blinked several times. "How many times did you guys do it?"

"Four—if you don't count the two times in my office yesterday."

"Your office? Oh my gosh, you did not!" she said with a chuckle.

"We did!"

"Making up for lost time, I'd say. This calls for new lingerie." She slipped off the stool and headed toward the area of the store where she kept the lingerie she'd helped design with a friend from New York. "We just got in this baby blue set that would make your eyes pop!"

I followed her and nearly gasped when I saw the lace nightie. "I love this! And you have it in my size."

"Yep. I already set aside this same one—in this color—for myself after I have the baby."

"I'm totally buying this. Maybe a new vibrator as well."

Sutton screwed up her face. "Why do you need a new vibrator? You own like twenty."

"Brax likes..."

I let my voice trail off when I saw the horrified expression on Sutton's face.

"Um, I'll just go on up and peek around for a bit," I said.

She nodded. "'Kay. I think I'll go throw up now."

Chapter Seventeen

Brax

I sat back in the chair as I took a drink of coffee. The newspaper that had been delivered only moments ago and was open to my article and ready to read.

The Seaside Chronicles

March 3, 2023

Friday's Catch

Dear Anglers,

As you've already heard, I did indeed head out on the fly-fishing trip I mentioned before. Thanks, Ms. Seaside, for making everyone aware of that. And for those wondering, no, I did not go alone. I went with my girlfriend, Harlee. Harlee Tilson, also known as the Princess of Seaside. Does this make me the Prince of Seaside now? I'm sure Ms. S will want to weigh in on that.

Oh, what was that, Ms. S? You didn't get to actually announce that Harlee and I are officially a couple? Sorry to steal your thunder from you. And give up on the couple names, for the love of God.

Harlee and I went down to St. George River and spent four peaceful days fly fishing. We were able to catch a decent number of fish and donated them to a family in need. I'm not always the bad boy, Ms. S.

I had the pleasure of teaching Harlee how to fly fish, and I dare say if she keeps up with it, she may get better than I am. I almost forgot how much I loved teaching people to fish. Harlee gave me a great idea about doing a fishing camp this summer for the kids in Seaside. Be sure to keep an eye out for details on that. I'm also keeping my fingers crossed she'll come work for me this summer—that is, if I can steal her away from Sutton's store, Coastal Chic (insert shameless plug for my sister's shop).

Enjoy the few pictures I snapped of our trip (mostly of the fish we caught...and one hell of a sexy photo of my new girlfriend), and if anyone has any questions about fly fishing (not about the sexy AF girlfriend), give me a shout, and I'll try to answer them in the next article.

Until next time, happy fishing.
Catch of the Season
AKA Prince of Seaside
AKA Harlee's hot AF Boyfriend

PS. This means I'm officially off the market, so good luck to the next round of bachelors Ms. S casts into the vote for Catch of the Season 2023!

"Braxton Bradley!" Harlee shouted as she made her way from the bedroom and into my kitchen.

I dipped the paper down and watched her approach. "Good morning, princess."

"The sexy AF girlfriend? Really?"

Laughing, I looked back at the paper. "It's true."

"And that picture! Why did you include that picture of me?"

"Cause you look hot in it."

She stood there with a blank expression. "My hair is a mess and my cheeks and nose look like I'm giving Rudolph a run for his money."

"I know. You're hot as fuck."

Her eyes narrowed, then her facial expression softened. "You think I look hot in that picture? I'm dressed in layers of clothing."

I put my coffee cup down, stood, and pulled her to me. "I think you look hot as fuck all the time. And now that you're mine, I can tell you that, or write that, anytime I want. And I can also do this."

I ran my hand up her thighs and under the long T-shirt she was wearing—and stopped when I brushed against her bare lips.

"Holy shit, you're not wearing any panties."

She smiled. "No, I'm not."

"Are you in a rush?" I asked as I moved my mouth to her neck.

Tilting it to give me better access, she whispered, "Why?"

"Because I'm going to make love to you right here."

"Right. Here?" she panted when I nibbled on her earlobe and pushed my sweats down.

"Right. Here." Walking backward at my urging, she bumped into a wall. I lifted her leg and slipped my fingers inside her. "Jesus, you're so wet."

"Yes," she panted, her fingers digging into my shoulders. "I want it hard and fast, Brax."

Moaning, I slid my fingers into her hair and tugged it gently. "You drive me wild, princess."

Right as she was about to answer, the doorbell rang, and we both froze.

"Who could that be?" Harlee whispered.

I shook my head. "I have no idea."

It rang again, then someone knocked.

"Fucking hell," I grumbled, tucking myself back into my pants while Harlee reached up and kissed me.

"I'll go get dressed," she said.

"No, go wait for me. Whoever it is, I'll get rid of them."

She smiled and turned to walk away. I gave her ass a hard slap, causing her to let out a scream before she quickly headed back to my bedroom.

Clearing my throat, I made my way to the door. I was going to kill whoever was on the other side. Opening it, I said, "What the hell do you want?"

I froze for the second time when I saw the woman standing there.

"Hey, Braxton."

It wasn't the woman I'd slept with last year standing on my porch who threw me for a loop.

It was the baby she held in her arms that made me nearly throw up what little bit of food I had in my stomach.

"Heidi?"

"Do you mind if we come in? It's cold out here."

For just a moment, I thought about closing the door. This was a woman from my not-so-distant past. A woman I had spent a night with and walked away from without a second glance. A classic one-night stand. Her boyfriend had just dumped her. She'd been pissed and had wanted revenge sex.

"Braxton?"

I shook my head. "Right, right. Come on in. I'm so sorry."

Heidi walked in and looked around for a moment before she turned to me. "Do you mind holding him while I take off my coat?"

I pointed to myself and tried not to notice how my hand was shaking. "Me? You want me to hold him?"

She nodded and laughed. "He won't break."

Without even waiting for me to respond, she placed the baby in my arms and started to take off her coat.

My mind instantly started adding up the months since I'd last seen Heidi. It had been the summer before. She'd been on a charter with a bunch of other women who'd been there for a girls' trip. College sorority friends or something like that. She'd flirted with me, I'd flirted back. Later, I'd run into her at the Salty Dog, and we'd had a few drinks. She'd told me her boyfriend had dumped her right before her trip and the next thing I knew, I was in her hotel room.

When had that been? May or June.

Holy fuck.

"Cute place you have here, Braxton."

Looking toward my bedroom, I held my breath. Harlee would hear a female voice and come out, and the perfect world we were slowly building together would crumble right before my freaking eyes.

I couldn't lose Harlee again. I *wouldn't* lose her again.

"Heidi, can you take the baby back now?"

She'd been standing over at a table in the living room that had pictures of my family spread across it. She turned. "Oh, sorry! Sure."

Right before she made it to me, I heard Harlee's voice.

"Who are our guests?"

I froze yet again, and Heidi just kept moving like it wasn't a big deal for another woman to come into the room and see her taking a baby out of my arms.

Turning to Harlee, she cheerfully said, "Hi, I'm Heidi Thornton." She then proceeded to take off the baby's coat.

Harlee raised a brow. "As in the Boston Thornton family?"

Heidi smiled bigger. "Yes! How did you know?"

Harlee looked at me, then back at Heidi. "My father owns the local paper, *The Seaside Chronicles*. Your family owns the *Boston Tribune*. You and I met at a conference in Boston a couple years back."

"I thought you looked familiar! How are you?"

Folding her arms over her chest, Harlee stared at the woman before she answered. "Well, considering we're all standing in my boyfriend's living room, and he looks like he's ready to bolt out the door, *and* you're holding a baby, I'm going to say I'm not doing as well as I was five minutes ago."

Heidi looked at me, then at Harlee, then back to me.

Then she laughed. She actually *laughed*.

"Oh gosh! No, wait. Such a misunderstanding we have here."

"Is it?" Harlee and I both said at the same time.

Heidi nodded. "This isn't your baby, Braxton. He's almost four months old."

My mouth fell open, and it felt like the entire house shifted. "You were...you were *pregnant* when we slept together?"

"I'm going to need some hard liquor," Harlee said, moving toward the bar cart.

Heidi glanced between us with an apologetic expression. "I didn't know I was pregnant at the time, I swear, Brax. I would never have done that."

My legs felt like jelly, and I looked around for something to hold on to. "That doesn't help."

"Brax? Whiskey?" Harlee asked.

I nodded. "Make it a double."

Heidi let out a nervous bubble of laughter. "But it's only eight in the morning."

"Heidi, read the room," Harlee said as she handed me the glass of whiskey. I downed it. "Better?" she asked.

My throat burned, though I managed to get out, "I'll take another."

Harlee didn't move to make me another. Instead, she turned to Heidi. "As fun as this is, you've really got me wondering why you're here."

"Right. Gosh, I'm making a mess of this. I'm really sorry. The father of my son—his name is Joshua—is being an ass about taking a paternity test. He found out I came to Seaside with my college friends, and even though I showed him the receipt from the bed and breakfast we stayed at, and the dates we were here, he's still insisting he's not the father. My own friend—whom he *left me* for—told him about you. That I slept with you for breakup revenge sex."

"Breakup revenge sex?" Harlee asked. She looked at me. "Is that even a thing?"

I shrugged.

"Oh yeah, for sure," Heidi said. "I've done it like six times because of Joshua."

Harlee slowly looked back at the woman. "Wait. Since your break-up?"

Heidi blushed. "We'd been together since high school, and I'll admit I went on a little sex bender after he broke up with me and started dating my friend—"

Harlee held up her hands to stop her. "You slept with six guys, including Brax, while you were pregnant?"

"I didn't know I was at the time! My periods have always been a little hit or miss, and I've always used a condom. Well, not with Joshua."

I looked at Harlee, who just stood there blinking rapidly at Heidi.

"Anyway, let me get to the point. Brax, I have an affidavit from my lawyer stating that you and I had sex one time, used a condom, and that it was in May of 2022. Yours is the last signature I need to get before the judge will force the dickhead to take the test."

I was positive I was giving her a *what the fuck* look. "Wait, *that's* a real thing? Affidavits for when you had sex with someone?" I asked.

Heidi nodded. "I know. I know. I'm so embarrassed even coming here, and Harlee, I'm so sorry for the way it makes Braxton look. And I know you probably think 'oh my God, she slept with six guys in a two-week period.'"

I choked on my own spit. Harlee reached over and hit my back a few times.

"Joshua was my first, so I had a lot of making up to do. I had a threesome the night after we were together, so that was like a two-for-one thing."

"I need another drink," I said to Harlee.

"Coming up," she said, heading toward the bar cart.

"Anyway," Heidi continued, "when I got back to Boston, I shared an Uber with this really hot guy, and we ended up—"

"I'll sign it," I quickly blurted out before we had to hear about any more of Heidi's encounters.

"Great!" Heidi exclaimed. "That way, I can finally get the mother-fluffer to take the test."

"Mother-fluffer? Oh my God. That's my new favorite word," Harlee said.

I read over the paper that Heidi had pulled from a bag, then looked at Harlee as she handed me a drink. "I guess I should be glad you're not freaking out and running away after all of this."

Harlee winked at me. "I don't spook that easily."

I smiled at her. I loved her so damn much.

After reading over the affidavit, I signed it and then handed it back to Heidi.

"Thank you so much for doing this, Braxton. And thank you, Harlee, for not freaking out. Most girlfriends wouldn't be so understanding."

Harlee gave her a warm smile. "I really do hope things work out with you and Joshua."

Heidi had put the baby's coat back on as I'd signed the paperwork. Now she stood, and this time Harlee took the baby while Heidi donned her own jacket. I watched as Harlee melted and started babbling to him.

It was the sexiest thing I'd ever seen. Harlee with a baby in her arms.

She looked up, and our eyes met. She had a huge smile on her face. I smiled back.

Oblivious, Heidi put her coat on and said, "Oh, I don't want that mother-fluffer back. I want to take him to court and get as much money out of him as I can. He's married to my ex-friend now—who, by the way, is the one who tried to accuse Braxton of being the father."

"Ouch," Harlee whispered.

"I'll take him." Heidi scooped the baby out of Harlee's arms and started for the door.

As I opened it, I asked, "Do you need any help?"

"Oh no, my driver's waiting for us."

Glancing out the door, I saw a Mercedes parked there. A man got out of the passenger seat and opened the back door.

"Wait, what's the little guy's name?" Harlee asked, peeking at the baby once more.

Heidi smiled at him, then at Harlee and me. "Braxton. I thought it was a cute name. Plus, it's driving Joshua mad that I named him that." She started down the steps and called back, "Toodles! And congratulations on your relationship."

I watched as the man took...er...baby Braxton and put him in the car seat as Heidi walked to the other side of the vehicle and slipped in. She finished strapping in the baby while the man got back in the passenger seat.

"That poor girl needs therapy," Harlee said, stepping into the house.

Shutting the door, I leaned against it and watched Harlee walk back to the bar cart.

"Another double?"

"How are you so calm and not throwing the whiskey bottle at me?" I asked, moving toward the sofa to sit down. That had never happened to me before, and I'd be lying if I said I didn't freak the fuck out for a good solid five minutes there. "And I want you to know I didn't lie to you, Harlee. I've never had sex with *anyone* without wearing a condom. I promise you that."

Harlee poured a drink, then walked over to me. She sat down on the coffee table and watched me take a long sip. I wanted to down it again, but I only drank half.

When I set the glass down, she took my hand in hers. "First off, I know that. The first time we slept together, you used condoms. And second, I know you haven't been celibate all these years. I also know things like this happen. But I will say I'm really, really glad little Braxton isn't your baby."

I closed my eyes and groaned while Harlee laughed. "I can't believe she named the kid after me. No wonder the dad thinks it's mine!"

"Not gonna lie, that moment had me speechless."

"You?" I said, reaching for the drink and downing the rest. "Thank you, though, for not freaking out on me."

"We're a team now, remember?"

I placed my hand on the side of her face. "I love you, Harlee."

Her eyes filled with tears, and she pressed her lips together tightly. I knew she was attempting to get her emotions in check before she spoke. A single tear slipped free, and I wiped it away with my thumb.

"I love you, too, Brax."

Standing, I pulled her up and threw her over my shoulder. "Now, let's get back to what we were doing before we were interrupted."

Gannon and Brody both stared at me with shocked expressions on their faces as I nodded, then tipped my beer back and took a drink.

Brody leaned over and put his arms on his legs. "Wait. A girl from your past showed up with *a baby*?"

"Yep."

"And you thought it was yours?" Gannon asked.

"What would *you* think if a woman you'd slept with about a year ago showed up with a baby in her arms, Gannon?" I asked with a laugh.

He rubbed the back of his neck. "I suppose I'd freak the hell out. Especially if Addie was there."

I motioned to him with my free hand. "Thank you. Not gonna lie, I had the urge to run out the door. And if it wasn't winter, I might have."

Brody laughed. "I'd feel the same. I'm not sure how Sutton would have handled it, though."

"I don't know," Gannon stated as he looked at his beer and then at us. "I feel like all four of those women are so confident in themselves and who they love that they wouldn't have jumped to any conclusions. It's one of the things I admire most about each of them."

"I agree," Brody said. "I think Sutton might not have been as calm as Harlee, but I don't think she would have run off."

Mason walked in and handed each of us another beer before sitting. "I agree with you guys. I see Addie every day at the clinic, and she's so freaking level-headed. And Palmer...I honestly don't know what I would do without her. She's completely changed my life, and Charlie's too."

"To Barbara and Keegan," Brody said, raising his beer.

Smiling, I replied, "To the best parents any kid could ever want."

We all clinked our beer bottles together.

"Dude—how did you not shit your pants, though?" Brody asked with a snicker.

"I'm not so sure I didn't, to be honest with you. Did I mention she named the kid Braxton?"

"No fucking way!" Gannon said, leaning over laughing as the other two at least tried not to laugh *quite* so hard.

"I was positive that one was going to push Harlee over the edge," I said.

Mason shook his head. "Let's hope Ms. Seaside doesn't find out about your little visitors."

I rolled my eyes. "Christ, it would be my luck. The woman clearly hates me."

Knowing Ms. Seaside like I did, I was positive this incident wouldn't make the column.

Gannon shrugged. "I don't think she hates you, but she does have a weird fixation on you."

Brody and Mason agreed.

"It was pretty early in the morning," I said. "If she has her spies out that early, then I'm not sure what they'd make of it. Harlee and I both literally stood at the door and waved them off."

"I'm sure she could put a spin on it," Mason said. "I'm just glad she's moved on from Palmer and me. I think the Dr. Zaddy thing has finally worn off. Although, some teenager did call me that when I was picking up lunch earlier."

Making a note to myself to ask Harlee where in the hell she'd come up with that name, I changed the subject. "So, with my mom and dad selling the Grill, and Addie and Sutton having babies, Palmer getting married and…" I trailed off.

"And?" Gannon asked with a smirk.

I grinned. "Not going to lie, I'd marry her tomorrow if I thought she'd do it."

"Who says she wouldn't? Anyone with two eyes can see the way the two of you looked at each other over the years," Brody said. "Take it from me, dude, don't wait. I regret ever letting Sutton go."

Exhaling, I knew exactly how Brody felt. "Sutton said I remind her of you. With the way I handled things with Harlee."

Brody shook his head.

Mason lifted his beer. "To finding the loves our lives. May we always make them happy and love them with every ounce of our beings."

We clinked bottles again and then took a drink. I sat back and let the moment sink in.

Harlee was mine, and I was never going to let her go. I might just take Brody's advice and ask her to marry me tonight.

"Gentleman," I said, putting my glass down, "Brody's right. Life is short, so if you'll excuse me, I need to go see a girl about a wedding."

Chapter Eighteen

Harlee

The Seaside Chronicles

April 6, 2023

From the Sandbar

Seasiders,

Spring is in the air, even though we're waking up to some chilly temperatures this morning! The forecast today at eight a.m. was 34. You have to love Maine weather. Keep bundled up, my fishes.

Now, do I have a juicy bit for you today. Word on the beach is there's a little debate among all of you about who's the favorite Seaside couple. I'd like it noted that I was not the one who promoted this little battle, but I'm here for all of it!

Couple number one is Palmer Bradley and Dr. Mason Bryan. Everyone adores how this love story is going, and with Palmer and Mason set to walk down the aisle this summer, they seem to be the front-runners—especially since their story has been going on a little longer than that of our second couple.

Couple number two is still together, even if the betting books had her dumping him within the first month. Harlee Tilson, our very own Princess of Seaside, and Braxton Bradley, our former Catch of the Season—who is no longer available to catch—are the couple running a close second from what my seagulls tell me. And no, Braxton is not the Prince of Seaside, no matter how many times he signs his column that way. Who in their right mind gave that man a spot in the paper, anyway? That is a debate for another day.

Personally, I'll give it to Harlee and Braxton. They're going strong after a solid month of dating, give or take a few days. Harlee seems to shine when she's with Braxton, and he practically falls all over himself in her company.

Speaking of Catch of the Season, stay tuned for this year's candidate announcements coming up next week! Voting will start the week after.

I'll be keeping my ear to the docks for the latest news on couplegate!

Fair winds and following seas!

Ms. Seaside

PS. Braxton, please stop referring to me as Ms. S, or I'll crown you with a new title that I promise you won't like.

The bell above the door rang as I stepped into the Seaside Grill for the last time. Well, not the last time. But the last time with Barbara and Keegan as its owners.

"Good morning!" I approached the table across from our normal Thursday and Saturday meeting spot.

Palmer looked up from a notebook and smiled. "Ahh. The competition."

With a roll of my eyes, I sat down. "I can't even with this woman."

"Or man," Sutton added with a giggle.

Lori, one of the new waitresses Ruby hired, took my order and hurried to get my coffee.

"Any progress on who Ms. S might be?" Addie asked before she took a bite of her bagel.

I shook my head. "No, and I'm honestly ready for Brax to give it up. I don't even care who she is anymore."

Palmer leaned back and smirked. "Not so fun when she's constantly writing about you, is it?"

My chest squeezed with guilt. A part of me wanted to tell Palmer the truth. I knew that was out of the question though. No one could know. Ever. "Fine, I will admit that it does get rather annoying," I said. "I think if Ms. S hears it, then she believes it to be true. I stopped by the library the other day and overheard two women in the cooking section throwing out bets on if Brax and I would have a baby before you and Mason. I poked my head around the corner and asked them both to stop with the baby talk because if Ms. S heard them, I'd be pregnant by next week."

The three of them laughed.

"Mason and I have agreed to enjoy each other for a bit before the B word is brought up," Palmer said.

I nodded. "I really just want to spend time with Brax before we bring a third party into all of this."

"Hey, why do I feel like you're dissing me and Sutton?" Addie asked.

"Not at all!" I quickly said. "In a way, I envy you both starting a family with the loves of your lives. But for me, I really just want it to be the two of us for a while. The last few years we've only been at each other's throats, so it's nice just being able to love him. And the sex is amazing."

"Please don't go there," Sutton said.

"I think a healthy sex life is a good thing," Addie argued.

Sutton looked at her. "Do you want to hear the details about how much Brax likes Harlee's new vibrator, then?"

Addie stared at Sutton for a moment before she looked at me. I gave her a wink. "He really likes it. A lot."

"Oh my God. My brain just got that visual, and I am not okay!" Palmer said.

Before I could add any more detail to see how far I could push them, someone cleared their throat, and we all turned to see Kris Jensen standing there. I tried to school the shocked look on my face. After Brax had asked me to marry him out of the blue, with no ring and the most romantic proposal on the beach where he declared his everlasting love, we both knew we wanted to get married right away. My mind quickly drifted back to the memory of that night.

"Are your eyes closed?" Braxton asked as he held my hands and walked us onto the beach.

Laughing, I replied, "Yes! They are closed, and you have a blindfold on me, Brax! What are you doing?"

He stopped, and I could feel him move behind me. His warm breath hit my neck, causing a shiver to run across my body. "Keep them closed, okay?"

I nodded, "Okay."

The feel of his hands moving up my arms made me draw in a deep breath. He removed the blindfold, and I realized I was holding my breath. I slowly exhaled as he said, "Open your eyes, princess."

Opening them, I gasped at the sight before me. "Oh, Brax."

A pathway lit up by candles led to an area that had a blanket with candles placed everywhere, giving the beach a serene and romantic feel. Rose petals were sprinkled on the blanket and the sand. A small table was set up with two glasses and a bottle of champagne.

Brax took my hand and led me down the path and to the blanket. I slowly shook my head as I took it all in. Lanterns filled with candles surrounded the blanket with smaller candles placed in between. It was beyond beautiful.

"This is so gorgeous," I whispered as I looked around.

Then Brax dropped to one knee, and I gasped. Tears instantly started to roll down my cheeks and there was no stopping them. My heart pounded as he took my hand.

178

"Harlee, I don't know why I've been so stupid these last few years. Why I've fought my feelings for you or why I pushed you away when I did. That's not true. I was scared, because I've never in my life felt this way about anyone. I love you so much, Harlee, and I don't want to waste another moment in this life without you by my side. I want to wake up every morning with you in my arms and drift to sleep with you curled up next to me. I want to watch your stomach grow big and round with our kids. I want to take you fishing as much as you'll let me."

I laughed and wiped a tear away.

"I want you, Harlee. Forever and for always. Will you do me the honor of being my wife?"

He held up a box and opened it. I blinked a few times and then looked at him. "Um, I'm not sure if you're aware that there is a bread tie in that box and not a ring."

He smiled the biggest smile, and my heart skipped a beat. "I want you to pick out the ring you want, Harlee. But I wanted to ask you first, so please take this as a temporary ring."

Laughing again, I dropped to my knees, cupped his face, and kissed him. When we broke apart our eyes met. "Yes. I want nothing more than to marry you, Brax."

His face lit up, and I was struck by how handsome he was in the candlelight. "I want to get married at the bed and breakfast," I said. "It seems fitting."

He pulled me closer. "I couldn't agree more. Now, I'm going to make love to you, Harlee"

My teeth dug into my lower lip as I nodded. Braxton gently laid me down on the blanket as we got lost in one another under the clear sky and the endless stars.

"Hey there, Kris!" Addie said, pulling me out of the memory.

"Kris!" I said as I stood and wrapped her up in a hug. "What a pleasure it is to see you!"

She let out a soft laugh. "It's good to see you all. Sutton, Addie, congratulations on the upcoming babies."

They both said thank you.

Turning her attention to Palmer, Kris added, "And congratulations, Palmer. I'm so happy to hear you're going to be getting married. I haven't met Dr. Bryan yet, but I've heard he's a very nice man."

Palmer smiled. "He is, indeed. And thank you, Kris. I'm going to be bringing Mason's son, Charlie, out to Lighthouse Island now that the weather is better. I'd love to swing by the B and B and see you."

"Please do. Anytime." Focusing back on me, Kris asked, "Harlee, do you have a second to chat?"

"Of course, I do." I followed Kris out of the restaurant and down the street. "Is everything okay?" I asked.

Kris looked around to make sure no one was listening, then focused back on me. "Someone was out on Lighthouse Island snooping around."

I frowned. "Snooping around about what?"

"The little side project you have going on."

"You've got to be kidding me."

"They booked two nights at the bed and breakfast. The first day, they were out exploring the island, which I wasn't too terribly suspicious about. Lots of folks from Seaside come to the island for a break from life. But that night at dinner, they were asking a lot of questions about you and Braxton. Things like, have you ever stayed at my place. Do we have many weddings on the island..."

Drawing back in surprise, I asked, "How in the hell would they have found out?"

She shook her head. "I don't know, but I think I threw her off."

"Who was it?"

"I hate to even tell you."

"Kris!"

She closed her eyes and said, "Your mother."

"What!" I nearly shouted. "How did she find out about the wedding?"

Kris motioned for me to keep it down. "I don't know, Harlee. I promise you, I've been super quiet about everything. I haven't told a soul who I'm planning the wedding for. I've never even mentioned your name or Braxton's. Do you think your mom is Ms. Seaside?"

I nearly laughed, but held it in. "No. I think she's a meddling mother who somehow found out. When was she out there?"

"The last two nights. I don't think she knows when, but she for sure has her suspicions. I just don't know how she pieced it together that the island is involved."

I placed my hands on my hips as I glared down Main Street toward the building that housed *The Seaside Chronicles*. "My father."

Kris tilted her head. "Why do I feel like I just had déjà vu? Oh, that's right, you said the same thing when Braxton first printed his reply in the paper."

"I'm going to kill that loudmouth," I said. "My dad had to be the one who told her Brax and I were planning a surprise wedding. The only reason he even knows is because he overheard me on the phone with you talking about it."

"This doesn't have anything to do with the whole who-gets-married-first thing with Palmer and Mason, does it?"

"No, we were planning this before the column even said anything."

Kris nodded. "And you're *sure* your mom isn't Ms. Seaside?"

"Ha. She's too busy trying to keep up with all the little projects she has going on. I swear she's already involved in more things than she has time for."

Kris smiled. "The apple didn't fall far from the tree with you, then."

I smiled back at her. "Thanks for letting me know. If she lets it slip that Brax and I are planning this, I'm going to...well, I don't know what I'll do."

"What about Palmer? Don't you want to tell her that your mom is on to the wedding? I mean, you're having a dual wedding?"

I sighed. "The last thing she needs is more stress since she's busy planning Charlie's birthday party for this weekend. I'll let her know, though. And I'll talk to my mom, get her to stop being so damn nosy. And hopefully you-know-who doesn't get wind of it."

Kris nodded. "Good luck. Oh, and don't forget about this afternoon."

"We won't. Everyone thinks it's a last-minute thing for Charlie's birthday party."

"Perfect!" Kris gave me a hug. "Now, back to the Island; I hate the mainland."

"See you later!" I called out as she got on her bike and pedaled off toward the ferry.

Hurrying back into the Grill, I rushed to the table and sat just as Lori was putting my breakfast down.

"What was that all about?" Palmer asked. I could see the concern in her eyes.

"Kris has an ad going in the paper for the bed and breakfast. She dropped her cell in the pond on the island and couldn't get it to turn on, so she had to make a trip over to replace it and was killing two birds with one stone."

Lord, how could I always come up with a lie like it was second nature?

Palmer raised her brows, then focused on her breakfast. She was probably thinking the same thing.

"I just adore her. I hate that we don't ever see her anymore," Sutton said.

Addie nodded in agreement. "She has to be so lonely out there. Do you think she'll ever date again?"

I slowly let out a breath. "I honestly don't know. She was so in love with Rick. They had their whole life planned out, and so much of it revolved around Lighthouse Island. I don't even want to imagine how she feels, losing him like she did. It just makes me so sad for her."

Addie and Sutton both sniffled, and I saw Addie dab at the corners of her eyes.

Palmer reached for my hand. "I imagine she feels close to Rick when she's at the house. With him being buried there and all."

I nodded. "She pours everything into the bed and breakfast."

"Maybe someday," Sutton started, "someone will come and stay at the bed and breakfast and sparks will fly."

"How wonderful would that be?" Addie added.

"It *would* be wonderful," I said before I picked up my fork and dove into my breakfast.

I set my purse and keys down on the table next to the front door and called out Brax's name.

When he didn't answer, I headed out to the backyard.

I smiled the moment I saw him hanging up the wind chimes we'd bought last weekend when we'd driven up the coast. "I like it there."

"Yeah?" he asked, stepping down from the ladder and making his way over to me. "Let's hope the bears don't tear it down."

Glancing back at the wind chimes, I asked, "Do you think they will?"

"Probably not. My mom had some out once and this one bear used to come and hit it all the time. I think she liked the sound it made. She even brought her cubs to hear it for a few years. It was cute watching her hit it while they looked up at it."

"That's precious." I walked over to him and wrapped my arms around his neck as I reached up to give him a kiss.

"How was your day?" he asked.

Sighing, I dropped my head on his chest. "Mine started off with chatter about the latest article, of course."

"Good one, by the way. But damn, why is Ms. S hating on poor little ol' me?"

I grinned. "I think she secretly has a thing for you."

With a sexy smirk, he replied, "You think? I wonder if she's pretty."

"I've heard rumors she's a princess."

Brax chuckled. "Nah, I've got the only princess in town." He kissed my forehead, then tilted my chin up to look at me. "What else happened?"

"Kris stopped by the paper, and they told her I was at the Grill. She swung over to tell me my mother has been snooping around the island, trying to get intel."

"On the wedding?" he asked.

"Yep. Palmer and I had to sneak away from Sutton and Addie to talk about it."

"Is Palmer upset that your mother is onto you?"

I shook my head and drew my finger along Brax's logo on his shirt. It was a fishing boat with a fish under it, and over the top of the boat it read *Bradley Charters*. "She wasn't. She's actually amused by the whole couplegate thing." Sighing, I said, "I'm getting so tired of this, Brax."

He wrapped his arms around me tighter. "Tired of what? Ms. Seaside?"

"Yes," I answered. "Your sisters and I started talking about babies and futures, and after Kris left, I really started to think. I want to spend as much time with you as I can. I love working at the paper and at Sutton's shop. Ms. Seaside doesn't take up a whole lot of time, but it's the sneaking around and the lying that I hate. I spun a lie so quickly today about why Kris needed to talk to me that it bothered me for hours."

"Do you want to start phasing her out?" he asked as he twirled a piece of my hair around his fingers.

I didn't answer for a few moments while I really thought about it. "I think I do. I'm ready for her to quietly slip away. I can't do this anymore, and I can't tell Addie, Palmer, and Sutton that Ms. Seaside is me. I'm scared to death they'll hate me forever."

He drew back and cupped my face in his hands. "They won't hate you. They might be upset at first, but they would never hate you."

I felt the tears sting at the back of my eyes. "I just want the column to slowly fade away."

Brax kissed me gently on the lips. "Then that's what we'll do. I should probably keep the Friday article, though."

"I agree. Once summer hits, it'll be easy to explain why you cut back if you don't want to do it each week. Unless you really want to."

He tilted his head as he thought about it. "I really like doing it. It's kind of cool having people tell me they're learning some things about fishing. But as far as how often I'll do it, we'll play it by ear."

"Then I say keep doing it for however long you want. As for me, I'm thinking I might like to learn a thing or two about fishing charters."

A brilliant smile lit up Brax's face. "I know just the guy to teach you."

Chapter Nineteen

Harlee

The Seaside Chronicles

April 7, 2023

Friday's Catch

Hey, Anglers,

I'm counting down the days until May 15 when the season opens again! If you haven't booked your trip yet, you can on our website—the link is listed below. If you've never been deep-sea fishing, then you don't know what you're missing out on. I'm certainly ready for some freshly caught cod these days, how about you?

Now, on to the not-so-fun stuff.

Ms. S, Ms. S, Ms. S.

Couplegate? Really? I feel like you might be running out of things to write about because surely you can find something more interesting than little ol' me! It leads one to think you might have a crush on this angler. If that's the case, I can tell you I'm one hundred percent in love with and committed to Ms. Harlee Tilson. Let's see

Doc Mason declare his love to my sister so publicly. Oh wait—he did! I might have to up my game the more I think about this. Surely my declaration in the column pulls us into the lead over Palmer and the Doc.

And a new title? How about I throw out some suggestions for you. The Angler King. Seaside's Prince of Fishing. The Chronicles's Hero. Ms. S's Bestie. Or we could go with my personal favorite...The Lucky Angler. Of course, these are merely suggestions, so I'll leave it up to you.

Until next time,
The Lucky Angler
AKA Prince of Seaside by default.

PS. I know something you don't know!

I couldn't help but smile as I set the paper down on my desk. I'd come into the office early in hopes of catching my father before he started his Friday morning meetings. He only worked half a day on Fridays, so if I didn't catch him first thing, I wouldn't be able to talk to him again until Monday. He and my mother were heading to Boston for the weekend, and I didn't want to have this conversation over the phone.

My cell buzzed with a text from the man himself.

Daddy: Got your text. I'm free right now.

Perfect. I stood and smoothed down the pencil skirt I'd worn today since I was attending a marketing meeting in about an hour. Clearing my throat, I straightened my shoulders and walked out of my office and down the hall to my father's.

"Good morning, Harlee!" Beth said cheerfully as I approached.

"Morning, Beth."

"Head on in, he's expecting you."

"Thanks." I opened up the door and stepped inside.

My father sat behind his large oak desk, his head down as he read something. When he looked up, he smiled. "The Lucky Angler? I think my favorite one is Ms. S's Bestie."

I chuckled and made my way over to one of the chairs that sat in front of his desk. "Brax is enjoying the weekly column."

Dad nodded. "I think once the fishing season starts, he'll really hit his stride. So far, everyone's loving his column, though. Especially the banter with Ms. Seaside."

"You know he'll start talking more and more about fishing when the season picks up."

"I know," Dad said on an exhale. "I still think the column will do well. I mean, we're a seaside town, so it only makes sense to have something about fishing in there." He picked up a pen and circled something in Brax's article.

"Dad, I wanted to talk to you about Ms. Seaside."

Not looking up, he shuffled some papers around on his desk and grabbed a file. "Okay, what about her?"

"I'm going to start slowly phasing her out."

That caused him to look up sharply. "What do you mean, phasing her out?"

"I'm going to start pulling back on her."

"On the things she talks about?"

I twisted my hands together as I nodded. "That...and start publishing less."

He leaned back in his chair. "I see. I thought you loved doing the column."

"I did. But now that I'm with Braxton, things are different."

"You don't have to keep writing about him, you know. There are plenty of other people in town, Harlee. I mean, last week you didn't mention him at all. You talked about Mrs. Pritcher and the library. And the week before that, you reported that Mr. Hall was seen on a date with an unknown woman." He chuckled and shook his head. "He was so pissed off about that. I can't tell you how many times he called and left me a message, demanding to know who Ms. Seaside is."

"For a man who thrives on gossip, he doesn't like getting a taste of his own medicine," I stated with a grin.

"No, he sure doesn't."

I drew in a deep breath and slowly exhaled. "Dad, it's more than that. I'm tired of lying...and the fact that I'm so good at it bothers me. I want to have a normal life without having to worry that I might say something that will give out a clue about who I am, or that someone will find out and the whole town will hate me."

He waved me off. "No one would hate you, Harlee. You do too much for this town. If it wasn't for you, we wouldn't have the new pet shelter. Or the programs you've set up with some of the local businesses and the high school. Not to mention all the holiday events you put on."

"Dad, that's all fine and dandy, but if everyone found out it was me, feelings would be hurt, and I could lose people from my life. I was willing to take the risk before. Now I'm not. I don't know, maybe I grew up more, or maybe I'm ready to stop lying to those closest to me. I want to focus on my future. And I really want to learn more about Braxton's business and help him with it."

He steepled his index fingers and nodded. "You always did enjoy fishing. I remember taking you when you were little, and you wanted to stay for hours out on the water. You were the only little girl who never complained about putting the worm on the hook."

Smiling, I looked down at my hands and forced myself to place my palms flat on my thighs. When I looked up, I knew he saw it in my eyes.

"I'm done, Dad."

With my declaration, he gave one nod and replied, "I'll let you handle it the way you want."

"I don't think stopping altogether would be wise for the revenue. I'm hoping it won't impact the paper too much."

He smiled. "It will some, but we'll handle it when we cross that bridge."

I nodded. "I think what I'll do is talk more about local events and such, and less gossip. When I finally write the last column, I'll let everyone know that Ms. Seaside is putting her pen and paper away for good."

"If that'll make you happy, then you have my full support. Although, your mother will be disappointed. She lives for Thursday mornings."

I laughed. "I still can't believe she hasn't figured it out. Speaking of Mom, I'm meeting her for lunch. I'm going to tell her about the wedding. The more I thought about it, the more I realized it wasn't fair of me to keep it from her. I know she only wants to be a part of it. She can be so...in my face about stuff."

"I've tried to ask her not to be overbearing with it all, Harlee. But you're her only daughter, and she wants what's best for you. I'm sorry I let it slip about the wedding."

"It's okay, Dad. It was rather selfish of me to keep it from her simply for my own sanity. Now that Palmer has told Barbara, the two moms can get together and plan things if they want. With limitations."

He chuckled.

"Let's be honest—Mom also likes to know everything first before anyone else," I said. "You know it burns her up that Ms. Seaside knows more than she does."

My father tilted his head and regarded me for a moment. "I've never asked—because honestly, I've never wanted to know—but how *does* Ms. Seaside get all of her information?"

With a smile that I knew was a bit on the evil said, I answered, "Rule number one in journalism, never reveal your sources. You ought to know that better than anyone."

He tossed his head back with a bark of laughter. "You've got me on that one!"

The bell above the door to Coastal Chic rang, causing me to glance up from where I was folding shirts at the counter.

"Hey, Palmer," I said as she dashed into the store.

"Did you see it yet?"

"Did I see what?"

With a frustrated sigh, she said, "The column. Ms. S. She didn't utter a single word about you, me, or couplegate. As a matter of fact, she didn't have any gossip at all!"

"What was it about?"

"Some board meeting for the city council to talk about adding more stores and restaurants to the pier. It was rather boring. Actually, the last *few* have been kind of dull, if I'm being honest."

I nodded and went back to folding. "That makes sense. It's going to be a pretty big meeting, since they're deciding if they're going to allow the expansion. I do think it would be fun to have like a mini-carnival type area by the pier."

"Well, Ms. S would disagree with you. She made it perfectly clear she doesn't like change. So, there's another clue for you and Brax."

Laughing, I said, "Brax and I have both agreed to give up our search for Ms. Seaside."

"Really?" Palmer asked as she leaned against the counter. "What brought that on?"

"For Brax, I think it's because fishing season is getting ready to start in a few weeks, and for me, I honestly don't care who she is. Maybe if we stop snooping around, she'll leave us be."

Palmer laughed. "I still think the woman has it out for our family." She held up her hand. "I know, I know, she talks about plenty of other people, but she sure does like the Bradley family."

"That's true. She even wrote about your folks and how sad she was that they sold the Grill. How are they doing, anyway?"

"I've never seen them so relaxed. Of course, Mom's thrilled about your wedding, and I think tickled that she knows something Ms. S doesn't. Your mom called her earlier and they're planning to go look at dresses. I'm so over the moon my dad is finally relaxing and enjoying life. I know they're both excited about the babies and the wedding."

I smiled. "My mother was thrilled when I confessed about the wedding as well, and I told her she could help if she promised not to drive Kris insane."

Palmer laughed. "Your mom loves to plan a party, just like her daughter."

"Can't argue with you about that. And she is good at keeping a secret."

"Again, apple doesn't fall far."

I flinched, hoping Palmer didn't notice my slip. But she said, "Given the fact that you and Brax have kept your engagement on the down low, I don't think *anyone* will see it coming."

"We're getting married on May thirteenth. I can't believe it! The only people who know are us, our mothers, and fathers, Kris, and Pastor Scott. I think we have a good chance of keeping it a secret."

She nodded. "I'm not worried about anyone slipping. I don't think your mom or my mom want Ms. S finding out, so they won't spill the beans. Our fathers are tight-lipped, too, and if we can't trust the pastor, then who *can* we trust?"

I laughed. "It's going to get harder the closer we get."

"And how do we notify our guests about the location without giving away the surprise?"

"Mason and Brax have been trying to figure out a way to do it at the last minute."

Chewing on the inside of my lip, I nodded and started to fold another shirt. "What if we ask my dad to help?"

"What do you mean?" Palmer asked with a confused expression.

I gave her a half-shoulder shrug. "I mean, my dad obviously knows who Ms. Seaside is. Maybe he can give her the information at the last minute and let her announce the wedding."

Palmer's eyes went wide. "Use her for our little bit of news!"

"Yes!" I said with excitement. "I mean, no one will see it coming. Everyone thinks you and Mason are getting married this summer, and no one has a clue that Brax asked me to marry him, or that you and I came up with this crazy idea to do a dual wedding in May."

Palmer rubbed her hands together. "This is so great. Do you think she'll do it?"

"Why wouldn't she? After all, doesn't she live for this kind of stuff? And to be the one to announce it is kind of perfect. Maybe she'll even lay off of Brax for a bit. Maybe we can even have the wed-ding invitations delivered to those who are invited—"

"With the paper!" we both said at the same time.

"Yep," I continued with a laugh. "I mean, it's really only family and some close friends, and we know they won't tell anyone if we ask that the location be kept secret. How hard would it be to have the invitations delivered with the paper? We'd have to make sure Dad doesn't tell Ms. Seaside where and when we're getting married, so the whole town doesn't show up."

"This could work!"

"It will totally work. Brax got Ron to reserve one of the ferries going over, so we don't have to worry about that."

"We're brilliant."

"Indeed, we are," I replied.

"What are you brilliant about?" Sutton asked as she walked up to the counter.

Palmer looked panicked, glancing from Sutton to me, then back to Sutton.

I quickly said, "We came up with a cute decoration idea for Ma-son's birthday party."

Sutton grinned. "Fun! What is it?"

"It's a surprise," Palmer quickly said. "But it's going to be the best surprise ever!"

"I love surprises. Does Mason know about it?"

I pointed at her. "No hints, Sutton."

She blushed. "A girl can try."

Chapter Twenty

Brax

"**M**om! Help! He has a spider!"

I watched three girls run by screaming with two boys chasing them at Charlie's birthday party at Mason and Palmer's house.

"Now that my eardrum is busted," I said dryly, "you're sure you want one of those?"

Gannon chuckled. "I think it's a little late now, don't you?"

"How's Addie doing?" I asked before taking a sip of my beer.

"Great. We went for an appointment the other day, and they did a sonogram. She's on track for her due date of July twenty-second."

I turned to look at him. "What if Sutton and Addie have their babies on the same day? I mean, Sutton's due on the eleventh, so it could happen."

"All I know is, I pray—for both my and Brody's sake—that neither of them go over their due dates."

"Why?" I asked with a curious laugh.

"The bigger they both get, the more things get... Well, let's just say sex has certainly gotten interesting."

Another group of kids ran by, but this time my sister Palmer was running behind them, shouting, "Do *not* put that down his shirt! The fish needs to be in water or it'll die!"

Gannon and I both watched, then looked at one another.

"So, do you want a boy or a girl?" I asked.

I swore my brother-in-law's face twitched as he looked back at the group of kids. "Um...doesn't matter. As long as they're healthy. And they listen."

Scanning the chaos in the backyard of Mason and Palmer's house, I screwed up my face. "Good luck with that."

"Are we having fun?" Harlee plopped down in the folding chair next to me.

I nodded. "If that's what you call a pounding headache, screaming out-of-control kids, and a mom who keeps touching me on the arm and squeezing it while telling me she'd really love private fishing lessons, then I guess I'm having fun."

Harlee laughed. "Oh my God. Which mom? Show me."

I rolled my eyes and pointed. Harlee busted out laughing, stood, and said, "I've gotta go tell Palmer. This is rich!"

And with that, my secret fiancée rushed off to gossip with my baby sister.

"Put me down for no birthday parties."

That came from Brody, who handed me a beer, then Gannon one, before sitting in the seat Harlee had vacated. "I mean, the only kid who's well-behaved here is Charlie, and he has an excuse to act like a crazy person. What in the hell did they give these kids, for fuck's sake?"

"Whatever it was, I hope it lasts well into the night and keeps their parents up," Mason said from behind us.

We laughed as he nearly collapsed into the chair next to Gannon.

"I will never let Palmer talk me into a birthday party with Charlie's entire class again. One kid put a toad in the punch. Another decided she wanted to know what flavor the icing was on the cake and decided to lick her finger before taking a sample."

"Gross!" Brody and I said at the same time.

"I'm not eating anything at this shindig. I saw a little boy use the palm of his hand to rub his snotty nose, then reach into the bowl of chips. I gagged. Which made Addie gag and nearly throw up." Gannon shuddered.

Brody looked at the bowl of chips in his hand and slowly put it down on the ground. "*And* I'm done with that."

I couldn't help but laugh.

"I'm not a hundred percent sure, but I think Palmer is signaling for you to go over to the cake table, Mason," I said.

He jumped up. "Thank God. It's cake, presents, then it's over!"

We watched Mason nearly sprint across the yard.

"You think he's ready for this day to be over?" Brody asked.

A screaming girl who was running away from a bee raced by, causing us all to cringe.

After taking a long drink from my beer, I said, "I'm honestly surprised he's even still here. I'd have left for the bar a long time ago."

Gannon hit me on the back as he stood. "It's called love, Brax. It makes you do crazy things."

Smiling, I searched for Harlee. When I saw her bending down to look at a flower a young girl was holding, I felt so much warmth in my chest that I lifted a hand and rubbed at the spot. Love did, indeed, make you do crazy things. It had also made me the happiest man on Earth.

Harlee turned and met my gaze. She lifted her hand and waved. I did the same.

The little girl took Harlee's hand and started toward the cake table. I stood. My eyes were transfixed on them both, and I started to imagine that she was walking with our own little girl. The thought nearly made me tear up.

My body swayed slightly, and I looked over to see Brody grinning at me like he knew something I didn't.

"Why are you grinning at me like that?"

He slowly shook his head. "No reason at all."

The Seaside Chronicles

May 12, 2023

Hook, Lone, and Sinker — Special Edition

Seasiders,

I don't know whether to be happy or slightly agitated that something so big was planned without my knowledge—and right under my nose! It makes this writer wonder if she's slipping somehow and losing her touch. I'll have to ponder that after finishing this column.

At any rate, my fishes, I have big news for you this beautiful spring morning: there is to be a wedding. And not just a wedding, but two weddings! You heard that right...two weddings. Do you see why I'm so concerned? How is it possible that two weddings were planned without my seagulls or me even being tipped off? That's a question to wrestle with later, as I'm sure you're all wondering who our two couples are. Hold on to your surfboards, fishes!

Palmer Bradley and Mason Bryan are getting hitched this weekend, along with—and this one I did not see coming—Braxton Bradley and Harlee Tilson! Who even knew they were engaged? Never mind the fact that they've only been dating for a hot second. I've been unable to find out the location of the double wedding, but I do wish both couples a very happy life together.

Don't worry, Seasiders, I'll be sure to have more information on the nuptials soon. Mark my word...even if I've yet to receive an invitation.

Fair winds and following seas!
Ms. Seaside

I drew in a deep breath and slowly exhaled as I looked at myself in the floor-to-ceiling mirror.

"Nervous?" Brody asked, walking up to me.

I shook my head, but a small part of me was exactly that.

Mason, who was looking out the window, said, "Yes."

Brody and I both smiled at each other before he said, "Turn around, your tie is off a bit."

"Probably from my hands shaking nonstop," I said. "Why are my hands shaking? I *want* to marry Harlee. It's the only thing I've been thinking about since we got together."

Brody chuckled. "I was nervous going to the justice of the peace with Sutton, and we were getting married for totally different reasons. I was happy, though, even if it wasn't how I would have pictured our wedding." He glanced over at the other groom. "Mason? You doing okay?"

Mason turned and leaned against the windowsill. "Nerves or not, I'm so ready to marry Palmer. The fact that Harlee asked us to be a part of this makes me really happy."

"Because you get to marry Palmer sooner?" I asked.

He gave a slight shrug. "That, and all of us doing it together. I don't know...it feels special. And Palmer said this place holds special meaning for you and Harlee."

I nodded. "It does. We got stuck here at the bed and breakfast back in February and, well...things changed for us here."

He smiled. "Thanks for letting us join you guys today."

"I loved the idea the moment Harlee asked my thoughts on it. Thank you for making my baby sister so happy."

Brody finished adjusting my tie and took a step back. "Please tell me you aren't going to start crying and hugging."

I smiled at him. "And thanks for being the best man."

"I'm honored you asked. But don't think I don't know I'm your second choice."

Laughing, I shook my head. "I still can't believe Thomas and Kelsey Roberts eloped and went to Spain for a month."

"That's a match I wouldn't have put together," Mason said with a disbelieving look on his face.

"How in the hell did Ms. Seaside miss that one?" Brody asked.

Mason shook his head. "She missed our weddings too."

Brody nodded. "Maybe she *is* losing her touch."

"Maybe so," I said as I put my cufflinks on and then looked at Mason. "Have you seen the setup yet?"

"I was waiting for you and to get the all-clear from Kris. I know Palmer and Harlee saw it when they walked through with their moms."

"Speaking of parents, where's my dad?" I asked.

Mason grinned. "He and Harlee's dad are with Mitch, helping him with last-minute preparations for the reception. In other words, they're telling him he's setting up the tables all wrong."

I rolled my eyes. "I thought the mothers were going to be the issue."

We all laughed.

Turning back to Brody, I asked, "You've got the ring?"

Brody tapped his jacket. "Right here."

"Mason, tell me you didn't give Charlie your ring to hold on to," I said.

With a subtle laugh, he shook his head. "Gannon has it. We told Charlie that Gannon was the stand-in best man and would carry the ring, to which Charlie said good, because he was worried he'd lose it."

"Smart!" Brody said.

Mason nodded, then asked, "How's Sutton feeling?"

"Last time I checked, she was in the kitchen with Kris asking for mayo to dip the cheese sticks Kris made for her. When I heard that, I turned and walked out of the kitchen."

Mason and I both shook our heads as I said, "That's disgusting."

"You're telling me. I was talking to Gannon, and he said Addie asked for ice cream and black beans again. I think it's something with your family's gene pool."

I laughed and shrugged as Brody went on.

"It really makes me wonder what this child is going to be like with all the crazy food combos his mother keeps eating. The other day, she told me she was craving dirt. *Dirt*, Brax! I asked if I needed to be worried, and she promised me she wouldn't eat any. What in the living hell?!"

I couldn't help but laugh again. Mason looked like he was deep in thought.

"You know, I've had other pregnant women tell me that they crave dirt as well," he stated, clearly going into doctor mode and thinking hard about why that might be.

Before Brody could reply, there was a light knock on the door.

"Come on in," I called out.

Kris poked her head inside. "If you guys are ready, you can come on down. The girls are finishing up getting ready, so you can take a look at everything."

Mason and I both nearly sprinted out the door. Kris let out a laugh as Brody extended his arm to her.

My breath caught when we walked down toward the bluff that overlooked the beach and ocean. When Harlee had come up with the idea of marrying on Lighthouse Island, I knew we had to have Kris be a part of it—and have it at the bed and breakfast. When we'd approached Kris with the idea, she'd asked to help plan it.

"Kris, I think you've missed your calling," Mason said as he walked down the makeshift aisle.

"Barbara and Melinda said the same thing," Kris stated with a flush on her cheeks.

White chairs were set up in rows with the aisle running down the middle. White petals adorned the pathway and added the perfect touch. Both brides had wanted simple, and even though this screamed simple, it was still beautiful.

At the end was an altar where we would say our vows. It was made out of wood that Mason and I had collected on the beach over the last few weeks, and Kris's brothers, Ron and Mitch, had made it for us. A stunning bouquet of flowers sat in the middle, with greenery weaving down the sides.

"Wow," Mason said as he walked up to the altar. "I never would have imagined a bunch of random wood could look this good."

I shook my head in disbelief. "Me either. What did the girls say?"

Kris beamed with pride. "They both got teary-eyed, then had Addie and Sutton yelling at them not to ruin their makeup."

"It's truly beautiful, Kris. Mitch and Ron did an amazing job."

"I'll tell them both you said so."

"Seriously," Mason said, turning to Kris, "have you ever thought about turning the bed and breakfast into a wedding venue? I mean, look at this view! You have the space and could even construct another building to have indoor weddings or receptions."

Kris nibbled on her lip for a moment. "I honestly never thought about it until I planned this wedding for Harlee and Palmer. I've had so much fun doing it that I've already talked to Mitch and Ron about building a venue. Chip said he could help as well. I know the three of them are busy with the lighthouse, the ferries, and Chip with the pilot boats, but it would be a fun project for us. Something else to bring people to the island and share our history with them."

Walking up to Kris, I took her hands in mine. "I really like that idea, Kris. And I *love* the idea that we're your first wedding."

Her eyes misted over. "I do, too, Braxton." She cleared her throat, then squeezed my hands. "We have a wedding to get to. There's a bar set up in the living room of the bed and breakfast for the wedding party. The girls are in the guest house behind the B and B, so if you two want to head on in for a bit before things get going…"

I gave her a kiss on the cheek. "Will do."

After making our way back into the bed and breakfast, we found Gannon at the bar.

"Anything need to be done in here?" Brody asked.

Gannon shook his head. "There are like six women in the kitchen, and they all told me to get out. Everything's set up for the dinner after the ceremony, and I found your dad and Mike listening to the Sox game on Keegan's phone. They were sharing Bluetooth headphones."

My eyes went wide. "They're listening to a baseball game?"

Gannon chuckled. "They assured me the phone would be put away for the ceremony."

Brody shrugged at me and Mason. "How about a prewedding toast?"

"I like the sound of that," I said, walking up to the bar.

Gannon took out four shot glasses and lined them up. "Whiskey?"

Mason nodded. "Sounds good to me."

I agreed.

Holding up our shot glasses, Brody gave Mason and me a wide grin as Gannon said, "To everlasting love. May you both have utter happiness with your future wives, and I hope life brings you everything you desire and deserve."

Brody added, "And may your future brides, who will eventually be the mothers of your children, never eat weird shit like my wife does."

"Hear hear!" Mason said, and I echoed him.

"Another toast," Gannon said, this time only pouring a shot for me and Mason. "To brothers-in-law. I couldn't have asked for better when it comes to you two."

"I'll second that," Brody said while Mason and I downed the shots.

"One more!" Brody exclaimed. "To second chances. It's the main theme for all four us. And to the women who gave them to us."

"Yes!" I said, downing my shot.

"One last one for the hell of it!" Gannon shouted.

"Why are *we* the only ones taking shots?" Mason asked, pointing between me and him.

Gannon and Brody gave each other a look. "Trust me," Gannon said. "You may be okay now, but the moment you're standing at the end of that aisle with everyone looking at you, you're going to be glad we took the edge off."

Mason glanced at me. "Kind of wish we hadn't taken those shots before we got dressed, then."

"What?" Brody and Gannon said in unison. "You've already been drinking? Why didn't you say something?"

"You said one shot, dude! How were we supposed to know you'd be shoving the whole bottle of whiskey down our throats?" I said.

Mason hiccupped, and all eyes turned to him. "I'm not much of a whiskey sinker." He shook his head. "Um, drinker."

Brody leaned over to Gannon and loudly whispered, "Palmer is going to kick your ass."

"Gentlemen?" Kris said from the entranceway of the living room. "It's time."

Mason and I turned and both bumped into one another, but it was only because my foot got hung up on his.

From behind me, I heard Gannon mumble, "Shit. We got them drunk."

I laughed when I saw the horrified expression on Kris's face.

Chapter Twenty-One

Harlee

Two brides.

Two grooms.

Two sisters who cried the entire ceremony while one of them kept sneaking bites of what looked like a cheese stick.

Two brothers-in-law who nearly got the two grooms hammered before the wedding.

Two sets of parents; both mothers crying happy tears while the dads cried out in unison, "Home run," during the wedding vows. Turns out Keegan hadn't stowed away his phone as promised.

And one stepson who asked at least six times during the nuptials if we were done yet.

All in all, it was the most beautiful wedding ceremony I'd ever seen. I might be biased, though.

Kris had taken care of nearly everything for us, from arranging the photographer to making the food for the dinner after the ceremony. We took pictures, changed, and joined our family and friends for the reception dinner that would put all dinners to shame. Kris had a large tent erected right next to where we'd gotten married. She'd even made sure there were heaters for when the sun set and the temperatures dropped.

My wedding dress was a simple white dress with lace. Palmer's was almost like mine, but it flared a little more at the bottom. We had both changed into more of a cocktail-type white dress for the dinner and the reception.

After walking around and trying to at least say hello to all those who'd attended, it was time to eat. In all, there were maybe sixty people present for the wedding and the dinner afterwards.

"Oh, Kris! It looks even more beautiful with all the candlelight," I gasped as I looked at the place settings on the table. Everything was white with a beachy theme. Even the candles and most of the flowers were white. A dash of blue was thrown in here and there among the flowers and with the light blue napkins.

The name cards had starfish tied to them with the same light-blue ribbon, something Palmer and I had done earlier that morning. Resting on each white plate was the menu. We had gone with more of a traditional seaside meal.

New England Clam Chowder
House or Caesar Salad
Steamers and Mussels
Mini Crab Cakes
Corn-off-the-Cob
New Potatoes
Steamed Lobster

"Everything is ready to serve," Kris said with a huge smile. I could totally tell she was in her element.

Glancing over at Brax, I nodded. He held up his glass and tapped it to get everyone's attention.

"Dinner is about to be served, so if you'd like to find your seats..."

Our guests quickly moved to their assigned seats. Myself, Palmer, Mason, and Brax were sitting at one table, with my parents sitting next to us at another table. Addie, Gannon, Sutton, and Brody sat on the other side. Kris had arranged it so those three tables were facing toward the room, with the other tables spread out evenly in the rest of the space. Our tables were rectangle, while everyone else's were round to allow for easy conversations.

We spent the rest of the evening eating, talking, laughing, dancing, and enjoying ourselves. I loved seeing my parents having fun, and I know Palmer did as well. There was something so special about sitting there watching your mom and dad dance and kiss.

After stepping away from talking to my parents and their best friends, I moved to the other side of the room where a bar was set up. I needed water for my dry throat.

Warm arms engulfed me as I waited for my ice water. Dropping my head back against Brax, I said, "When can we leave? I'm exhausted."

His breath tickled my neck when he laughed softly. "We can leave whenever you'd like."

The bartender handed me the ice water, and I took a long drink before I set it down and turned in his arms to face him.

"Did you know we have the entire bed and breakfast to ourselves?"

He raised a brow. "How did that happen?"

"Kris booked the honeymoon suite on the top floor for us, and Palmer and Mason are going to stay on the second floor. There aren't any other current guests."

"And how did we luck out with the top floor?"

Giving him a sexy smile, I replied, "I have my ways."

He leaned down and brushed his lips against mine. "Do you think anyone would notice if we slipped away?"

Looking past his shoulder, I saw Palmer and Mason standing together, his arm around her waist. They looked so happy, and that warmed my heart.

"We can't leave Palmer and Mason to handle all the rest of this."

Brax sighed. "You're right, of course."

At that moment, Kris signaled for everyone's attention.

"As fun as this has been, there are only three ferries left that will be leaving the island tonight. The schedule was posted on the invites for everyone. Now would be a good time to start saying goodbye."

"She's my new hero," I said softly.

"You know," Brax said as he looked around, "a number of people have already left."

I nodded. "I said some goodbyes to people in the last hour or so. And everyone has come up to me to thank us for the invite."

"I've had a lot of that too. And Sutton and Brody left about an hour ago. Sutton claimed exhaustion, but Brody had a feeling she was craving fried chicken from that place right off Main that opened not too long ago."

"Kenny's Fried Chicken?"

He pointed at me. "That's the one."

"Harlee, Braxton."

The sound of my mother's voice caused me to turn. She was standing alongside my father.

"It was such a beautiful wedding!" she said.

I hugged her and kissed her cheek. "Thanks, Mom. It was fun keeping a secret like that from everyone."

She laughed. "You could give Ms. Seaside a run for her money!"

Brax let out a bark of laughter. "Can you imagine Harlee as Ms. Seaside?"

My mother tittered. "Not at all. Not that you don't have it in you, sweetheart, but I just don't see it."

I glanced over at my father, who simply grinned and gave me a half shrug. "We're taking off, kids." Engulfing me in an embrace, he whispered, "Well done, Mrs. B."

I hugged him back tightly. "Thank you, Daddy."

When we drew back, he gave me a quick nod and then reached for my mother's hand. "Come on, darling. I don't want to miss the ferry."

After Kris's announcement, the tent was soon empty of almost everyone but the people who were cleaning up. Kris, of course, was running around directing them.

Palmer was sitting in a chair, rubbing her foot with one hand. When she looked up at me, we both exchanged grins. "Not used to wearing heels like that," she said.

"Me either. All I really want is for Brax to massage my feet."

Sighing, Palmer looked around. "It was so beautiful, wasn't it?"

"It really was."

"Mason and I are going to go change, then take a walk on the beach."

"That'll be nice," I said as I slipped my own heels off and wiggled my toes.

"Did you and Brax want to join us?"

I slid my gaze to the right to look at her. "As much as I loved sharing my wedding day with you, Palmer, I'm not sharing my wedding night with you as well."

She laughed. "I meant to relax for a bit."

"No, thank you. The only way I want to relax is with a foot massage and then having your brother—"

Shoving a hand in front of my face, she begged, "Don't say it! For the love, Harlee, don't say it!"

I pushed her hand away. "I was going to say, then having your brother sneak down for some food."

"Oh."

"*Then* I'll have hot wedding sex with him all night."

She rolled her eyes. "I can't with you."

"Kris told us to leave since she hired people to help out with all the clean-up. So I vote for leaving," Brax said as he bent down to grab my heels—then pulled my sneakers out from behind his back.

"Oh my God! If I didn't love you a lot before, I really, really, *really* love you now."

Palmer raised a brow at Mason.

His cheeks turned pink. "I have failed you, my wife. I will, however, carry you to our room if you wish."

Palmer stood and kicked off her other heel. "I can walk barefoot."

Wrapping his arm around her waist, Mason looked back at us. "Enjoy, you guys."

"We will!" Brax and I both said.

"And you too!" I called out, watching them walk out of the tent and toward the bed and breakfast.

I slipped on my sneakers and laced my fingers with Brax's as we waved and called out our goodbyes and thanks once again to Kris.

As soon as we got up to our suite, I collapsed onto the bed. "I'm so exhausted!"

"So am I," Brax said, sitting on the bed, then dropping back.

Turning my head to look at him, I found myself taken aback by how handsome he was. My husband. All those years, I'd secretly told myself I wasn't in love with him, only to actually fall more in love with him than ever before.

Brax had his eyes closed, and I watched his chest rise and fall, his breathing seeming to slow down a bit. I rolled onto my side and propped my head on my hand.

"Do you want to shower and maybe sleep for a bit?" I asked.

He turned his head. "I want to make love to you. But I also really want to relax."

I laughed. "I feel the same way. Shower?"

Brax nodded, then kicked off his dress shoes. I did the same with the sneakers he'd brought me.

We stood, and he placed his hands on my shoulders and turned me around. He unzipped the white dress and let it fall to the floor to pool around my feet. His soft lips kissed my shoulder as his hand came around to cup my breast.

I dropped my head back and moaned. "I thought we were showering and going to sleep for a bit?"

"That was before I saw you in these lace undies with this push-up bra."

"Does this mean you've gotten a second wind, Mr. Bradley?"

He turned me around to face him again. His gaze swept over my body, taking it all in as he licked his lips. "I have, indeed, Mrs. Bradley."

With his fingers moving swiftly, he reached around and unclasped my bra and gently pulled it down my arms. He tossed it onto the chair in the corner and motioned for me to sit on the bed. My heart kicked up as I did. There was nothing that I loved more than Brax warming me up before we made love.

He smiled and dropped to his knees. His fingers ran up the sides of my legs and gently pushed them open wide.

"Do you want me to make you come with my mouth?"

I nodded.

"Tell me."

I felt my cheeks heat for some reason. I'd never been timid, especially with Brax. "I want you to make me come with your mouth... and your tongue."

A wicked smile grew across his face. "Anything for you, wife."

"My panties?" I asked.

"Do you want them off?" he asked as he reached up and pushed them to the side. He leaned in and licked, causing me to let out a hiss of pleasure.

When I lifted up, he slipped my panties off and dropped them to the floor. Then he was back, his head between my legs, bringing me to an orgasm so fast and so hard, I felt like I could hardly breathe.

"Fuck the shower, Harlee," he said as he quickly undressed and climbed over me. He slid inside with one solid push, filling me completely.

"Braxton!" I gasped, aware that his sister and Mason were somewhere on the floor below us. Kris had assured me that this room was much more soundproof than the others, but I was still conscious of how loud we were.

"Jesus, Harlee, you feel so good. So fucking good."

I wrapped my legs around his waist and pulled him in deeper while I lifted my hips to meet his thrusts.

"Brax. Oh God, Brax!"

He buried his face in my neck and moved faster and harder, yet somehow still sweet and gentle. I could feel him growing larger in me. When he lifted his head and his eyes met mine, he smiled, and I fell in love with him even more.

He reached between us, and all it took was one touch and I came. Brax followed me as he moaned my name, then crushed his mouth to mine. My body trembled and my heart felt like it might leap right out of my chest

"I love you. God, I love you so much, Harlee."

I moved my fingers softly over his back, my legs dropping open as he lifted his weight off of me but still stayed inside. "I love you, too, Brax. More than you'll ever know."

He kissed me gently on the lips and then whispered, "I *so* know, and I love you just as much.

The Seaside Chronicles

May 18, 2023

Drop the Hook

Seasiders,

Color me shocked. A seaside wedding for our two happy couples, and on the beautiful little haven of Lighthouse Island. I'm told by a little fish that the island was picked because it holds a special place in Harlee and Braxton Bradley's hearts. One has to wonder what that means! At any rate, let us all wish them a lifetime of happiness. I guess now Braxton really is the Prince of Seaside... It pains me to write that, you have no idea.

Speaking of our prince, the fishing season is upon us, and a seagull told me that they saw Harlee heading out yesterday morning with her new husband. Could she be joining the ranks and working for Bradley Charters now? Harlee seems to be picking up where Palmer left off with all the jobs! Let's hope she doesn't get seasick.

News on the docks is that the city council is well on its way to ruling in favor of a carnival-type expansion of the pier. Our little town is growing, but let's hope not too much.

Fair winds and following seas!

Ms. Seaside

Chapter Twenty-Two

Harlee

"**W**hy do we have to be here before sunrise, Brax?"

"Haven't you ever heard the phrase the early bird gets the worm?"

"Does that apply when we're not on land?"

He winked. "It certainly does. Look, there are our first customers of the season!"

I followed him as we walked down the dock toward two couples. One was older, and they looked to maybe be the parents of the other.

"Good morning!" Brax called out. "I'm Captain Brax, and I'll be taking you out today for your fishing tour."

"I'm so excited!" the younger woman said as she wrapped a hand around the younger man's arm.

The older woman shot her a frustrated look, but it was so quick I was positive I was the only one who'd caught it.

"This is my first mate and wife, Harlee. Harlee, this is Bradley and Wendy Peterman, and their son Rick and his fiancée, Trish."

I reached my hand out to shake everyone's before we started to make our way toward one of Braxton's boats. It wasn't one of the larger ones, since he was doing a private charter for this family. Thomas was still in Spain on his honeymoon, so Lance, another guy who worked for Brax, was taking out a larger group of people on one of the boats a little bit farther down the dock. I was truly so happy for Thomas, as was Brax.

Once we got to the boat, Brax went over the trip itinerary, safety rules, and other things that pertained to the charter. He also informed them that because this was a smaller boat, there wouldn't be restrooms.

"How long will it take us to get to the fishing spot?" Bradley asked.

"About an hour, maybe a little less."

"Bait?" Rick asked.

"Clams and squid," I explained.

"Okay, let's go get some fish," Brax said as he nodded at Bobby, his second mate. Brax normally had two to three more crew members with him, but since this was a small, private group, it was the three of us working today.

After making sure everyone knew where to find drinks and snacks, we were off and heading out to sea.

Brax smiled as he said, "Hopefully we'll see some white-sided dolphins on the way. Keep an eye out for them up toward the bow."

"How big is this boat?" Rick asked me.

My mind went over everything Brax had told me last night about the particular boat we'd be using today.

"Twenty-eight feet. Three-hundred-and-fifty-horse diesel. She carries a hundred-and-fifty gallons of fuel..." My voice trailed off. "Oh, and twenty-seven miles of radar! It has that too."

Brax looked at me and winked.

Once we were out of the bay, he picked up the speed and I quickly got lost in being out on the water. Brax had already taken me out a few times as he got each boat ready for the season. I had never had so much fun as when we were skimming across the water with the wind blowing through my hair. It was freeing. One look at Trish, and I knew she was feeling the same way.

"Are you having fun so far?" I called out to her.

She nodded. "This is going to be the best day ever!"

"I don't feel so well, Rick," Trish said, holding a hand over her mouth.

"Did you take the stuff I gave you?" Rick asked, clearly annoyed she was taking him away from fishing time.

One quick glance over at Wendy told me she was already frustrated with Trish, and we had only started fishing thirty minutes ago. Brax had mentioned there was a stiff northeasterly wind and since we were in about three-hundred-and-fifty feet of water, the boat was rocking pretty good.

"What if we can't get back?" Trish asked as she sat in the back of the boat looking even more green than she had minutes ago.

"Trish, do you need anything?" I asked, sitting down next to her. Rick took that as his cue to get back to fishing.

She shook her head and leaned toward me. "I hate fishing."

My eyes widened. "Then why are you here?"

Bradley called out, "Fish on!"

"I'm here because of Rick. He loves fishing, and so do his parents."

"That doesn't mean you need to like it. You're allowed to have your own separate likes, and the same goes for him."

She looked so unsure, my heart broke for her.

"When Rick's parents mentioned chartering a boat for a private fishing trip," she said, "I pictured something completely different, like much bigger. I thought it would be fun. But it's freezing, the boat is all over the place, and I hate the smell of fish."

"Okay, well, you're certainly not in the right place then. Do you need a jacket? I have one with me."

"Bobby, we need the gaff up here!" Brax called out. "We've got a great cod!"

I watched Bobby make his way to the front of the boat to get Bradley's fish.

"What's a gaff?" Trish asked.

"It's a handheld pole with a sharp hook," I said. "You use it to retrieve the fish from the water when it's too big for the line to pull it out."

Trish stared at me with a blank expression.

"It's a big hook you stab into the fish."

"Oh, okay."

I watched as Brax reeled in a fish of his own. There was something about watching him do what he loved that made me want to jump the man. Would that feeling ever get old? If we were alone, he would be very distracted right about now.

"Fish on!" Rick called out as he also reeled in a fish.

It was then that Trish leaned over the boat and threw up. I rubbed her back softly while Wendy glanced over and shook her head. Rick didn't even realize his fiancée was sick.

"Your girlfriend's sick," Wendy said to her son.

Rick looked back, though he kept reeling in his fish. "You doing okay, babe?"

I glared at him while Trish threw up again. Then I shot Wendy a look, wanting to correct her that Trish was Rick's *fiancée*, but I kept my mouth shut.

It was a choppy sea, no doubt about it. Six- to eight-foot waves were hitting the boat. Even I had to take a deep breath a few times. Wendy was lucky Ms. Seaside wasn't in *her* town to write up what a mean future mother-in-law she would be.

After throwing up again, Trish took me up on my offer of a jacket and found a spot out of the way to curl up. The rocking of the boat put her to sleep within minutes. Or maybe she passed out from sea sickness or fear of the boat sinking.

Making my way over to Brax, I smiled as I watched him reel in yet another fish. "That's a big one," I remarked, looking out into the water.

"That's what she said," he replied with a laugh.

I shook my head and checked to make sure the Petermans weren't within hearing distance.

"Brax...Trish is really sick. And Rick doesn't care at all."

"Has she never been on a boat in the ocean before? I mean, seas are rough today. Hence the good fishing."

I glanced over toward the family. "I think she thought she was going out on a yacht."

He laughed.

"She only came because her fiancé and his parents like to fish," I said. "She's trying to impress them, but I think all she's done is make the mom mad."

The fish surfaced, and Brax flashed me a wide grin. "Look at that cod."

"It's beautiful," I commented.

"Bobby!" Brax called out. "Will you take this for me?"

Bobby took the fish and rod. "Sure thing, boss."

Brax turned to me and gave me a gentle smile. "I love that you're worried about her and about her need to fit in with her future in-laws...but Harlee, you're going to meet a plethora of people on these trips. Including women who're going to shamelessly flirt with me, Bobby, Thomas, Duke, all of us. Just like I'll see guys flirting with *you*. It's a job. We smile, and we help them have the best fishing experience they can have—within limits. If anyone ever touches you, I expect you to punch them or tell me." He smiled again. "But honey, Trish isn't going to be the last girlfriend to climb onto one of our boats to impress a boyfriend. Same goes for guys, believe it or not. I've seen some women who can out-fish *me*."

"You mean a woman is the crazy fisherman with a boyfriend who can't fish?"

He laughed. "Fisherwoman. Yes. You'll meet all types when we do the larger charters, but these small ones are mainly for people who really love to fish."

Sighing, I nodded. "So what you're saying is, it's not my job to fix everyone's problems."

"Personal problems. As for fishing problems...you can only fix the ones you know how to fix."

"And considering my current knowledge of fishing, that means getting them drinks and food."

Drawing me closer, he kissed me—and we both nearly stumbled when the boat rocked.

"Jesus, how does Gannon do his job?" I asked as I reached for the rail. "I think I'll go make sure no one's thirsty."

"Hey," he said as he took my hand in his. "You're worth more than getting drinks for everyone. You know that, right?"

I nodded.

"I love you, Harlee."

My stomach did a little flip. "I love you more."

"Impossible."

"Fish on!" Rick called out, and we both got back to work.

It turned out that after Trish had a nap, and whatever she took finally kicked in, she actually enjoyed fishing and caught three of her own. Let me add—three bigger fish than any that Rick, Bradley, or Wendy managed to catch. I was so proud of her. After that, she and Wendy chatted up a storm.

I couldn't help but wonder if anyone had ever met and fallen in love on one of Brax's charters. Wouldn't Ms. Seaside love that?

My smile faded as I thought about the task I knew I needed to do...and soon. Ms. Seaside would be coming to an end. And a new chapter would begin for me and Brax.

Chapter Twenty-Three

Brax

The Seaside Chronicles

July 6, 2023

Tide's Out

Seasiders,

This is probably the hardest column I've written to date. You may have noticed my columns have been...changing, if that's the right word to use. The love I once felt for writing these weekly "informational" pieces has been slowly slipping away. As much as I love a good gossip piece, this writer is finding herself at a crossroads in her life. Do I keep doing the weekly column and special editions, potentially upsetting my subjects, or do I move on to the next chapter in my life? I do believe it's the latter. It's time I slide my pen and paper into a desk drawer and go out with the tide.

I have faith that whatever column replaces mine, you will all adore it as much as you have adored me. Plus, you'll still have Friday's Catch, and I have to admit, Braxton Bradley does add his trademark humor to it, which makes it rather enjoyable to read. (Though I'm not sure if he'll be able to keep that up when I'm no longer dangling at the end of his fishing pole.)

At any rate, I want to say thank you for being such loyal readers. I hope you know that I truly love Seaside and each and every one of you. Well...maybe not every one of you, but I do like most of you. I'll miss keeping you up to date with my version of the news, but never fear, my fishes, I'll still be around, watching and listening!

For the last time...

Fair winds and following seas!

Ms. Seaside

The doorbell ringing combined with a loud knocking sound caused Harlee to fly out of bed. "What is that?"

I swung my legs off my side of the bed and stood. "Someone's at the door."

I started for the bedroom door, but stopped when Harlee called out, "Brax, you're naked!"

With a quick glance down, I laughed. "Oh yeah."

After slipping on sweats and a T-shirt, I made my way to the front door and the loud knocking that wouldn't stop. Harlee and I were taking the next few days off to go to Boston. We had yet to plan a honeymoon, and since we were smack in the middle of our summer season, we were booked solid with charters. Still, we both needed some time away, even if it was a short trip.

"I'm going to kill whoever this is," I muttered—before I looked out and saw Palmer standing there. "Somehow, I knew it was going to be her."

I hadn't even fully opened the door when she pushed inside.

"She's quitting!" Palmer shouted. "She's actually *quitting!*"

Staring at her like she'd lost her damn mind, I asked, "Who is?"

Lifting the paper, she shook it in my face. "Ms. Seaside! She announced it in today's paper!"

I knew I was looking at my sister with a face full of genuine disbelief. Harlee hadn't mentioned anything to me about this being her last column.

"What's with all the yelling?" Harlee asked as she appeared in the living room.

Turning, I gave her a questioning look. She ignored me and focused on Palmer. The little minx.

"Ms. Seaside is hanging up the column," Palmer said. "She's done! She's not writing for *The Chronicles* anymore."

With wide, surprised eyes, Harlee took the paper Palmer nearly shoved in her face. "Why would she do that?"

Palmer threw her hands up. "How am I supposed to find out who Mrs. Pritcher is dating? And what about that house on Captain's Row that sold to some millionaire? She was supposed to find out who it was! I still say it's Taylor Swift, by the way."

I groaned while Harlee chuckled.

"And what about her hinting that she ate at Pete's Place once a week? Oh my gosh—she's not going to be writing about the babies!"

"Babies?" Harlee and I asked at the same time.

It was right then that Harlee's cell phone rang. It was plugged in on the kitchen counter, so she went and retrieved it. "It's Sutton. Hello? Yes, we heard. No, Palmer's here. Yes. No—wait! Sutton! Wait, we're leaving for Boston and—" She pulled her phone away from her ear, then looked at me. "Well, apparently Sutton is on her way."

"Here?" I asked.

Harlee nodded.

Palmer started to pace. "Addie and Sutton must be beside themselves."

"I'll get some coffee on," Harlee said as she winked at me.

"Why would they be, Palmer?" I dropped onto the sofa and scrubbed a hand down my face.

Palmer stopped and looked at me like I'd hit my head. "Ms. Seaside isn't going to write about the babies. I mean, it's practically a family tradition for the Bradleys to be featured in her column! And now the poor babies won't get that."

I stared at my sister in disbelief. "You *hate* being talked about in the column."

"No, I don't."

I closed my eyes and counted to ten.

"But back to the bigger problem," she said. "Readers are going to miss out on more funny stories when Addie and Sutton go into labor. Like last week, when she mentioned how Addie got stuck in Mom's car and couldn't get out."

Laughing, I said, "That *was* funny."

"Wait," Harlee said as she sat down in the oversized chair she loved so much. I'd often find her curled up in it with a book, a blanket, and a glass of wine. "I thought you guys hated Ms. Seaside writing about you, and now you *want* her to write about you? And worse yet, the babies?"

Palmer waved her hand at me. "Please, she would never say an ill word about those babies."

I shook my head to clear my thoughts.

The doorbell rang, and Palmer rushed to answer it. Sutton waddled in with her swollen belly.

She took a few deep breaths, then looked around the room at each of us before she said, "Ms. Seaside is no more!"

"I know!" Palmer replied.

Sutton's expression was a mix of sadness and anger. "This means she won't write about the babies!"

The door flew open and in walked Addie, with Gannon helping her. I swore, she was even bigger than Sutton.

"She quit! That bitch *quit* right before the babies are born!"

Gannon looked exhausted. Poor Brody limped in behind them.

"Sutton, you forgot your breakfast tacos."

I sliced my hand through my hair as I looked at Harlee, who simply smiled and shrugged.

"Women confuse the hell out of me," I mumbled.

There was nothing better than fall in Maine. The trees started to turn, the wind got cooler, and the smell of baked apples seemed to fill the air everywhere you went. It had to be my favorite time of year, no doubt about it. This year, the crisp temperatures were welcome after a particularly hot summer. And man, oh man, were the fish currently biting.

I only had a few more weeks before the season ended, and we were fully booked. After the summer fishing camp Harlee and I had hosted in August, we'd had an influx of people signing up for charters, a lot of them families. It was the best season yet, and I knew it was all because of Harlee.

"This is so stunning. I can't believe it's ours!" Harlee said softly as we both stood in the massive front yard of the house we'd recently closed on. We'd sold both of our houses and had moved into the guesthouse behind Harlee's folks' place until we'd found a home of our own. A place where we could make new memories and grow old together. A place where we could raise our kids, which we'd started to talk about more and more. We'd thought we wanted to wait, but it quickly became clear that a baby was the only thing missing from our world.

I watched Harlee stretch her arms out and spin. "It's going to be a beautiful place to raise a family!" She stopped spinning and looked at me. Those big blue eyes were sparkling, and she wore a smile so wide, it made me smile in return.

The house was located on its own peninsula on Seaside Cove. The three-bedroom, two-and-a-half-bath house was originally owned by Captain Jerald S. Pendleton. It was the typical old Maine cape that had been completely updated, which was great for us. The view was amazing, as the peninsula sat on the banks of the Penobscot River right before it opened up into the bay.

The best part: It sat on seven acres of land. Of course, the best part for *Harlee* was the history behind the old home. Built in 1800, it had only been owned by three different families and had survived plenty of storms, and even a few hurricanes. She'd already done extensive research on the house and the story behind it. My little history buff.

A bell rang in the distance, and we both turned to see the twelve-week-old German Shorthair Pointer we'd adopted only a few days ago come racing toward us. We knew he'd need plenty of room to run, so this would be the perfect place for him too.

Harlee grinned from ear to ear as Moose went running by, only taking a moment to bark before he continued on. "I think he gives it his bark of approval."

I laughed. "I think so."

"Oh, Brax, can you imagine the parties we can have here?" She gasped, then did a weird little hop. "We could do a haunted tractor ride all through the island for the kids! Maybe we can have a fundraiser for the elementary school's art program. Palmer would love that!"

I nodded and reached for her. Taking her hand, I drew her in close and placed a soft kiss on her lips. "Are you happy, Harlee?"

She brought her hand up to my cheek as she looked deeply into my eyes. "I've never been this happy in my entire life." Reaching up onto her toes, she sealed her mouth over mine, and we soon got lost in each other.

A horn honked, and we broke the kiss to see Gannon and Addie parking their car.

"I can't wait to show Addie!" Harlee said as she rushed toward the driveway.

When Addie got out, she looked at the view, then looked at the house and smiled. Harlee made it to her side before they both screamed and hugged one another.

"Need any help?" I asked, walking up to the SUV Gannon had traded his Jeep in for.

Gannon looked down at his almost three-month-old baby in the backseat. "She's fussy."

"Give me that baby." I unbuckled Hannah from her car seat and carefully picked her up. Bright grayish-blue eyes looked up at me, and a little smile played at the corner of my niece's mouth. "Come here, baby girl. Uncle Brax has you now."

I held her close as we walked toward the house. Her fussing instantly stopped.

Gannon shook his head. "Dude, how do you do that? Seriously, I need to know."

"Ahh, I'm not going to share my secrets. Am I, sweet baby girl?"

Hannah made a weird bubble laugh.

"Man, this place is amazing, Brax," Gannon said as we walked up the steps and into the house. Addie and Harlee, as well as Moose, were behind us, the girls chatting a mile a minute about paint colors and finding the right ones to make the house historically accurate.

Once inside, Harlee gave them the tour, then met me and Hannah back down in the living room. She gave Hannah a kiss and stared at her with longing eyes. I knew how she felt.

"It's beautiful, Brax!" Addie said while she hugged me, then reached down and kissed her daughter on the forehead.

Another honk drew our attention outside.

"Palmer, Mason, and Charlie are here!" Harlee said, rushing out to the front porch.

We followed. The moment Palmer got out of the car, she screamed in excitement, and little Hannah made a grunt of disapproval.

"I feel you, little one, but they like to scream, so the sooner you get to used to it, the better," I whispered down at her.

Palmer reached back into the car and pulled out *The Seaside Chronicles*, waving it in the air.

"What is she doing?" Harlee asked with a laugh.

"She's back! Oh my God, I knew she wouldn't be able to stay away!"

With all four of us confused, we asked in unison, "Who's back?"

Palmer nearly skipped to the front porch. "Ms. Seaside! She's back, and she wrote a column this morning about Harlee and Brax."

I snapped my head over to look at Harlee, who had a stunned expression on her face. When she looked at me, I knew immediately she hadn't been the one to write the column.

"Let me have that baby!" Palmer stated, heading toward me with her hands already out.

Clearing her throat, Harlee said, "Um, it's such a beautiful day, who wants lemonade on the porch? The realtor brought some, along with some homemade baked goods." There were two big swings on the front porch, and a few rocking chairs that the previous owner had left for us.

"Let me see that paper," Addie said, grabbing it from Palmer before I handed her the baby.

"Do you need help, Harlee?" Addie absentmindedly asked as she flipped through the paper until she found the column.

Letting out a nervous laugh, Harlee replied, "No, you guys enjoy the fresh air. Brax, can you help me?"

"Sure." I followed Harlee into the empty house. Once we were in the kitchen, Harlee spun around, her face white as a ghost.

"So it wasn't you?" I asked.

"No! My father?"

"But why? Why in the world would your father start writing the column?"

She chewed on her nail, shaking her head. "Actually, he wouldn't."

"Then...then who is?" I asked.

Her eyes, filled with confusion, met mine. "I have no idea."

Three days earlier...

On the other side of Seaside, sitting next to a warm, cozy fire, a woman sat with a pen in her hand and paper on her brand-new writing desk. With a smile on her face, she began to write...

The Seaside Chronicles

October 1, 2023

High Tide

Seasiders,
    Did you miss me?

Epilogue

Harlee
Christmas

"**A**nd he won't tell you?" Brax asked for the millionth time.

I pulled the ham out of the oven and set it on a cooling rack. "He won't tell me."

Leaning against the counter, Brax sighed. "The writing is definitely not the same. Do you think other people have noticed?"

"Well, Palmer, Sutton, and Addie have noticed," I replied as I slid the rolls into the oven and set the timer.

"I mean, I get why your dad did it, it sells papers, but why won't he tell you who it is? And it's so random. It doesn't even come out every week. She only did two articles in October, three in November, and so far, three in December."

Turning to face him, I crossed my arms over my chest. "I was just as pissed off as you, Brax, when we first found out. But I don't own *The Chronicles*, my father does. He can do whatever he sees fit to benefit the paper. And clearly, that column brings in readers."

"So did mine."

I smiled. Brax had stopped writing his weekly column, Friday's Catch, last week. He'd enjoyed it, but once I'd told him our little news, he knew it was time to hang it up.

Sutton walked into the kitchen with her five-month-old son, Granger, on her hip. "Palmer wants to know if you have any saltine crackers."

"Yep," I said as I turned and headed to the pantry. I pulled out a sleeve and handed it to Sutton. "Morning sickness again?"

She nodded. "Charlie asked Palmer why it's called morning sickness when she seems to be sick all the time."

I chuckled. Brax and I hadn't yet shared the news of our own little bundle of joy, since I was still pretty early in my pregnancy. Palmer had told everyone at Thanksgiving. She was due May 27th. My due date was August 10th. I'd been feeling a little queasy, but nothing bad so far. I was thankful fishing season was over, though. I was pretty sure I wouldn't have been able to take being on the rocking boats during the first trimester.

"Thanks!" Sutton called out as she and Granger headed out the door.

I focused back on the food.

"I don't like it," Brax continued. "I want to know who in the hell it is."

"Who *who* is?" Barbara asked, walking into the kitchen to grab more items to put on the large table in our formal dining room.

"No one," Brax said with a huff.

Barbara gave him a look, a green bean casserole in one hand and mashed potatoes in the other. "Don't tell me you're searching for her *again*."

He rolled his eyes.

His mother let out a frustrated sigh. "One day. I want *one day* where no one in this family talks about Ms. Seaside. One day, Brax."

Ms. Seaside still wrote about the Bradleys, though not nearly as much. But when she did an article about Barbara and Keegan—being caught by the police making out in their car down at the pier—well... Barbara's attitude toward the gossip columnist had quickly changed, and not for the better.

Holding up his hands, Brax replied, "Fine. I won't say another word."

"Besides, she hasn't written about any of you kids in weeks. I think she's moved on." And with that, Barbara turned on her heels and marched out of the kitchen.

Brax started to say something, and I shook my head. "There's no talking about her, Brax. Let it go."

He reached for the ham and started out of the kitchen. "I'll let it go, but only for today!"

Grinning, I turned and peeked at the rolls. I took them out, placed them in a basket, and covered them with a cloth. Pushing all thoughts of Ms. Seaside from my head, I smiled wider, ignored the urge to throw up, and headed into the other room with the rest of the family.

Little did I know, on the other side of Seaside, a woman sat at a desk, making a list of newsworthy things to talk about...and at the very top of that list, underlined in red, was Harlee Bradley's pregnancy.

The End...or is it?

Other Books by Kelly Elliott

COMING SOON

Love in Montana (Meet Me in Montana Spin Off)

Fearless Enough – March 21, 2023
Cherished Enough – June 6, 2023
Brave Enough – August 29, 2023
Daring Enough November 21, 2023

Holidaze in Salem

A Bit of Hocus Pocus
A Bit of Holly Jolly
A Bit of Wee Luck - March 17, 2023
A Bit of Razzle Dazzle – July 4, 2023

The Seaside Chronicles

Returning Home
Part of Me
Lost to You
Someone to Love

Stand Alones

The Journey Home*
Who We Were*
The Playbook*
Made for You*
*Available on audiobook

Boggy Creek Valley Series

The Butterfly Effect*
Playing with Words*
She's the One*
Surrender to Me*

Hearts in Motion*
Looking for You*
Surprise Novella TBD
*Available on audiobook

Meet Me in Montana Series
Never Enough*
Always Enough*
Good Enough*
Strong Enough*
*Available on audiobook

Southern Bride Series
Love at First Sight*
Delicate Promises*
Divided Interests*
Lucky in Love*
Feels Like Home *
Take Me Away*
Fool for You*
Fated Hearts*
*Available on audiobook

Cowboys and Angels Series
Lost Love
Love Profound
Tempting Love
Love Again
Blind Love
This Love
Reckless Love
*Series available on audiobook

Boston Love Series

Searching for Harmony

Fighting for Love

*Series available on audiobook

Austin Singles Series

Seduce Me

Entice Me

Adore Me

*Series available on audiobook

Wanted Series

*Wanted**

*Saved**

*Faithful**

Believe

*Cherished**

*A Forever Love**

The Wanted Short Stories

All They Wanted

*Available on audiobook

Love Wanted in Texas Series

Spin-off series to the WANTED Series

Without You

Saving You

Holding You

Finding You

Chasing You

Loving You

Entire series available on audiobook

*Please note *Loving You* combines the last book
of the Broken and Love Wanted in Texas series.

Broken Series
*Broken**
*Broken Dreams**
*Broken Promises**
Broken Love
*Available on audiobook

The Journey of Love Series
Unconditional Love
Undeniable Love
Unforgettable Love
*Entire series available on audiobook

With Me Series
Stay With Me
Only With Me
*Series available on audiobook

Speed Series
Ignite
Adrenaline
*Series available on audiobook

COLLABORATIONS
Predestined Hearts (co-written with Kristin Mayer)*
Play Me (co-written with Kristin Mayer)*
Dangerous Temptations (co-written with Kristin Mayer*
*Available on audiobook

Made in the USA
Middletown, DE
03 May 2023

29954411R00144